Praise for *Bad Apples*

'Just finished Will Dean's *Bad Apples*. A delicious return to Tuva.'
Ann Cleeves

'Fiendish, funny, scary as hell. *Bad Apples* is the stand out in a
truly outstanding series.'
Chris Whitaker, author of *We Begin at the End*

'*Bad Apples* is a chilling outing for Tuva Moodyson – unsettling
from beginning to the very end but leavened with dark humour.
A compelling thriller that devoted fans and new
readers will adore.'
Jane Casey, author of the Maeve Kerrigan series

'[Tuva] is admirably resilient, full of warmth and humour... Her
travails may well give sensitive readers nightmares, but that's a
small price to pay for spending time in her exhilarating company.'
Literary Review

'The fourth in the excellent series of Tuva Moodyson thrillers.'
Choice

Praise for *Black River*

'Dean's series about deaf Swedish reporter Tuva Moodyson is a must read – and this book is his best yet... *Black River* is eerie, unnerving and buckets of fun.'
Observer, thriller of the month

'Just finished Will Dean's *Black River*. Splendid to catch up with Tuva Moodyson and that very special world... Such a BRILLIANT central character... great on women's friendships.'
Ann Cleeves, author of the Vera Stanhope novels

'A peerless exercise in suspense.'
Financial Times

'The relentless pace drives you forward until you are hanging on to the pages by your fingertips, afraid to go on, but terrified to put it down. Another masterpiece from Mr Dean.'
Liz Nugent, author of *Our Little Cruelties*

'My favourite Tuva novel yet... Atmospheric and chilling.'
Jane Casey, author of *The Cutting Place*

'An atmospheric and electrifying return.'
****Heat

'*Black River* what can I say? Will Dean raises the bar yet again. Suspenseful, distinctive, each page crackles with menace. Everything you could want in a thriller.'
Chris Whitaker, author of *We Begin at the End*

Praise for *Red Snow*

'For all those who loved *Dark Pines* by Will Dean I can tell you that the forthcoming sequel, *Red Snow* is even better. Scandi noir meets *Gormenghast*. Just wonderful. Can't get enough of Tuva Moodyson.'
Mark Billingham, author of the Tom Thorne novels

'A complex plot suffused with the nightmarish quality of *Twin Peaks* and a tough-minded, resourceful protagonist add up to a stand-out read.'
Guardian

'Makes the blood run even colder than *Dark Pines*. Will Dean goes from strength to strength.'
Erin Kelly, author of *He Said / She Said*

'This is just what crime fiction readers want: the old magic formula made to seem fresh.'
Telegraph, best thrillers and crime fiction of 2019

'Great Scandi noir with an excellent heroine. Though beware – liquorice will never taste the same again.'
Ruth Ware, author of *One by One*

'Total Scandi vibes, a cracking plot and a hugely likeable heroine: the dream.'
Grazia

'This is a crime novel of poise and polish, peopled with utterly compelling characters. Claustrophobic, chilling and as dark as liquorice. Brilliant.'
Fiona Cummins, author of *The Neighbour*

Praise for *Dark Pines*

'The tension is unrelenting, and I can't wait for Tuva's next outing.'
Val McDermid, author of the Tony Hill and Carol Jordan novels

'Memorably atmospheric, with a dogged and engaging protagonist, this is a compelling start to what promises to be an excellent series.'
Guardian

'The best thriller I've read in ages.'
Marian Keyes, author of *Grown Ups*

'Atmospheric, creepy and tense. Loved the *Twin Peaks* vibe. Loved Tuva. More please!'
C. J. Tudor, author of *The Chalk Man*

'A remarkably assured debut, *Dark Pines* is in turn tense, gripping and breathtaking and marks out Will Dean as a true talent. Definitely one to watch.'
Abir Mukherjee, author of *A Rising Man*

'Dean never lets the tension drop as his story grows ever more sinister.'
Daily Mail

'Bravo! I was so completely immersed in *Dark Pines* and Tuva is a brilliant protagonist. This HAS to be a TV series!'
Nina Pottell, *Prima* magazine

'Will Dean's impressive debut shows that Nordic noir can be mastered by a Brit.'
The Times

ALSO BY WILL DEAN

Dark Pines
Red Snow
Black River
Bad Apples
The Last Thing to Burn
First Born
The Last Passenger

WOLF PACK

WILL DEAN

POINT
BLANK

A Point Blank Book

First published in Great Britain, Australia, and the Republic of Ireland by Point Blank,
an imprint of Oneworld Publications, 2022
This mass market paperback edition published 2023

Copyright © Will Dean 2022

The moral right of Will Dean to be identified as the Author of this work has been
asserted by him in accordance with the Copyright, Designs, and Patents Act 1988

Point Blank would like to thank sensitivity reader @deafgirly
for her tremendous help across the Tuva Moodyson series.

ISBN 978-0-86154-201-7
ISBN 978-0-86154-200-0 (ebook)

Typeset in Janson MT 11.5/15pt by Geethik Technologies
Printed and bound in Great Britain by Clays Ltd, Elcograf S.p.A.

This book is a work of fiction. Names, characters, businesses, organizations, places, and events
are either the product of the author's imagination or are used fictitiously. Any resemblance to
actual persons, living or dead, events, or locales is entirely coincidental.

Oneworld Publications
10 Bloomsbury Street
London WC1B 3SR
England

Stay up to date with the latest books,
special offers, and exclusive content from
Oneworld with our newsletter

Sign up on our website
oneworld-publications.com/point-blank

For Emma and Evie. Always.

1

Birch buds glow neon green as sunrays pick out blood drops on the road.

I touch my brakes.

Something injured. Fallen. Down in the long grass.

In the shade of the pine trees lies a creature on its side, losing blood, losing its life. No other traffic on this route. I'm north of Visberg where the hill forest meets Utgard and I am completely alone with this wounded beast.

I pull off the road and turn on my hazard lights. Clear asphalt ahead and clear asphalt behind. But a thousand dark trees either side of me, some of them tall enough to eclipse a church steeple.

Birdsong as I open the door of my Hilux pick-up truck. I can't hear it well but I know it's there. Chirping and cheeping as something lies dying quietly on the verge.

I approach. The hairs on the back of my neck stand up as I dodge the red splatter.

I can't see well; it's in the shade, protected by buttercups and weeds.

Movement.

Still alive. Hanging on.

Another twitch.

I make out the size and shape of the dog. A spiked collar round its bloodied neck, a coat shrouding its torso. I run to it and then I stop. Some primal instinct kicking in. Some animal response buried deep inside my genes waking from its slumber and instructing me to pause. To look around. To wait.

Trees rustle.

The dog whimpers in the long grass and a buzzard circles overhead, waiting, watching.

I approach the dog, and a man bursts out from the treeline in full camouflage and he's carrying a rifle.

'You,' he says, out of breath.

I point to myself.

'What have you seen?'

I frown and say, 'There's a dog by the road. It's hurt.'

He follows my gaze, and then he runs to the dog. To *his* dog. I can tell from his gait and from the horror on his face that this dog is his.

He kneels in the grass and lays down his rifle and says, 'Bronco.'

I approach.

'I found him a minute ago. I was going to call someone.'

The man says nothing.

Overhead the buzzard glides lower and I see its beautiful shadow dance across the surface of the road.

'He's alive,' says the man, his voice cracking. 'Bring your car closer.'

I don't question him. I do as he asks.

The short drive back to the hunter and his wounded dog is all the time I need to understand what has happened today in this forgotten Värmland forest. The dog's distant cousin, some wolf descended from those who crossed the Russian border through Finland to Sweden many years ago, has tracked this domesticated dog, this beloved pet, and savagely attacked him. Canine versus canine. Wild against tame.

I take the blanket I keep on my back seats through winter in case of breakdowns, and I offer it to the man. He ignores me.

'Open the door,' he says, and then he scoops up the injured dog as gently as a mother might lift her newborn for the first time. He supports the animal's neck, stained, and he holds the dog close to his chest. Blood drips down the man's hands and through his fingers.

I stand with the Hilux passenger side door open but the man says, 'The back door.'

He gets inside. He uses the blanket to cover the dog, to conceal its wounds.

'The vet?' I ask.

'In Gavrik town,' he says. 'Put your foot down.'

I make a U-turn in the road, my tyres squealing, and drive on past the dried blood. The dog's breathing is fast and shallow.

'Kevlar armour did its job,' says the man. 'Collar did its job. Now it's time for the vet to do hers.'

I look through my rear-view mirror and the man has tears in his eyes and he is stroking the dog's ear, reassuring his friend.

I speed up and say, 'Shall I call them, to tell them we're coming?' but the man ignores my question and the dog whimpers and the man starts to sing. In a low tone, barely audible, the man starts to sing an ancient lullaby to his dying companion.

The most private of moments.

A haunting glimpse into the bond between these two. I stay quiet. I drive and I think about Noora. Shot in my own apartment. How she didn't jump back into the wall or scream or throw her arms back, but rather how she just went down where she stood. Crumpled on the spot. The lack of drama in that hideous moment. The silent panic on Tammy's face.

The man keeps on singing in his deep whisper and his dog groans and whines and the man smiles and looks up at me through my mirror.

'Thank you,' he says.

'Wolf attack?' I say.

'Goddam wolves,' he says. 'Menace.'

'You left your rifle in the grass back there.'

The man lets out a long sigh. 'It'll still be there when I go back to pick it up. That's the way it is round these parts.'

'Is the dog in pain?'

'He's in shock,' says the man. 'Bronco's his name. Still in shock.'

'Tuva Moodyson.'

'You what?'

'I'm Tuva Moodyson.'

'Oh,' says the man. 'Bengt Nyberg. Call me Nyberg.'

And then he carefully moves his dog on his lap and the dog yelps.

'There, boy,' says Nyberg. 'I'm sorry. You just rest yourself real easy, you let me do all the worrying for the both of us. Shush yourself and rest easy, my boy.'

The twin chimneys of the Grimberg Liquorice factory present themselves like a vanity statue built by some narcissistic despot. They rise and rise as we approach and then they stand, resolute and dominant, over the town of Gavrik.

I park right outside the door to the vet, next building over from Doc Stina's Vårdcentral surgery, and then I open the door for Nyberg and his dog.

'What breed is Bronco?' I ask.

'Swedish elkhound. Finest hunt dogs ever bred.'

We go inside and the receptionist sees the dog and runs off to find a vet. Three come out and usher Nyberg into a room, and a minute later Nyberg emerges without his dog. His face has aged a decade. He looks distraught and alone.

'I…' he says, swallowing hard. 'I'll leave them to their work. Thank you, Tuva. I want to thank you.'

I wave that away and sit down on a plastic chair by the organic, dry cat food and gesture for him to sit down next to me.

'What did they say?'

'Just that they'll take it from here and all I can do is wait.' He looks at me and he seems smaller now. Diminished. 'They say he's lost a lot of blood.'

'They're very good vets. Great reputation.'

He nods.

'I should have said before, I work for the *Gavrik Posten*. After Bronco's made a full recovery can I write something about this? Talk to you again?'

'I don't know,' he says, shaking his head.

'Because that collar and suit he was wearing probably saved his life, right? I think more people around here need to know about that. Maybe I could interview Benny Björnmossen from the hunt shop with you.'

'That's who sold me the Kevlar jacket and the collar,' says Nyberg.

'Might save some more dogs,' I say. 'Worth a try.'

'When you put it like that,' he says.

I pass him my card.

'What were you hunting this time of year?' I ask. 'Just between you and me.'

'Wasn't hunting,' he says. 'Can't hunt much in April. I was out looking for my cousin's girl, only twenty years old, she is.'

'She's missing?'

'Been missing a while,' says Nyberg. 'Works up at Rose Farm. You know the one? With all the solar panels and windmills and the moat. They've had wolf trouble in the past, as well. The farm with the big fence, you know it?'

I nod my head.

'Elsa's been working there on and off since she finished school. Well, they got a man called Abraham Viklund who runs the whole place.' Nyberg looks down at his bloodstained hands. 'And that's why I was carrying my rifle around in April. On account of Abraham.'

2

On the drive back to the office I pass two cross-country skiers. They spend all winter using their poles to push themselves around the local forest trails, and then when spring mercifully arrives they push themselves along the roads instead. Long, thin skis with wheels attached. Bloody hazards, the lot of them.

I park in my usual spot. There's no sign saying, '*Gavrik Posten*, Deputy Editor'. If there was such a sign, Nils would most likely deface it within a week.

In front of the Grimberg Liquorice factory the janitor sweeps under the arch entrance and nods solemnly to me as I pass by. We both remember what happened in that spot, although we've never talked of it since.

The doorbell tinkles as I step into the office and Lars says, 'Just in time for *Fika*.' He's arranged the cinnamon buns and cardamom buns and the coffee pot on Sebastian's desk and he's lit an Ikea tealight candle. He turns slowly to me and adjusts his bifocals and says, 'Have you been in a scuffle, Tuva? Are you okay?'

I look down at the blood on my cuffs.

'Dog blood,' I say.

'You've got a dog?'

I've worked with this guy on and off for almost half a decade and he knows full well I don't have so much as a gerbil.

'Killed it,' I say.

His mouth slowly drops open.

'Damn thing wouldn't stop barking.'

'You…'

I drag my finger across my throat.

'You…'

'She's winding you up, you daft old goat,' shouts Nils from his corner office, which doubles as the office kitchen. His door is open and I can see his socked feet up on his desk. 'Kommun wouldn't let Tuva Moodyson own a dog. Wouldn't allow it to happen.'

'I'm confused,' says Lars as he carefully rearranges the buns.

'Just an accident,' I say. 'Sorry, Lars. Dog was attacked by a wolf in the forest, north of Visberg, north of the sewage works. I think he'll be okay, but he lost a lot of blood.'

'I don't like blood,' he says. 'That's why I never went into medicine.'

'That's not the only reason,' yells Nils from the other room.

'*Fika* o'clock,' says Lars, breaking, slowly, very slowly, into a broad smile.

I wash my hands and Nils joins us from his corner office. His hair is gelled into spikes and he smells very powerfully of the cologne his wife bought him for Christmas. Someone came in trying to sell expensive laser printers last month and she told Nils he smelt very masculine. She told him it was a good, *musky* scent. And since then he's doused himself in the stuff each morning and inflicted it upon us each day. Oh, and, coincidentally, we now have an expensive new printer.

'That mutt gonna live?' asked Nils.

'Thanks to his coat and his collar,' I say.

'You make him sound like a vicar,' says Lars as he loosens the waistband of his elasticated cords.

'Kevlar armour,' says Nils. 'Benny Björnmossen told me it's one of the most high-margin items in his shop. Reckons high-calibre ammunition, German-made knives and dog armour are his best items.'

'Might sell more of them after this incident,' I say. 'Looks like the coat saved the dog's life.'

'Hunt dog, was it?' says Nils. 'Proper hunt dog, working dog, not a poodle in camo. The real deal was it?'

'Swedish elkhound, the owner told me.'

'Solid dogs,' says Nils. 'Reliable. Great stamina.'

Nils is one of those guys who knows everything about hunting but has never actually hunted anything. He's an expert in rifles and different patterns of camouflage but he's never so much as trapped a mouse before.

Lars pours us all coffee and I look over at Sebastian's mug.

'Told you he wouldn't stick around long,' says Nils.

'I thought he showed real promise,' says Lars.

Nils snorts and takes a cardamom bun.

'You didn't like him because he made you look short,' says Lars.

Nils straightens his back and looks like he'll say something, but then picks the pearl sugar from his bun and nibbles it between his front teeth.

'When's Lena back?' asks Nils.

'Tomorrow lunch,' I say. 'She's not just renegotiating the print costs, she's dropping by to see Noora, as well, to say hello.'

Both men look down at their plates. It's not their fault they don't know what to say about Noora. I hardly know what to say myself. Or what to think, even. I'm numb with the unending sadness of it all. Sometimes I'm paralysed by it. Speechless.

We eat in silence and we drink the last of the coffee.

'*Fika*'s over,' I say. 'Back to work, gentlemen.'

Usually Nils would say something about me not having rank over him despite my promotion, about how he only reports to Lena, but today he swallows it down and goes back to his office and closes the door.

'Have you ever heard of a man called Abraham Viklund, Lars? Lives on a farm north of Visberg hill.'

Lars deals with this request the same way he always does. Like a search engine attached to a 1994 dial-up modem. He frowns and looks at me and then looks away. Then he looks at me again and his eyes widen and then he dismisses the thought. He reaches down and scratches his shin. And then he says, 'Not that I know of.'

'Nyberg? Bengt Nyberg?' I ask.

'Sven's boy?'

'In his sixties, I'd say.'

'In that case, no.'

'Any chatter about a missing young woman today? Anyone said anything?'

'Missing?'

I nod.

He frowns and looks up at the ceiling for a moment. Then he scratches his nose and says, 'No.'

So I pick up my phone and place the octagonal foam attachment on the headpiece to my hearing aid and I ring the police station.

'Gavrik police, Thord Petterson speaking.'

'It's me.'

'Tuvs, I don't have long.'

'Missing girl, out Visberg way. Nyberg?'

'Sven's girl?'

'I don't know.'

'Nothing reported here, yet. This happens all the time. Maybe give it twenty-four hours and then chase it up.'

'What about...'

'Tuvs, I have to go, I'm sorry. Showing the Chief's boss's nephew around one of the Volvos. Kid wants to turn the sirens on. Anything important call me back in thirty minutes, okay?'

He calls off.

I google Bengt Nyberg. Retired technician. Thanks to Swedish tax returns and home addresses being public, I put his family tree together in less than a minute. He said it was the daughter of his cousin who went missing. I see three cousins. Two of them live down in Skåne. The other lives close to Rose Farm.

Her name is Elsa Nyberg.

She is twenty years old.

Give it twenty-four hours, said Thord.

Took a rifle because of Abraham, said Bengt Nyberg.

'Rose Farm,' I say out loud.

'What?' says Lars.

'Rose Farm, out Visberg way. Somewhere close to Snake River but not close to Snake River Salvage. Solar panels and high fences.'

'I heard what you said,' says Lars. 'And I know exactly where that place is.'

'You do?'

He looks out the window and then he looks back to me and shudders.

'You don't know?' he says, his tone flat.

I shake my head.

'You're not familiar with the story?'

I shake my head again.

'It was the year I arrived here in Gavrik. One of my first big stories at the *Posten*. When I think back to that funeral, I still don't know how to process it. Not out here in the sticks. That kind of thing isn't supposed to happen all the way out here.'

'What happened at Rose Farm, Lars?'

He starts to talk, but then he blows from his mouth and says, 'I need to take a walk round the block, get some air.' He looks nauseous. 'I'd buried those memories deep, Tuva. I'm sorry.'

Lars walks out with no coat on, which I have never seen him do in my life, not even in summertime, and the bell above the door tinkles.

I google Rose Farm, Visberg.

1987.

Newspaper reports in all the nationals. Front-page spreads. There's a one-hour documentary on YouTube about the farm. About what happened there. And there's a PhD thesis written by a student in Lund covering the psychology of the family in the lead up.

A horrific murder-suicide. Johan Svensson lived on Rose Farm with his wife and three children. On May 2nd 1987 Johan murdered his wife and their two eldest children.

Then he turned the shotgun on himself.

Only the newborn survived.

3

I save the address of Rose Farm and grab my coat and run out of the office.

Storgatan, the main street in town, is empty. Just because it's April doesn't mean it's warm. Last night we dropped down to minus seven, and tonight it's forecast to get colder still. There are still mounds of salted snow in the shadowy corners of the ICA Maxi car park, their chill trapped for another month or more.

I climb into my Hilux and switch on the heater. There are feathers tied to the dead bushes on the roundabout near Eriksgatan; feathers signifying Easter is two days away.

The drive east is quiet and featureless. The periphery of a childhood nightmare. Most of the plants are still dormant and the Värmland skies are as white as snowdrop petals. Thinking of Noora makes me numb. I've been numb for months.

When I reach the country lane dividing the easternmost part of Utgard forest from the westernmost part of Visberg forest, I slow my truck. I try to make out the blood splatter on the road but I can't see it. Dried from the cool easterly breeze. Soaked into the salty residue from last winter. I can drive at 5kpm here because there is no traffic. Not a single bus or saloon car. When you're approaching the edge of the map, it's not unusual to find yourself completely and utterly alone.

And then I see it.

Not the blood, rather the flattened grass on the verge where Bengt Nyberg's elkhound lay whimpering earlier today. The shape of the animal.

I pull over. History repeating itself. I get out and walk to the verge and I see the blood now, staining the bleached couch grass and ice-burnt foliage. The shape of a canine on its side. *Bronco.* Next to that, the twin indents in the earth of a man who knelt to give comfort to his wounded friend. And next to that, the long and unmistakable shadow of a rifle.

The gun has been taken.

By Bengt? Would the dog be awake by now after his operation? Would Bengt have had time to recover his firearm?

The sky is vast and it is as blank as a bedsheet.

I might be imagining it but I can smell gunpowder in the cool, spring air. It takes me back to that hellish day. My apartment, the place I had to leave for weeks because I couldn't face going back there. When the gun was fired that day and Noora fell to my kitchen floor, the sickly aroma of gunpowder filled the room and it was as if it replaced the oxygen and held the horrific scene in stasis. Time stopped. That 9mm bullet changed the world. My world, Noora's world, so many worlds. They all stopped spinning when the bullet left the barrel. And now Noora lies in a different bed. The ventilator has mercifully been removed and she can breathe on her own but that's about all she can do. No talking or moving. The woman I love is trapped within herself.

I walk back to the street, my cheeks damp. I never cried this easily before. When I was fourteen and Dad died, I didn't cry much at all. I couldn't. When Mum died, after all those years of sadness, it unleashed something. Broke the dam. So now I cry whenever I need it, and I'd give anything to see Noora cry, to see any sign that she was still with us.

Nine more kilometres to Rose Farm.

I've heard some people mention the farm but I've never visited. A friend of Tammy's goes there to get her hair cut and coloured, and Tammy went there for lunch one time and told me it was actually pretty good. Comfort food, lots of steaming-hot potatoes and sauce. It was well cooked.

The forests thicken.

Light leaves the sky and the shadows of pine trees rush to fill the void.

I'm not at the farm yet but I know it's coming. There's a fence, you see. Most places in Sweden are pretty relaxed about property boundaries. Lots of people don't bother with walls or fencing in the rural areas. But these guys sure do. On the side of the lane is a deep v-shaped ditch leading to a steep bank, topped off with a tall barbed-wire fence. Looks like a prisoner-of-war camp. Are they focused on keeping something out or keeping something in?

Could be wolves, I guess. If they're farming livestock, a pack of wolves could decimate their herds and flocks in minutes. A pack of efficient, ruthless killers working together. Domesticated doesn't stand a chance against wild. It never has and it never will.

The entrance is marked by some kind of gate with signs and CCTV cameras powered by their own individual solar panels. The gate is locked. Beyond is a spiked barrier laid across their access track. There are three signs on the gate. One says 'Open weekends. Weekdays by appointment only'. One says, 'You got the right to roam but best do it someplace else'. The third one says, 'Welcome to Rose Farm'. Inside the 'o' of Rose is a perfectly formed and realistic-looking bullet hole.

I take the hint and pull back on to the main road and park on the opposite side in an unfenced paddock. The paddock is more elevated than the lane and it affords me a better position to be a snoopy little bastard.

My Hilux smells of dog. It smells of blood and adrenaline and wolf scent and sweat.

Opposite me, Rose Farm is laid out like some kid's Lego creation. Bright colours and clear boundaries.

The access road, if you manage to gain access through their barriers, leads up to an ornate driveway flanked by old trees. On the left of the road is a brick stable yard and on the right side is a large red barn. I retrieve my binoculars from my glovebox and adjust the focus. The stable yard on the left has been split into two units. One has a mint-green sign that says, 'Ruby's Spa'. Next to it is a dimpled copper sign that reads, 'Rose Farm Organic Café'. To the right of the road is that dark red barn and other farm buildings and machinery. But if you drive up past the stable and farm you reach the house proper. Almost a manor house, but not quite. One large, pink wooden structure with two distinct wings. A manor *farm*. The shade of pink is subtle, almost a taupe. The house looks to be at least a hundred years old.

There are three wind turbines dotted around the property and numerous solar arrays. A man with stubble walks three guard dogs close to the red barn, and I wonder if the missing girl is here someplace. But then my mind turns to the historic murder-suicide. 1987. A father slaughtering his own family and then turning the weapon on himself.

A fist at my truck window.

4

'You lost?' he says, tapping on the glass.

His giant fist leaves an oily smudge on my window. The truck shakes. He must be two metres tall, this guy.

'I'm fine,' I say, smiling, locking the doors.

He walks round my Hilux with his snarling guard dog, like he's checking my tyres as some sort of inspection. And then he gestures for me to wind down my window.

'Asked if you were lost.'

'No, I said I'm fine.'

He stares at me. Large head with sad, doleful eyes. A scraggly ginger beard, short and patchy. Overalls. A little younger than me: twenty or twenty-five. A seed stuck in his moustache whiskers.

'You don't look fine.'

I open my window a crack. 'I'm fine, really. Came here for a walk is all.'

'For a walk?'

'I'm in rehab.'

He frowns at me.

'Back injury,' I say. And it's half true. My back has been spasming of late.

'Rehab's for drunks and junkies,' he says. 'You a drunk or a junkie?'

Both, shithead.

'Bad back,' I say.

He doesn't look convinced.

'You live around here?' I ask.

He nods towards Rose Farm.

'Farmer?' I ask.

'Walk someplace else,' he says.

This rankles me. It's a constitutional right in Sweden for every person to be able to walk wherever they like as long as it's not too close to someone's dwelling. You're even allowed to camp for a night or two on private land in rural areas if you're responsible.

'I'm going for a walk,' I say. 'Won't be on your farm.'

'Isn't my farm,' he says.

I can smell him through the window crack. Engine oil and sweat.

'I won't bother you,' I say.

'You already bothered me.'

With that I open the door of my Hilux and climb out and lock the door and start walking. With what I've been through this past year, what I'm still going through, I'm not in any mood to let an overgrown meathead order me around.

'Where you going now?' he asks.

I keep walking up the road, away from the entrance to Rose Farm.

'I said,' he says, running to catch me up, 'where you heading, lady?'

His dog barks twice and then pulls on its leash, trying to get closer to me.

'A walk,' I say. 'Just a walk.'

He passes me by and keeps the dog on a short leash.

'Andreas Olsson,' he says, his expression softening. 'Didn't mean to be unfriendly back there. Just that we're private people, is all.'

My neck loosens and I say, 'Tuva Moodyson.'

'Do I know you?'

'Reporter at the *Gavrik Posten*. We took over the *Visberg Tidningen* last year.'

'You took old Ragnar Falk's job, didn't you?'

It's more complicated than that. Lena and her husband bought the paper from Ragnar and combined it with the *Posten*. But I say, 'Yeah,' because it's easier.

We walk on for a hundred metres without either one of us saying anything. Then the dog stops to sniff a hole in the verge and Andreas says, 'Anatolian shepherd dog.'

'Sorry?'

'Jack here, he's an Anatolian shepherd dog. One of the best protector-dog breeds there is, if you ask me.'

'He's cute,' I say.

'He's not too cute when he sees a grey wolf threaten his territory, I'll tell you that much.' There is glee in Andreas's voice, some pride in his dog's ability, but his eyes are still tired and furtive.

'Lots of wolf attacks up here?'

'Kommun don't give us enough quotas, see. If we could hunt them right we'd keep them at bay. Thin out the packs. It's the government at fault. Meddling. They aren't hill people.'

'Are you a hill person? You live closer to Snake River than you do to Visberg.'

'Raised in Visberg town,' he says. 'Moved out to Rose Farm two years back.'

'What do you do if you don't farm?'

He scratches his beard.

'I mean, if you don't mind me asking.'

'I'm a groundsman, is all. Keep the gardens and ditches clear. Maintain the perimeter fences. I build stuff.'

'Talking to the police earlier about a missing girl,' I say.

He smiles.

'What?' I say.

'You got an agenda. I knew you would have.'

'Just saying, I heard a girl went missing on the farm.'

'Not *on* the farm.'

'No?'

'Elsa works here a few days a week but she hasn't gone missing on the farm. We run a tight ship in there.' He points through the high barbed-wire fence.

'You're not worried about her?'

'Elsa? No. She'll be in Ronnie's Bar flirting with some guy from the pulp mill, same as usual. She's a flirt, plays with guys, you know the kind.' Then he says something I can't understand.

'Sorry, what did you say? I'm deaf. Can't hear you clearly.'

'You're deaf?' he says, stopping in his stride and patting his dog's head.

I nod.

'Deaf, deaf?'

I nod again.

'And yet you can hear what I'm saying?'

'Hearing aids.'

'So you aren't real deaf? Just a little smidge.'

'I'm deaf.'

'A bit deaf.'

He'll be lucky to avoid a kick in the dick at this rate.

'Police reckon Elsa Nyberg went missing on Rose Farm,' I say, lying to see his reaction. 'They're sure of it.'

'They don't know one end of a farm from the other,' he says. 'Incompetent, the gang of them. One policewoman got herself shot to death just last year. You ever heard of such a thing, thought the cops were supposed to be armed and ready but not the Gavrik police, nope.'

Now I'm the one who stops walking.

'Noora Ali is my girlfriend. She's not dead, she's just very, very sick.' My voice breaks. 'And she wasn't on duty when she was attacked, so mind what you say about her in my company.' I spit the last few words out and he senses the rage in my eyes.

'Didn't mean nothing by it,' he says. 'I never knew all that. I'm real sorry.'

I swallow. 'Okay.'

'I'm not a stranger to sudden losses. I am sorry, Tuva.'

I set off walking again and he hangs back a little way.

'What's that in the distance?' I say.

'That hut down the river a piece?'

'Yeah.'

'Just an abandoned fishing cabin is all. Locked up. Can't get to it from the road, marsh all around, only access is from Snake River itself.'

'Could Elsa be hiding out there?'

'Nope.'

I look at him.

'How can you be so sure?'

'Because I monitor this whole place twenty-four-seven is why. I'm patrolling with my dogs or else someone is. Elsa's a nice person, but she isn't hiding in Rosebud Cottage and I can tell you that like it's gospel.'

'Rosebud Cottage?'

'The fishing cabin. She isn't there.'

'Can I come on to your farm, Andreas? Just for an hour. I'd like to check out the spa and get a coffee in the café. Buy you a coffee maybe?'

'Closed,' he says. 'Open weekends only.'

'Or by appointment,' I say.

'You don't have no appointment,' he says.

A trio of geese squawk and beat their wings and glide down to the surface of the river and settle neatly into the ice-cold waters.

'Do you work for Abraham Viklund?' I ask.

Andreas rubs his brow.

'Is he your boss?'

'That's not how it is,' he says.

'Maybe Abraham is taking care of Elsa Nyberg, could that be it?'

Andreas bites his lip and his dog starts to growl and froth from its jowls.

'She isn't…' he says, blinking fast, 'she isn't with him.'

'How can you be sure?'

He exhales through his nose. 'Because nobody's seen Abraham Viklund for six whole years, that's how.'

5

Andreas watches me drive away, back towards Visberg. In my mirrors I see him standing there, all two metres of him, with his angry dog, staring, waiting for me to get well away from him and Rose Farm.

The afternoon is turning into evening and whatever warmth there was has been sapped from the air.

I hope she turns up, this Elsa Nyberg. I hope she's taken a lover and run away to a cheap hotel in a faraway town. That they're lying under crisp sheets that have been industrially laundered so many times they're wearing thin. Her in the crook of his arm. Him telling her stories and her telling him better ones. The pair of them alone, as far as humanity is aware. Two lovers intertwined and worrying about nothing whatsoever.

The road is empty.

Orange plastic poles, still deep in the earth, each side of the asphalt from last winter; markers that delineate the safe and man-made from the dangerous and wild. You have to stay inside of the guide poles. You have to stay on the road.

I drive and I feel out of balance, worse than before. A missing girl, and my love, who's being fed through a tube directly into her stomach. And some people say there's a god.

The Grimberg factory chimneys glow warm in the setting sun.

I park outside my office but I do not go in. Instead I cross the street to the hunt store. The stuffed brown bear, some unfortunate giant shot by Benny Björnmossen and stuffed by Sally out at Snake River Salvage, gawps at me with his rictus smile.

No customers in the shop.

'Oh, it's you.'

'Hi, Benny.'

'Hi, yourself.'

'How's business?'

'How's *business*?'

'Yeah.'

Benny takes the cap off his head and scratches his hair and then replaces the cap and says, 'Been better.'

'I've just been out north, close to Rose Farm.'

He straightens a pack of clear fishing line on the wall and says nothing.

'Have you ever been out there at Rose Farm, Benny?'

'Not that I recall.'

'You know what kind of operation they run up there? Looks like Fort Knox from the outside.'

'Farming,' says Benny. 'It's a farm. Clue's in the name.'

'They had a massacre up there in the '80s.'

He stops arranging the fishing hooks, looks at me and says, 'Yes, they did.'

'Shotgun.'

He grumbles something.

'From your store?'

'Why are you asking?'

'Just curious.'

He licks his lips and puts his hands inside his Marlboro Man jacket and says, 'All that was well before my time, see. Lived out Trollhättan way, back then.'

'You hear about the girl gone missing?'

'I heard it.'

'What do you think?'

'Does it matter what I think?'

I shrug.

'I think we'll see, is what I think. Old Bengt Nyberg told me about it just this past hour on the telephone. Told me you helped try to save his Bronco, too.'

'Did what I could.'

'Good dog, Bronco.'

'The girl?'

'Nyberg was out looking for her up in the river plains around Rose Farm, she works up there doing this thing and that. He ain't too concerned, says she's gone AWOL a time or two before this. Not like when your friend from the food van went missing last Midsommar, this'll be different, mark my words.'

'I hope so.'

'It'll work out alright. If she'd had a dog with her, I might have worried about the wolves out there, but she doesn't have a dog. She'll turn up.'

'What do you know about Rose Farm?'

'Why don't you go bother them about it instead of asking me?'

'Nils told me your ads are up for review this summer. New payment plan, new deal. Reckon I can swing you something sweet, now I'm deputising Lena.'

He blows air through his teeth and changes the sign on the door from 'Open Season' to 'Gone Fishing'.

'Better take a seat then.'

He points to two folding, camp chairs, each with integrated cup-holders, arranged by a tent and a fake campfire, consisting of strips of yellow paper blown up by a small fan.

'Comfy,' I say, sitting down.

'You break it, you buy it.'

'The farm?'

Benny wipes his nose on the sleeve of his jacket and then stretches his legs out towards the fire – some kind of muscle memory.

'People,' he says. 'Some people don't know much or care much if the outside world exists one day to the next. Folks up on that farm live by themselves for themselves. Well, that's to admire in a certain way, self-sufficiency and all. Self-reliance. Living as a pack. But when it comes to it lack of interest is as good as lack of care when all is said and done. They look inward, you get my meaning.'

'Like a commune?'

'I didn't say that, you did. It's just that if all this ended, all of us went up as dust, that Rose Farm team wouldn't likely find out about it for weeks. And when they did hear the news they'd likely shrug and carry on with their business. I'm a country man, you know that. I'm all for the old ways. But you gotta think about community when it comes down to it. No man is an island and no group is diverse enough to sustain itself ad infinitum.'

I check the price tag of the chair I'm sitting in: 300 kronor.

'They call their boss Abraham.'

'I ain't never met the man.'

'You've heard about him, though.'

'I only had contact with Linda Larsson, she runs the café up there. Decent food, as it goes. And I sold some merchandise to big Andreas as well, the gardener.'

'I met him today.'

Someone rings Benny's mobile and after a while Benny replies with, 'Thirty-five calibre hollow points but you better move quick on them.'

'You like Andreas, the gardener?' I ask.

'Like him? Like's got nothing to do with it.'

'He seem okay to you?'

'No comment.'

'Oh, come on.'

Benny breathes in deep and takes out a pocket knife and starts to clean his nails with its tip.

'Between you me and the wind, he's got some history up in Visberg town, few years ago now I'm talking. Some kind of misdemeanour with a young girl, back when they was both at school. Formal complaints. Reckon the Sheriff up there handled it.'

'Sheriff Hansson, the taxi driver?'

'Unless you know of another sheriff in hill town?'

Fair point.

'Andreas was a big lump even back then, had to duck just to get through my door. You seen him, so you know. And the talk was he wasn't too gentle with this girl, and she got scared. Don't think it was much more than that, but you know small towns, an incident like that is all you need to stain you for life. For your children's lives, too. So that's why Andreas moved out to Rose Farm. Sanctuary for him in a way. He gets a quiet life, and the girls of Visberg town don't have to worry no more. I'd say everyone was satisfied with how it all played out.'

'Until now,' I say.

Benny nods and locks his knife shut. 'Yeah,' he says. 'Until now.'

6

I step out on to Storgatan and the Grimberg chimneys look heavy against the plain grey sky.

Inside the office Lars has already gone home for his Friday-night lactose-free, gluten-free, vegan tacos and his Netflix comedy special. You have to love the man.

Nils is working on the owner of the health food shop, trying to talk him into some special bulk-discount deal for his adverts, droning on about circulation numbers and community engagement. But credit where credit's due: he's still hard at it past 5pm on a Friday. That's what living in a marginal, isolated town will do to you. Think about it; it's not like he could just waltz into a newspaper ad-salesman job somewhere else in Toytown now, is it?

I dredge social media for the friends of the missing girl, Elsa Nyberg. I find the two girls she shares most of her selfies with, pull their names, cross-reference, note down their mobile-phone numbers. I pull up her father's number and address. He lives a few kilometres east of Rose Farm. Nearest building, in fact. Next-door neighbours.

'Leif Nyberg.' His voice is gruff.

'*Hej*, Leif, it's Tuva Moodyson calling, from the *Gavrik Posten*.'

'It ain't convenient.'

'Can I just ask you a few…'

'I said, it ain't convenient.'

He hangs up.

I call Elsa's friend, Kristina.

No answer.

I dial again.

Nothing.

I text her *Hi, I'm Tuva Moodyson from the* Gavrik Posten *newspaper. I'm trying to look for your friend, Elsa Nyberg. Please text or call.*

The bell rings above the door.

A man steps in off the street and he's carrying a rifle. His hat obscures his eyes.

Nils opens the door from his office, sees the man with the gun and goes back inside and closes the door.

I stand up, lifting my hands in the air.

The man shakes his head.

'Please,' I say.

He shakes his head some more. Adjusts his hat. It's Bengt Nyberg.

'I don't know what to do,' he says. 'I should never have…'

'Please,' I say again. 'Put down the gun.'

His lip is shaking.

'Mr Nyberg.'

'Bronco didn't survive the surgery, see,' he says. And then he starts to weep.

I take a breath.

'I'm so, so sorry.'

'He was eleven years old. It was too much for his system, the vet said.'

'He was a handsome dog,' I say.

'Too much for him to take.'

Bengt looks at me and smiles through his tears.

'Could you just place the rifle on my desk. It's making me nervous.'

He places it on my desk.

'Those wolves can go to hell.'

I nod and walk over and pat his shoulder. 'I'm sorry.'

'Had him since he was a pup. Eight weeks. I wanted to come in here to say thank you, Miss Moodyson. I just wanted to say that to your face, see.'

'You don't need to…'

'Oh yes, but I do. Bronco wasn't in any pain thanks to you, still under the anaesthetic when he slipped away. Didn't feel nothing, the vet told me. No pain.'

I don't say anything. In this moment, in this office, the world has shrunk down to just the two of us. An old man and a young woman joined together through the death of a Swedish elkhound. The man is feeling his own pain and I'm feeling mine. Conflicted, and guilty as hell that in some ways, if I'm honest with myself, it may have been better for Noora to have gone this way. To have died, with no pain. Back when the ambulance took her to hospital, the kind paramedic talking me through what I could do to help – monitor her vitals, remove a syringe from its packet, talk to her – I yearned with my whole body and my spirit for Noora to live. And now, sometimes, when I can face the thought, I wonder if I yearned for completely the wrong thing. Now, as she lies in a bed in her parents' house in Gothenburg, them caring for her 24/7, feeding her through a tube, watching for any signs of consciousness, awareness, I wonder what would really be best for the person I adore.

I feel myself starting to lose it and Bengt steps back away from me and clears his throat and says, 'Didn't mean to upset you. Maybe I shouldn't have come in here. I'm not thinking straight.'

'It's fine.'

'I'll never forget it, you know,' he says. 'You letting a stupid old man and his bloody dog muck up your nice new truck. No questions asked. I'll never forget that kindness.'

'Will you be okay?'

He nods. 'Lost my wife, Klara just last year, see. You'd think I'd feel nothing for the old dog. But he was my companion. Daft bugger I must sound to you, but Bronco was a gentle dog. Used to lie across my slippers when I'd watch the ice hockey. He'd sleep. Snore something terrible. I liked the weight of him there.'

'Pop into the office anytime you fancy, if you want a chat in future,' I say. 'Usually there's not much news in this town so feel free to drop by.'

Bengt gestures to Nils's door. 'Scared him, did I?'

'Yeah.'

'Sorry.'

'Not the bravest.'

'Gathered that.'

I smile.

'Sorry, nonetheless. I'll leave you in peace now.'

He touches the brim of his camouflage hunt cap and picks up his rifle and leaves into the dusk.

Nils emerges.

'You've got bad friends,' he says.

'Thanks for saving me, shithead.'

'I was preparing my ambush.'

An hour later I'm back in my apartment.

It took me six weeks to be able to step foot back in here. I doubted I'd ever sleep here again. If it wasn't for little Dan next door, I'd have moved out immediately. It's awful. The knowledge that Noora was shot in my own home. The aftermath. But in a perverse way I feel close to her. I can't explain it but it seems right for me to be here. And at night, when I wake from a fitful sleep, dozy and warm, I imagine she's in the bathroom or making hot milk in the kitchen. And then the realisation dawns on me that she can't do any of those things. She can't focus her eyes or eat from a spoon. She isn't really here anymore. Not really.

I remove my hearing aids and feel the instant relief.

Hot shower. Clean T-shirt and pyjama bottoms. ICA Maxi meatballs, toast and lingonberry jam.

There are no arguments from the next-door apartment because the excuse for a husband has moved out. Dan and his mum are doing better these days. I'm tempted to check on him more often. More for me, if I'm honest, than for them. But I know they need time to rebuild their safe haven and to reconnect. They need the space to relax. I take Dan for a night or two each week to let his mum work or do whatever she needs to do. And they are my favourite nights of the week. Sometimes I get Tammy over at the same time and the comfort that brings me is unimaginable. My best friend and my favourite kid. They watch a movie and I just watch the two of them. Pure goodness, both.

I see my phone ringing so I grab my hearing aids but by the time I've inserted one of them the phone call has ended.

It was Thord.

I call him back.

'The missing girl you talked about, Elsa Nyberg.'

'I thought you said she wasn't missing,' I say.

'She is now.'

7

I sit on my IKEA sofa staring at a wall I haven't had time to decorate. White space. The absence of anything personal or ornamental. I may as well be gawping into the abyss.

Thord said Elsa Nyberg was last seen two days ago. He said she never turned up to work at Linda Larsson's organic café on Rose Farm, and she never turned up to work at Kurt Holm's Barns on Rose Farm. Linda told Thord it wasn't uncommon for Elsa not to turn up – said she was a miscreant and a lazybones. Kurt told Thord that Elsa's a reliable worker and a friend of the farm. Someone's lying.

I open a can of red Coke because I don't plan on getting any sleep anytime soon. The sweet bubbles slide right down and I wish they had rum with them. I don't drink on Fridays. Them's the rules. I'm the kind of high-functioning I-don't-even-know-what that forges deals with herself. I negotiate. I negotiate hard. And the end result this time was that I get to drink on weekends. As much as I damn well please. Except for the weekends when I visit Noora at her parents' house and then I don't touch a drop. She sleeps in her parents' bedroom now. She has her own hospital-type bed with a special mattress that prevents sores. Her parents watch her continually. Noora's had two seizures since she moved back home, and even though both her parents were medics back when they lived in Iraq it's hard for them. They know exactly what to do on a technical level, but it's their own daughter for God's sake.

Thord also told me how Elsa's father – a cousin of Bengt Nyberg, the elkhound man – found a one-ounce gold coin in his daughter's bedroom. Said she has no money, makes minimum wage and has no savings. And yet he found a gold Kruggerrand under Elsa's bed. It was in a clear plastic capsule.

I google *one-ounce kruggerrand* and find the current market price is seventeen-thousand kronor. My phone screen says seventeen-hundred dollars but the exchange rate at roughly 10:1 makes things easy on me. That's a lot of value for a twenty-year-old waitress and farmhand. It's more value than I have in my bank account right now.

The clock says eight-thirty, so I have another hour until it's time.

I lie on my bed and force myself not to look at the photos on my bedside table. It's not the one of Tam and me down by the reservoir that hurts. It's not the one of Mum and Dad that I brought home from my storage locker in Karlstad on Christmas Day, when everyone else was eating ham and singing with their families and I was huddled in an ICA ski jacket reading letters from Dad to Mum from the '80s, and laughing, and sobbing through the laughing. It's not that photo I'm avoiding today. It's the one of Noora. A selfie she took last year outside Ronnie's Bar on Storgatan. Her goofing around with snowflakes settling on her hair. An image I asked her to message me. An image I had printed. An image I cherish. An image so beautiful it'll wipe out the whole weekend if I give into temptation and pick it up and hold it and stare at it. So I keep my gaze low.

I research the murder-suicide of 1987 on my iPad. I tap into three regional newspaper articles and a well-written story in *Svenska Dagbladet*. From what I can glean, the father was having financial difficulties. He had a wife and three children and an idyllic manor farm by a river in rural Värmland. He was a speculator in the options markets, operating by phone and later on by fax machine. The man wrote pieces for prestigious Nordic financial periodicals and was guest speaker at the Stockholm School of Economics. He was the kind of person who had it all, at least that's what it looked like from the outside. In practice his speculations swung from success to failure, and despite his wife pleading with him to stop, pleading for him to downsize, to reduce the stress on the family, he perceived any such downsizing as a failure. He wouldn't countenance the idea of giving up Rose Farm, or his family's expensive ski holidays in Verbier, or his wife's new BMW, or the beautiful horses they kept on the property. The lies spun out of control. The debts grew. The interest rates rose. It seems that the father felt trapped in a web of his own making. And, despite an infinite number of better options, he chose to end his life instead of ending his lifestyle. And he took his wife and their two eldest children along with him on that horrific journey.

I open another red Coke and a fresh pack of digestive biscuits.

There was a lot written about why the father spared the youngest, a child of four weeks. Perhaps it was that they were too angelic-looking at that age, too obviously innocent, and he couldn't bring himself to pull the trigger. Or maybe it was that some hideous bargain was struck between him and his wife: some unthinkable agreement where she begged for the lives of her children and he rejected her pleas. And then he came to the cold, rational conclusion that whereas his older boys would know of their father's failings, would remember them and talk of them, the baby would never know. Not directly. Perhaps that agreement was made before the first shots were fired. Perhaps evil does walk the earth after all.

Rose Farm, in total some four-hundred hectares of arable land and riverside forest, was sold to a company out of Norrköping the year after the tragedy. Then, in 2013, it was sold to another company, this one registered in Stockholm. I bring up the company records. Two directors: Therese Viklund and Abraham Viklund. A few clicks later I've ascertained that Therese used to be a successful and highly sought-after management consultant in central Stockholm, specialising in company rescues and turnarounds. She was seen as a leader in her field, despite her young age. I can find no recent photographs of her, but back then she was very attractive, in an ice-queen kind of way. A straight fringe, thick brown hair, very little make-up, cheekbones to die for, full lips. Abraham is three years her senior. He studied or worked at the Sibelius Academy of Music in Helsinki, the Conservatoire de Bordeaux in France, the Hochstein School in New York and the Franz Liszt Academy of Music in Hungary. Back in his twenties, he composed several celebrated violin concertos. And then he dropped off the map. I check his details and it looks like he doesn't work, doesn't claim unemployment benefit, doesn't have a driver's licence, doesn't earn any money or pay any taxes. So what *does* Abraham Viklund do? Who is this man?

Google Maps allows me to view Rose Farm from the air.

The main manor farmhouse, pink, with its two freestanding wings a few metres from the main building. Above it is Snake River. Below it, to the left, is the old stableblock I spotted today: the café and the spa. Below the main house and to the right is the big red barn and myriad sheds and vegetable gardens. There's a smaller dwelling close to the river surrounded by a wall, and then Rosebud Cottage a mile or so to the east, sat upon what looks like an island shrouded in reed beds.

I search all the inhabitants registered at the property. I already know about Abraham and Therese Viklund, the owners. The other residents are Ruby Gunnarsson, thirty-eight, a South African citizen and owner of the spa and beauty salon in the stables. Ruby is married to Niklas Gunnarsson, thirty-four, a travelling salesman. Niklas is also an admin of a popular survivalist forum. Linda Larsson, fifty-five, is the proprietor of the Organic Café. Kurt Holm, sixty-one, is the owner of Holm Seeds, an heirloom producer based in that big red barn. And then Andreas Olsson, twenty-seven, is the giant groundsman I met. Andreas also runs a very basic website where he sells a litter of Anatolian puppies every six months or so.

The property looks like any other Swedish farm.

Until you look closer.

I zoom in and I have never seen so many barriers and fences. Complex systems of ditches and dykes more sophisticated than the ones I spotted from my truck. There are small sheds on top of rocks and some of them have tall antennas.

The alarm on my phone goes off.

I turn off my iPad and brush my teeth and get ready for bed.

Then I lie down and glance at the photo of the woman I miss. My phone vibrates. A FaceTime call comes through from her mother.

'Tuva, how was your day?'

'It was fine, thanks,' I say, smiling; forcing the smile. 'How are you all? How was Noora today?'

'Oh, fair,' she says. 'Left hand a little better. Some more focus when we stand at her side, we think. It's difficult to say. Feeding well, though.'

'Good,' I say. And the word feels all kinds of wrong as the word leaves my lips.

'I'll leave you two alone,' she says. 'Goodnight to you both.'

I watch as she kisses the forehead of her twenty-seven-year-old police constable daughter and leaves the room. Noora is lit from a bedside table lamp. It's a warm, gentle light.

'Hello, my love,' I whisper, tears swelling my eyes. 'I missed you today.'

There is no reaction. I still search for it, for a flicker of her pupil or a muscle movement at her mouth. But there is nothing. The doctors say there's a slim chance she might be able to hear us, to understand. Despite the substantial damage to her brain from the injury and the swelling. She might be able to process thoughts. But they doubt it.

I imagine myself in Noora's situation, friends reading to me, talking to me in case I could understand. Only, I'd probably never know. Would the medical team put my hearing aids in? Tammy could be saying things, reassuring words, and I'd be all alone. The thought of it makes me shudder.

I kiss the screen of my phone. And then I start to read.

Stories are too difficult. Too long and too troubling, somehow. So I read poetry to Noora. I read sonnets from Shakespeare and Yeats, and poems from Mulla Effendi. I read to her and I'm not sure if I want her to be able to hear my words, or if I want her not to be able to know what's going on. One doctor, a wise, old Polish man, told me that science understands the deep cosmos far better than we understand our own minds. They are the last true frontier: the cells where the dividing lines between evidence-based science and spirituality blur. If there is a soul, he told me, you'd find it deep inside the brain.

I stop reading.

'Goodnight, my love.'

I lay my head down on my pillow. The phone is wedged close to my nose. We are together in some wretched sense of the word.

We are together.

8

I wake up renewed.

My phone is programmed to switch itself off after a certain time. The screen is blank. Her parents would have turned off her light. Kissed her forehead one last time.

I shower, eat the one digestive I have left, and leave my apartment.

Gavrik town is hushed: early morning strollers out with their kids still resting on sheepskin rugs in their buggies, and joggers out running past the Toytown shoe shop with their dogs keeping rhythm.

I head east towards Visberg and then, after Svensson's Saws & Axes, but before the big hill, I turn north into what looks like oblivion.

In a wilderness country like Sweden you get a strange feeling in the pit of your stomach when you consciously decide to turn off the road and head deeper into nature. Some primal instinct honed over millennia warning you to be on your guard, to watch your peripheral vision, to stand ready for predators crouching in the shadows and the hollows.

The pines of Utgard forest on my left and Visberg forest on my right. Each tree as formidable as a cold-war nuclear missile or the mast of a Spanish man-o'-war from a different age.

I emerge from the woods and follow the meandering curves of Snake River for a while. We're far from the salvage site and the waterway is narrower here.

Narrow and deep.

Nature doesn't make much sense this time of year. On my right there's a field. I'm not saying that the wild things are green yet, that's all just starting up. Mostly the landscape is still browns and greys, backdropped by pure white. But the weeds are presenting themselves. Fighting skyward. The dandelions and switch grass are probing for sunrays and the birch leaves, tiny and mostly still in tight bud away from all but the sunniest positions, are a hazy cloud of pale lilac.

The field is there, the white field.

Locals call it the ice cube or *snowberg*.

The municipal trucks and ploughs, used throughout winter to scoop up salted ice and snow from Visberg and Gavrik, transport it here, week after frozen week, and dump it in this field. I drive closer. Much of the snow has melted but there's still a thousand tons here, maybe ten thousand. It's eight degrees outside, but this nonsensical man-made glacier persists, thanks to the chill trapped within itself. Puddles form on top, some the size of carp ponds. But the baseline is ice-cold. The structure persists because of itself, and the earth below will still be permafrost come Midsommar.

The barbed wire of the Rose Farm perimeter fence sparkles in the sun as I approach.

I slow my Hilux close to the single entryway and the barriers are open and the road is clear so I drive on at 5kpm because there's a homemade sign instructing me to do just that.

My truck trundles forward on gravel, my boot off the accelerator.

Ahead of me, the elegant pink manor house with its wings. Six chimneys on the main building. An ornate chimney on each wing. To the left are the brick stables and to the right is the red barn. I choose left.

Ruby's Spa is closed and shuttered, so I park up and wander over to the organic café. It's called Rose Farm Organic Café, it has no other name as far as I can tell.

The windows have been recently cleaned. I peer in through the glass. Around a dozen tables inside and a counter and a kitchen beyond. Surprising this place can break even way out here. Come to think of it, it's a miracle any of these businesses break even.

'You looking for a hearty breakfast, my dear?' says a voice I cannot place.

'Er, yes, please,' I say, looking around. 'Where are you?'

'Up here.'

I look up and there's a woman on the roof of the stables with a harness around her waist and a cleaning brush in her hand.

'Gutters,' she says. 'I'll be down presently.'

I wait a while and then she emerges from inside, opening the doors wide and announcing, 'Beautiful day, isn't it. Where have you come out from?'

'Gavrik.'

'Ah, big-city girl.'

'Less than nine thousand residents,' I say, smiling.

'We got seven residents and sometimes that's six too many.' She smiles a warm smile and squeezes her eyes together and beckons me in.

'I got fresh granola I made just last night if it's of interest, else there's coffee cake warm from the oven, or maybe a fruit salad. And then there's whatever else you see here.'

What I can see is a counter full of filled rolls, sliced meats and cheeses, and cinnamon rolls.

'A slice of that coffee cake, please. And a coffee.'

'Woman after my own heart. Let me help you with that.'

There are no prices on anything and I can't see a cash register anywhere.

'My name is Tuva Moodyson,' I say.

'Linda Larsson,' she says. 'There you go, my dear.' She places a plate with coffee cake topped with coffee icing and sliced walnuts on the counter and starts to make me fresh coffee from the machine. She has a sleeve of tattoos all up one arm, the kind a special forces commando might be proud of. 'Sit anywhere you like.'

I take it outside and sit facing the red barn in the distance.

The cake is amazing. The coffee flavour is strong and the bitterness complements the sweet icing perfectly. A light-texture bake with a little crunch from the walnuts. All washed down with hot coffee.

The spa is still closed.

A huge figure on the hill walks around aimlessly with a plank of wood on his chest; it's attached around his neck with thick rope.

'That's our groundsman, Andreas,' says Linda. 'He's in training.'

'Training for what?'

'Exercising, I mean. Carries that wood around. Sometimes I do the same, it's a good workout.'

'Think I'll need a workout after eating your cake. It really is delicious.'

'Thank you. That's kind.'

'One of your neighbours told me a girl's gone missing. Sorry, not a girl, a young woman. Elsa Nyberg?'

Her posture changes.

'We don't have any neighbours.'

'Someone from down the road, then.'

'Don't know anyone down this road, truth be told. But I do know Elsa. Complex girl. Not the first time she's taken herself off on an adventure without telling anyone. I don't expect it'll be the last, either.'

'She works here?'

'If you can call it work. She sulks around the cakes and looks at her telephone a lot.'

'So you're not worried about her?'

'Elsa? No, not in the slightest. That girl flirts all day and every day. Doesn't even care who she's flirting with most of the time.' Linda glances up at Andreas patrolling with his plank of wood. 'Seen her up on that snowberg one time, laid out on blanket with a married man from Visberg. I asked her what had gotten into her head, and she told me she was recreating the ice-hotel experience, because it's not like she'll ever do it for real, not on what I pay her each hour. Cheeky l'il bitch.'

'Do you know if the spa will be open today? Want to buy a package for my friend.'

'Maybe in an hour,' says Linda. 'Ruby isn't one for early mornings. She's from South Africa, see.'

'So?'

Linda smiles and says, 'They got it easier over there with all the sun and good living. Not used to rising as early as us Swedes. When the land is frozen solid half the year, you gotta get up early and go catch yourself a worm. I'm here by five most mornings.'

'Five. Wow. Where do you live, Linda?'

She points to the wing on the left of the manor farmhouse.

'Nice place.'

'It's okay,' she says. 'But I spend most of my time here in the stables. I'm not much of a house cat.'

'Does someone live here at the stables? I can see a small, private garden and hot tub over there.'

'You sure do ask a lot of questions.'

'Sorry,' I say. 'I'm reporter at the *Gavrik Posten*. Just curious, I guess.'

'Just curious, you guess.'

'So nobody lives here?'

'Ruby and her man Niklas live there, upstairs. This is a community on Rose Farm.'

'Does that work out okay, living and working together?'

'Ruby I got no issues with. Niklas, on the other hand, he's got a mean streak I don't like one bit.'

'What do you mean?'

She scratches the area above her lip and says, 'I shouldn't talk out of turn.'

I stay silent. One of Lena's best tricks. Instead of talking I look up at the apartment above the spa, and then back to Linda.

'You know how some men will choke a dog a little bit to let it know who the boss is?'

'I guess.'

'Well, that's all a matter of degree. It's a matter of self-restraint. Andreas over there, Andre the giant I call him, he's very handy with dogs, they like him, trust him. But Niklas, on the other hand, I saw him punch a dog square in the face one time and ever since then I haven't trusted him one iota.'

9

A couple arrives for coffee and cloudberry pie. When they've both sat down with their trays I walk up to Linda and say, 'I'm kind of restless today. Okay if I walk around the farm a little?'

She looks me up and down. 'Free country.'

I nod.

'Outside of our perimeter, that is. Inside it you're our guest. You can walk over to the spa, see if Ruby's dragged her butt out of bed yet, but I wouldn't stray much further than that if I was you. This place is a business, sure, but it's also home to seven of us. It's our home.'

'I'll go see Ruby, then.'

'Yeah, you do that.'

I head through an old stable yard and push against the gate. The spa is still closed. The sign on the door says, 'Welcome To Ruby's. Open.'

I try the door.

Locked.

I step out on to the dirt track I drove in on. The manor farmhouse up the hill glows soft pink and the green copper roof gives the place an air of the unreal: a fairy hall built for river sprites out of spruce resin and pine needles.

Across the way is the red barn, or barns, each one adorned with something or other. Can't tell from this distance. I walk closer. There's a man in the distance sat on a deckchair with a small table next to him.

I keep on walking, the morning sun heating one side of my face.

'Hello,' I yell. 'Is it okay if I come over?'

No response.

I can see now that he's painting with a long artist's brush. Painting on to a flat, wooden board. Painting dark shades with flicks of his plaid-shirt-coated wrist.

'You mind if I approach?' I say, which seems ridiculous in Sweden, but Linda was pretty clear.

Still no response. Perhaps he's deaf like me. The painting isn't of his livestock, at least I don't think it is. The wooden board is almost completely black. Flourishes of grey and vermillion, sprays of incandescent yellow, but on the whole the composition is like the bottom of a well. I'm careful not to startle him, but I move into his field of vision; not between him and his cows, just closer.

'Sorry to bother you,' I say.

'You been botherin' me ever since you left Ruby's beauty parlour over yonder.'

'I'm Tuva Moodyson,' I say.

'Don't mean much to me.'

'I'm a reporter at the *Gavrik Posten*.'

He smirks and pushes the heel of his hand across the board, leaving black paint all over his skin and an arc across his paining.

'Mainstream media,' he says.

Hardly, mate.

'Community newspaper,' I say.

'You here about the maniac killed all his kiddies back in the '80s, are you? New documentary on the TV, is it? He ain't here no more. Banker blew his own head off. You gotta look deep underground to find his soul, may he rest in eternal damnation.'

Black oil-paint drips off the man's hand and lands in the dirt.

'That supposed to be cows?' I ask, gesturing to his work.

He smiles. 'Maybe it is. Never know what I'm working on till I got it done finished. Except this piece was interrupted.'

'Shame,' I say. 'I liked it.'

'You paint, lady?'

'I used to, a little. Watercolours, mainly.'

'On paper?'

I nod.

'Could never get used to all that bleeding. The way the colours morph and settle, mix and move. Never the same from one minute to the next. Makes me uncomfortable.'

'That's what I liked about it.'

He stands up and wipes his hand on his dungarees and then he offers it to me.

Do I take it?

I take it.

'Tuva.'

'Kurt Holm. Folks round here tend to call me T-Bone.'

I frown.

'Kurt Holm, T-Bone, I guess.'

'Coolest name ever,' I say.

'No complaints.'

'This your farm?'

'Is this my farm?'

'Is it?'

'I don't own nothing, haven't done since Pernilla passed.'

'But you work here?'

'Guess you could call this here a situation of mutual convenience, on more levels than I'm at liberty to talk of. I work here, run the farming operations for the Viklund family. Specialise in heirloom seeds. I get board and benefits, prefer a simple life myself. I'm built for it. The solitary, the quiet, the animals rather than the people. Me and my art. I cannot abide a crowd, never have been able to.'

His hair is dyed jet-black and is combed back and held in place with pomade.

'I don't like crowds, either.'

'Bully for you.'

'Because of my deafness. Can't hear straight if too many people are talking at once.'

'I'm similar. Only I can't *think* straight. My mamma told me I thought in straight lines, one subject at a time. Deal with it and file away. Next one coming up. That's what she said.'

I rub at the black paint on my hand. It's already partly dry.

'Spirits, or some kind of wipe,' he says. 'I got them in my place.'

'In the barn?'

'Not in the barn, no, Tuva. I agree, we're all on the same level as the beasts, but I don't particularly want to live like one. I live in the east wing up there.'

I frown.

'The little pink house to the right of the big pink house.'

'I know what east means.'

'You know what trespassing means?'

'Didn't see a sign,' I say.

'We got about fifteen.'

'Not here.'

'True enough. Maybe I should make one, with the paint I got spoiling out here in the sun talking to you about precisely nothing.'

'I'm here because I heard a girl went missing.'

One of the cows makes a long, strained moo noise and three more follow its lead.

'Elsie, you mean? Yeah, young Elsie goes missing every few months. She's a free spirit that one: like some kind of grasshopper child, you never can see when she's ready to jump on to the next reed along the riverbank.'

'Elsa. Elsa Nyberg?'

'I call her Elsie and she calls me Bone.'

'Bone?'

He burps.

'You're not worried about her?'

'More worried about whoever she's with, truth be told.'

One of the cows tries to mount its neighbour.

'It's all natural,' he says, looking over at them. 'Even though they're all females.'

'Oh, I know that.'

'What newspaper you said you work at, now?'

'*Gavrik Posten.*'

'Only local rag I ever read was the *Visberg Tidningen,* run by old Ragnar Falk.'

'My paper bought his newspaper. It's all the same now.'

'It's all the same now, is it? Wonder what Falk thinks about *it's all the same now.* Wonder what you'll think when some big Karlstad outfit buys the *Posten.* And so on. And so on. Such is the wicked and unending cruelty of Babylon.'

'Babylon?'

'Big cities, big problems. You a Christian woman, Tuva?'

'I'm not anything.'

'I didn't think you was.'

'When did you see Elsa Nyberg last, Kurt.'

'T-Bone.'

'T-Bone.'

'I don't know, a few days ago. She helps me with the feed, with the water troughs. She helps me with the egg collections and suchlike. Don't work for me, though, and I don't pay her. You'd have to talk to the Viklunds about all that.'

'Did she seem okay to you?'

'Did she seem okay to me? Yeah, sure she did. She completed her work and she cleared off. We don't sit around talking like old hens all day, like you and me right now; the farm would reverse to nature soon as you can say black magic.'

'You see her, any sign of her, you call me?'

I hand him my card.

'Call you? On what, exactly?'

'You don't have a phone, T-Bone?'

'Who would I call on it?'

'Could you use Linda's phone? I saw one in the café.'

'Yeah, I guess I could do that.'

An alarm bell rings out on top of a small artificial hill, a hundred metres closer to the river, and then Kurt 'T-Bone' Holm's walkie-talkie crackles to life in his pocket.

He holds it up.

A voice says something I can't make out and then, 'Police department, half a mile southbound, over.'

He presses the button on his walkie-talkie and says, 'I got it, over.'

'Best you leave now, young woman,' he says. 'We don't see eye to eye with big-city newspaper people up here at the farm, but that ain't nothing compared to how we feel about the police. Go get back in your van and leave.' He taps his nose twice. 'Go do it.'

10

I start to walk back to my Hilux and then I pause and turn around.

'What is it now?' asks T-Bone.

'You're worried about the police disrespecting your rights. Maybe you need an independent journalist here, to hold them to account.'

'You gonna do that, are you? Hold the police to account?'

'Reckon I keep them in check. I pushed along the Medusa case back in Utgard forest. And I was instrumental in the police searching Snake River Salvage for those two missing women.'

'If you stick around for a half hour, you best keep Rose Farm's interests front and centre.'

'I focus on the common man. On the victim, always have.'

'No victims on this farm.'

'I mean Elsa Nyberg.'

'Elsie ain't so likely to end up a victim as you or me are. Look, here comes the cavalry, watch your step.'

There's activity on the compound: dogs being unchained and spiked barriers erected to block bridges over ditches. If the police want to get up to the actual Rose Farm manor house they'll need a tank not a Volvo.

And, as it turns out, they don't even have a Volvo. These aren't real police.

Sheriff Hansson's taxi drives in slowly and parks, its chassis shaking on its wheels. Brown with badges and rooflights like a vintage cop-car from the Midwest. He steps out and adjusts his hat and spits into the dead bracken.

'T-Bone,' he says, looking up.

'Sheriff.'

'I won't take up any more of your time than is strictly needed. Chief Björn asked me to drop by as a courtesy to you and Abraham.'

'A courtesy, is it?'

'Instead of the police department, you know. Just a friendly neighbourhood watch greeting, is all.'

'You watch your own neighbourhood, Sheriff. And I'll watch mine.'

'Fair.'

'You reckon.'

'You hear Elsa Nyberg hasn't been seen in over two days. You know anything about her whereabouts, T-Bone?'

'Moodyson from Ragnar Falk's newspaper here asking me the exact same question. You two should work together. Partners, ain't that the way? Regular Starsky and Hutch, you two'd make.'

'Tuva,' says the Sheriff.

'Sheriff.'

'So you haven't seen nor heard from young Elsa, then, I assume?'

'Could do with her here to help me swill out the big barn, that's all I know.'

'Mind if I look around a while?'

'Would me minding make any difference?'

Sheriff Hansson smiles and approaches us, his hands in his pockets. The man has a swagger to him but he keeps it in check. He doesn't walk bow-legged like Benny Björnmossen, he doesn't quite have that much attitude. But you can tell his homemade uniform, complete with epaulettes and badges, and a radio attached to his lapel: it all lends him some modicum of authority. Like a kid's drawing of a law-enforcement officer.

'Need some rain,' says the Sheriff.

'Yes, we do.'

'Didn't get enough snow in the winter to fill the wells proper. Dry as a maiden aunt out here, excuse my language, Tuva.'

'Excused.'

'You painting metal or timber?' says the Sheriff, looking at T-Bone's hands.

'Timber, of a sort.'

'Best time of year to do it. Good and dry.'

'Young Elsie ain't here, Sheriff. And if you look around you'll see all the tracks and pathways are temporarily inaccessible. We gotta apologise about that.'

'That's okay, I know you people are private and I respect it. Never caused me no problems all the time I've worn this badge. Not like the teenagers up in hill town. It's like they're out looking for trouble.'

'They are,' says T-Bone. 'Looking for trouble I mean. If they weren't you'd have more reason to be concerned, Sheriff. It's the natural order of things if you think on it. Say the kids start doing what their pappas tell them and they stop trying to break the rules and they quit asserting themselves in the neighbourhood they happen to live in. Then what? Anarchy is what. And not the good kind. Nature's way is for the young to challenge the old and then to dominate. I see it with Andreas's dogs up there,' he points to the small yellow dwelling close to the river. 'Them big old dogs try to hang on to their place because they fought to get there, and you never forget that kind of struggle. But it's happened for a thousand generations and it'll happen for a thousand more. Same with wolf pups out in the forest. The young take on the alpha. Always do. Kids in town are rebelling and I'll drink to it whenever I hear of it.'

'Well, you might be right. But you're not the one who has to keep order.'

'I keep myself to myself.'

'Elsa didn't tell you where she was going? If someone was threatening her? A boyfriend?'

'We didn't chat much. We had too much work to do.'

The Sheriff looks up at the pale-pink manor house with its two timber wings.

'Abraham home?'

T-Bone smiles and says, 'What do you think?'

'I know.'

'You don't know.'

'I know that, too.'

'Moodyson's here in case you infringe my constitutional rights as a sovereign citizen and free man.'

'Is she now.'

'Free press.'

'I want to find this young girl, T-Bone. In all seriousness, I want to help find her.'

'If I hear something I'll make sure it gets back to you. Best I can do.'

'I appreciate it.'

The Sheriff takes T-Bone aside and says a few words into his ear and then heads back to his taxi. He drives away leaving a cloud of dust in his wake.

'Man's a fool but he means well. Not got a bad bone in his body, the Sheriff.'

And then T-Bone's head snaps around to face the manor.

'You hear that?'

'No,' I say.

'Listen closer.'

'I'm deaf.'

'Just concentrate harder.'

Normally I'd bite back at that comment, but I can hear something faint in the distance.

'Music?' I say.

'Violin. Eighteenth century, made in Austria.'

'Wow, you know your music.'

'Not really. I just know *his* music.'

I stare at the manor house.

'Who? Where is he?'

T-Bone closes his eyes and looks like he's meditating. Then he opens his eyes, the sunlight dancing across his pupils, and he says, 'Abraham plays his violin at the rear of the main house. He's got a terrace for the purpose, all shielded with the right kinds of trees for good acoustics. If you were to be on a riverboat passing by you wouldn't see him or nothing but you'd be treated to the best concert of your entire lifetime.'

My phone vibrates in my pocket.

The violin music intensifies and blends with the song of blackbirds and the caws of hooded crows.

A message from Elsa's friend, Kristina; the one I found on Facebook. The message says, *It's me.*

The violin grows louder still and the dogs start barking in their gated compound.

Another message from Elsa's friend.

T-Bone looks at me as I read it.

They're all lying to you, she says. *Every last one of them.*

11

I climb into my Hilux, sync my phone to my hearing aids and call Kristina.

'Tina.'

'*Hej*, it's me. Tuva Moodyson.'

'That was fast.'

'You said they're all lying? About Elsa? What do you mean?'

'I can't say over the... Like this, I mean.'

'You want to meet somewhere quiet?'

'I don't have a car.'

'In Visberg? Maybe in the square?'

'The Grill. One o'clock.' She ends the call.

In front of me, through my filthy windscreen, I can see a young woman in full camouflage walking away from the spa. Well, not full camouflage, half and half, I'd say. She has a desert camo jacket and shorts. And strong highlights: platinum blonde and honey and black. Red nails and lips. A cigarette in a cigarette holder, also camo pattern. Her legs are shiny and tan. Her face is tan. She smokes rings from her holder and then she pulls the cigarette out and drops it to the dry earth and extinguishes it with her leopardprint boot.

As I drive by she gives me a look of pure poison.

The road is empty save for a pick-up truck with a small house strapped down in its flatbed. Some kind of dog kennel painted elaborately to resemble a full-size human home. The windows have imitation geraniums, and inside there are net curtains. The roof has fake clay tiles, all of them joined together in one plastic whole. There's even a letterbox in the tiny door. But the house is rotting away. Its gable ends are full of spider webs and there's mud sprayed up one wall. It's either an old dog's last home or else a young child's first. Life imitating life, and then decaying to the point where it becomes necessary to dump the miniature cabin deep in the woods for it to be consumed by nature.

I pass the man-made glacier, gleaming, shining in the sun, and drive on.

The drive up Visberg hill is not an easy thing for me to complete. The first time I tried it after Noora was shot, I had a full-on panic attack: hyperventilating, pulling over to vomit in the pristine snow of the ditch. That vomit stayed for three weeks, although gradually depleted by vermin and birds. I would drive up the big hill to work on a story about a new nature pond and the extension at the retirement home, or an article on how the rotating bee atop the Hive self-storage building has been renovated by a man down in Vänersborg, or how the snowberg was attracting Instagrammers and amateur ice-carvers, and I'd see the remnants of my panic attack down in the snow, frozen solid, and I'd go on.

Past the white bike, past the cross, over the abandoned train tracks.

Cresting the hill, entering the town. The place the world forgot. Never even knew it well enough to forget about it. The town Gavrik residents are afraid to visit. Visberg.

The town square is beautiful.

Full of apple blossom.

Clouds of whites and soft pinks bubble out from the gnarled apple-tree branches all over the square, eclipsing the bandstand and the statue of Edlund, the industrialist who founded the town. The petals move together in the April breeze like sea froth.

I drive round the square one time before parking because that's become a tradition now, a coping strategy, another compulsion that I obey in order to get from the beginning of each day to the end.

Past the Grill and the gamer café and Konsum mini-supermarket on the bright side of the square, round past the Hive, a whole block's worth of self-storage units, and then turning right to the dark side of the square, the dentist and the closed-down newspaper office and the empty pop-up shop and the clockmaker's. I park outside the Grill.

The sign says 'Visberg Grill, Pizza, Hot Dogs, Burgers. Established 1998.'

I open the door and the aroma of pizza-dough steam hits me straight in the face. People swivel to stare at me, eating with their mouths open, paper napkins tucked into plaid collars, motorcycle helmets resting on chairs, an infant in a pushchair beginning to scream and bark for her mother.

The menu screen is backlit. Every kind of pizza you'd never consider ordering, and a few you would.

I look around the place for Kristina. But I can't see her.

'Ah, Tuva, nice to see you, welcome. What can I get you?'

Luka Kodro's in his trademark jeans and white T-shirt, always pristine.

'I'm meeting a friend,' I say.

'In your own time, take a table if you like. No rushing, no panic.'

And then a young woman at the back, sat at a window table overlooking the vast forests of Visberg hill, the vista rolling out as if from an airship or balloon, stands up slowly and raises her hand as if in class. She isn't blonde anymore, she's a redhead.

I walk over.

'Tuva?' she says.

I offer her my hand and she just looks at it.

'Hi, Kristina.'

We sit down.

She looks down at her hands, tearing a paper napkin into smaller and smaller pieces.

'Are you hungry?'

She shakes her head.

'Well, I'm starving. Mind if I eat?'

I'm not particularly hungry, although Luka's pizzas are very good if you stay well away from the crayfish and pineapple and peanut toppings. But Lena taught me that it's important to put everyone at ease. And you have to adapt to each person, there is no single approach that'll work for all nervous sources.

'I could have a pizza, maybe,' she says. 'A small one.'

'Perfect.'

Luka strides over.

'One American Hot Sausage, please,' I say.

'I'll have a Steak Béarnaise, with mango, easy on the salt, though,' says Kristina.

I can't help but smile a little.

'Salt can give you kidney disease. Left ventricular hypertrophy,' she says.

Of course.

I lower my voice. 'What you said on the phone.'

She shakes her head emphatically. 'I was just telling you the facts.'

'Tell me what you know. Mind if I record?'

I pull out my digital Dictaphone.

She looks aghast so I say, 'I'm deaf. I don't always catch all the words.'

'No recordings,' she says. 'Fuck, I shouldn't have come here.'

'No worries, I'll switch it off, look.' I show her I'm switching it off but she still looks like she might run out before her disgusting pizza is cooked, so I make a display of removing the battery from the Dictaphone and that seems to placate her.

'Elsa's missing,' she says. 'Proper missing.'

'Go on.'

'I don't know where she is or who's behind it, that's the thing.'

'Tell me what you do know. All off the record.'

'What record?'

'I won't put your words in my newspaper without your clear consent.'

She chews on the inside of her cheek. 'I told her not to work up there on Rose Farm. I told her not to get involved, but did she listen?'

I frown and fill our water glasses from a jug on the table.

'Rose Farm isn't a normal farm. It's preppers.'

'What do you mean?'

'I mean they're like a cult up there, some kind of Waco-style community, you know the kind. A wife-sharing group. They reckon the end of the world is coming, so they better get ready. Like an army base that place is. Elsa told me all about it.'

The pizzas arrive so we both clam up.

'*Buon appetito*,' says Luka.

'They're planning for a siege or a takeover, paranoid about the government taking their stuff or whatever. Elsa thought it was just T-Bone, the farmer, but turns out it's all of them.'

'Ruby at the spa? Andreas the groundsman?'

'Elsa told me Ruby's in charge of water. She's not to be messed with. And the weirdo dog-guy, the massive guy, some kind of giant, he's in charge of radios or something.'

'Radios?'

'That's what Elsa said. Radios and dogs.'

'What about the owners, Therese and Abraham.'

'Elsa never said too much about them, never even saw Abraham once, reckons he most likely died years ago and nobody noticed. Reckons he could have been pushed down the river in a Viking burial or something.'

'I think people would have noticed that, Tina.'

She chews on her steak pizza and raises her eyebrows and makes an apologetic gesture because she can't answer, and then she swallows and takes a sip of water and says, 'Not out there, nobody would have seen a thing. It's like Siberia out there.'

'But why do you think Elsa's missing? Where do you think she could be?'

Kristina ignores me and touches her eyebrow piercing and says, 'They got lots of money up there, all gold and silver bars. They're preparing for something, some kind of recession or bank run. So maybe she found out too much. T-Bone told her things he shouldn't have told her, he was fond of her, making a fuss of her and letting her go home early.'

'You really think she's in danger?'

'Oh, I'm sure of it.'

She chews on some more steak and mango.

'Where can we contact her? Where should we look?'

'That café owner as well, she was always a bitch to Elsa, always giving her the worst jobs: the toilets, the dishwashing, the drains. Elsa hated her.'

'Where do we look?'

'I don't know. I've talked to our friends from college, the group we hang out with on weekends in McDonalds. But they haven't heard from her. I even called her dad and he was worried sick, and he was already sick before this happened.'

'I'll go talk to him.'

'Thing is,' says Tina. 'That cult at Rose Farm have been planning for trouble for years. They're set up for it. Elsa reckons the place is like a training camp or something, all tunnels and hidden gun positions and food stores. She says they've planned for an attack of some sort and they will not back down.'

'You think Elsa's still on the property?'

'Might be, but she's smart. I reckon she got out just in time. Could be up in Dalarna someplace camping. She was a scout. Maybe she's on a campsite someplace with her sim card out and her credit card zipped away.'

I take a sip of water.

'But you think the Rose Farm people have driven her away? Threatened her?'

'I don't know. I just want her back. I want the police to protect her or something.'

'Do you have any idea which campsite she might have gone to? Any clues?'

'There is one place outside Ludvika. We went there twice back in school. I think she might feel safe there.'

I input it into my phone. Three-hour drive.

My phone rings in my hand.

'Thord,' I say.

'Tuvs. We found the missing girl's Volkswagen. Parked in thick shrub, concealed.'

'Good.'

'It's on the edge of Rose Farm.'

'Oh, shit,' I say, staring at Kristina.

'What?' she mouths.

'Thing is,' says Thord. 'And this is kind of awkward to say out loud, not exactly convention, in fact I'd describe it as—'

'What are you trying to say?'

'The residents are reluctant to talk to me down here unless you come to observe it all for the record. They're distrustful of agents of the government, so they say. Want an independent bystander to hold us to account. That's what they're talking about.'

I hear some shouting in the background but I can't make out the words.

The phone sounds muffled all of a sudden, like he's covering the receiver with his hand. 'I wouldn't ask normally, but there's seven of them, Tuvs, and one of me. And I don't want to get heavy-handed. You think you could swing by?'

'I'm already on my way.'

12

I pay for the pizzas and thank Kristina.

'I want to come,' she says.

'You can't come.'

'I want to.'

'You come, and they won't let me on their land and you won't find out anything new. Let me talk to the police and I promise to fill you in, okay? I know this seems counter-intuitive, but—'

'Counter-what?'

'I mean, it's a good thing they've found her car. Feels like a bad omen but it's a positive thing – the police can backtrack and work out her timeline, understand where's she's been. They might have her GPS data.'

'You call me if you find out anything, an eye for an eye.'

I think about explaining to her that the phrase doesn't mean what she thinks it means, and in fact it's coming across like a threat, but I swallow it down and say, 'Eye for an eye. Sure.'

The drive down Visberg hill is a blur. I have too many raw memories tied up with this hill and I've only been covering the town for half a year. My truck passes the bike memorial and I turn right and head north.

White birch trunks against an ominous sky.

I reach the edge of Rose Farm and the perimeter fence is almost a kilometre long so I keep on driving. Past the deep ditches and the CCTV cameras, past the pink manor house itself up on a hill, past the red barn and on. The property is closer to the riverbank here. I see where the grass has been flattened by a vehicle. I turn left and let my truck do some off-road driving, up an uneven and weather-beaten track sloping down gently to the marshland flanking Snake River.

Up ahead: a police car, parked. A quad bike, parked. Seven stern-looking people and a policeman. I see no abandoned Volkswagen.

I park in front of a tangle of thorny brambles and get out.

They all look at me as I walk towards them.

'Tuva Moodyson,' says Thord. He never calls me that.

'Hello everyone.'

'You're here to bear witness,' says T-Bone, his slicked-back dyed hair gleaming in the sun. 'Big government infringing on our civil liberties enshrined to us by the Lord Almighty on high.'

'I need to tape off this area,' says Thord. 'Police business. I'm not stepping on nobody's liberties.'

His gun's right there on his hip.

'I'm not even sure this is your land or if it's the Kommun land so close to the river. Maps aren't clear. Just back up now a little, all of you, just give me some room and the sooner I start the sooner I'll be out of your hair.'

'Planting evidence more like it,' says a guy with shaved head. He's standing next to Ruby from the Spa, so I deduce he's Niklas, her travelling-salesman husband.

'I'll record it all,' I say. 'If I record everything and oversee as an independent bystander then the constable can do his job and leave you in peace.'

An elegant woman with thick, brown hair, the only one of the group not wearing any camouflage or military-style clothing, steps up to me and says, 'My name is Therese Viklund. My husband and I run Rose Farm.'

I see Linda Larsson, her tattooed arm slung across her chest, roll her eyes.

'Hi,' I say. 'I'm Tuva.'

'We just need to make sure this gets done according to due process.'

'I understand.'

Andreas is here with two snarling Anatolian shepherd dogs straining at their leashes. T-Bone has a metre-long curved, serrated blade hanging from his belt like a machete. Ruby from the Spa has a compound bow – camo colours to match her outfit – and it's slung on her back together with a quiver of three arrows. Her husband, Niklas, who hasn't bothered to introduce himself, carries a Mora knife on each leg. I can see why Thord wants to keep the whole thing friendly. I understand his predicament.

'I'm gonna tape up now,' says Thord.

Niklas films him doing it on his iPhone.

'An ungodly agent of Babylon,' says T-Bone under his breath, his hands still black from the painting. His voice changes to that of a southern Baptist preacher, emphasising certain syllables, and he says, 'And I command, come out of her thy people.' A heron takes off behind him and beats its mighty wings and extends its neck and flies east toward Falun. 'Come out of her, my people, that ye be not participants of her sins and are not victims of the plagues.'

'We don't need big-city folk poking their noses in to our business,' says Niklas. 'We never needed it before and we don't need it today. Private property. The end.'

Thord stays professional. He disappears into the scrub and I notice the Volkswagen back there as the branches get disturbed. A dark grey Volkswagen hidden by overhanging willow leaves.

'I ain't sure that's even Elsie's car,' says T-Bone.

'I can confirm it is her car,' says Thord, emerging from the tree. 'Plates match.'

'Plates can get swapped,' says Niklas. 'I seen it done in Jo'burg. Nothing to it.'

Thord glowers at Niklas, at his desert camo boots and his tight black T-shirt, and then he pulls out a pair of latex gloves from his police-issue trousers and snaps them on.

I start recording video on my phone.

'Now's when he plants the evidence,' says Niklas. 'Right under our goddam noses.'

Thord gives me a tired look, and then a minute later Sheriff Hansson joins us in his taxi cab.

T-Bone greets him with a handshake and a slap on the back, 'Sheriff, nice to see you again. How's Marie?'

'She's doing well, gave up her stick, oh, I'd say a good ten days ago now. Like a new woman.'

'Well ain't that something.'

The Sheriff looks at Thord and Thord looks back at him.

'If you can explain what exactly I'm doing, Sheriff, and I'll be done as quick as I can.'

With T-Bone by his side, the Sheriff walks up to the group and says, 'The police will be through soon and you can go back to your day.'

'Tuva's here, just to ensure there's no breach of protocol,' says Therese.

'Who found the car out here?' asks the Sheriff.

'I did,' says Linda. 'I'd closed after lunch and was out here taking a walk, like I sometimes do. Saw the tyre tracks. Called it in when I realised it was Elsa's little Volkswagen.'

'Called it in right away?' says the Sheriff. 'Didn't try to open the door or whatnot? Could be important, so best you fill me in now.'

'I didn't touch it,' says Linda. 'I went to the others. Therese told me to call the police so I did.'

'You did good,' says the Sheriff. 'Thord's a fair man. I vouch for him. Any sign of Elsa?'

'No,' says Linda. 'I shouted after her for a while, but heard nothing over the sound of the river water.'

Thord emerges from the alders wearing his latex gloves and holding a leather handbag and a phone. He walks it over to his police Volvo and places them inside plastic Ziploc-style bags. Then he walks back over.

'Thank you all for your cooperation,' he says. 'Now, I've called this in, and there will be other officers arriving shortly to remove the vehicle and to search the area.' T-Bone starts to get agitated and Thord adds, 'Just the immediate area for now, not past the ditches, not on your farmland. It's the best I can do. Priority has to be that we find Elsa Nyberg as soon as possible.'

'I think we can all agree on that,' says Therese.

'Okay then. If you all stay on the other side of that ditch until we're done searching that would be appreciated. Therese, I've got your number, I'll call you if we find anything, okay? Now, who lives in the hut over there?'

He points to Rosebud Cottage, the shack all on its own surrounded by reed beds and inlets.

'Uninhabited,' says Therese.

'*Uninhabitable*,' says Niklas. 'Place can get flooded, just a wreck of an outhouse.'

'We'll need access,' says Thord. 'Is it locked?'

The group look at Therese and Therese nods. 'It's locked. I can come open it up if needed.'

'Needed it is,' says Thord. 'Can I drive to it?'

'Man, you can't even walk to it,' says T-Bone. 'River access only. Flat-bottomed boat and knowledge of the rocks and the reed beds. You can try to drive your Volvo but that's the last you'll ever see of it and maybe the last we'd ever see of you. I seen these marshes swallow a whole tractor one time. Ate it right up.'

A phone starts to ring.

It's the phone inside the clear plastic bag in Thord's hand.

It's Elsa Nyberg's phone.

13

We all stare at Thord and at the iPhone flashing inside the bag.

'You should probably answer that,' says Niklas. 'Might be important.'

Thord looks flustered. Maybe protocol is not to reopen a sealed bag? But he does open it.

'Back off,' says Thord, firmly.

'Fascist,' mutters T-Bone.

Thord turns his back on us and holds the phone well away from his face so not to breathe on it, but he's too late. It's locked.

'Might be the kidnapper,' says Niklas. 'Toying with you. Messing with your head.'

Thord ignores him and pulls the Sheriff to one side.

Too far away for me to hear them but I can lip-read most of what's said.

'You stay here until I call you. Keep them to the other side of the ditch. Make sure nobody comes close to the car. Can you do that?'

The Sherriff nods and then he stops nodding.

'How long, do you think?'

'How long, what?'

'I got a taxi client booked at three.'

'Can you call somebody?'

'I don't know.'

'Sheriff.'

'It's not like I get paid for this, you know.'

Thord looks apologetic and says, *I'll do what I can but you might have to cancel that fare.'*

The Sheriff nods.

Thord turns to us, me somehow now part of this strange Rose Farm gang.

'I'm going to leave Sheriff Hansson in charge of the scene until more officers arrive. I'll ask you to keep to the far side of the ditch and not approach the vehicle or cross the police tape. I won't hesitate to make an arrest.'

'Deep State,' says T-Bone. 'Neo-Socialists.'

'Don't,' says Thord.

'Globalist,' says T-Bone.

Thord drives away.

'You think she's still around here?' asks Therese.

'Nope,' says Niklas. 'I think she's on a road trip with her boyfriend, is what I think. She told me she was seeing an older man, some kind of successful businessman. Reckon she and he'll be long gone.'

'Without her phone or her handbag?' says Ruby. 'No way I'd leave my phone or my bag.'

'And don't I bloody know it, says Niklas. 'If you spent half as much time working as you do on Instagram we'd—'

'You really want to go there, Nik?' she says, smiling, showing all her perfect white teeth. Her accent has strengthened. 'You want that argument, is it? You want to go there, right now, right here, do you?'

'I don't care,' he says.

'Oh, is it?' she says.

'Maybe you should all go your separate ways and cool off a little,' says Sheriff Hansson. 'It's been an upsetting day. Go back to your homes and make some coffee. Ain't too much that looks as bleak after a good, hot cup of fresh coffee.'

Niklas and Ruby storm off, still arguing under their breaths, her beating on his arm.

Andreas looks down on us all from his immense height, then starts to take his dogs down to the river until the Sheriff says, 'Other side of the ditch, my man. Them's the orders, don't shoot the messenger.'

Andreas turns and jumps the ditch, unlocks a gate with broken glass on its upper edge and takes his dogs back on to the Rose Farm compound.

Linda Larsson says, 'I got stew to brew.'

T-Bone says, 'You call on me if there's anything, Sheriff.'

The Sheriff says, 'I appreciate it.'

Which leaves Therese and me.

Therese says, 'Mind if I take a quick look at the driver's seat, officer?'

'If it was down to me but it ain't.'

I can feel this story slipping from me, all the pertinent people drifting away, so I say, 'Therese, do you mind if I chat with you for twenty minutes? I'm writing this up for the *Posten*, Elsa's disappearance and all, and I'd love to get your viewpoint.'

'Sorry,' she says. 'We prefer to keep a low profile on Rose Farm.'

'Just to avoid misrepresentations, I mean.'

'Misrepresentations?'

'I want to get the facts straight. Don't want to portray you all as some kind of survivalist cult or anything like that.'

'That's not what we are, Tuva.'

'Exactly. Fact checking. Would be good to talk so I can write an accurate piece, a piece you'd approve of.'

'You're giving me editorial control?'

'My boss would skin me alive.'

'What then?'

'I'll let you read the piece before I publish. How's that?'

She thinks about it and then she says, 'You can ride with me on the quad back to the house but I don't have a second helmet.'

'That's okay,' I say. 'I can drive.'

'The routes aren't clear,' she says. 'Not for a truck. You won't get through.'

'Okay, then. I'll come with you.'

'Jump on.'

I do as she says, and just as she's about to tighten the chin strap of her helmet she pulls it up off her head, turns to me and says, 'You can have it. Safety first.'

'You sure?'

She nods.

We set off.

Not up the main road and past the spa and the café and the barn, but through the gate Andreas took his dogs through. Therese slows her quad and I can see how the lock mechanism works on fingerprint recognition. The unit is powered by a mid-size solar panel. The gate swings open and we drive through and my jaw drops.

So, this is the inner compound.

I knew the public area with the businesses was secure, but this is something else. And yet Therese doesn't seem to mind me being here? Doesn't mind me seeing all this? A dog pen next to Andreas's yellow house. Six dogs inside. We drive past the building and the dogs erupt in frantic barks and growls. One of them, perhaps the leader of the pack, snarls so aggressively saliva falls from its jowls to the dry earth below. And now I think I see why Therese tolerates me in here. This is a warning of sorts. A show of strength. And her showing me means there's a fairly high chance I'll tell others and the word will get out not to visit Rose Farm. To leave them be.

We head past wind turbines and well installations and solar arrays. We pass the back of T-Bone's red barns and through a network of ponds and lakes that seem to be fed through pipes connected to Snake River in the background. As we drive closer to the manor house I see it clearly for the first time. The soft-pink painted timber. The light grey shutters. The green copper roof. It's a beautiful house. Something from a period TV series.

The rear of the main building is shrouded in thick tangles of rambling roses and honeysuckle and oak. It looks wild and messy and thoughtfully arranged all at the same time.

We park outside the house and I look over the estate from Therese's point of view, my back to the front door. Looking downhill towards the road, in the distance I see the red barns on the left and the stable block on the right. I see the ditches and fences and barricades delineating the public areas from the private. I see the aerials climbing high out of wooden huts, and the target-practice boards arranged out at fifty metres. I can tell because it has a '50 metres' sign next to it. I can't read the others but I expect they say '100 metres', '200 metres', '300 metres', judging by the distances.

'I have a conference call in forty minutes, but you can come in for elderflower cordial or tea.'

I step inside. She takes off her expensive-looking boots so I remove my ICA Maxi trainers. The hallway is homely, but elegant. It's not a big-scale house like I used to visit sometimes on weekends, back when I studied in London. It always seemed to me that within a half hour train ride of Zone 1 you could visit a thousand different, fascinating historical properties, many of which are older than the city of Gothenburg. This room is lived-in. Black-and-white tiles, a log basket full of mossy birch, a set of antlers on the wall, a wooden staircase leading up.

'Follow me.'

The back of the front door has some kind of heavy steel-bolt device all the way across it. The only time I've ever seen such a thing was in a movie. I think it was the home of a drug kingpin. The metal bar could be secured in place to reinforce the entrance, so that even a specialist police unit or military breacher would have difficulty breaking through. Maybe they have some rare antiques.

We walk through to the kitchen.

Therese boils water and places four *Havrekakor* biscuits on a plate and says, 'Cordial or tea?'

'Cordial, please.'

She turns off the kettle and pours us both elderflower cordial in long glasses. She adds large ice cubes and slices of lime and sprigs of mint.

'Delicious,' I say, taking a sip, trying to connect with this rather cold and handsome woman.

'Our own crop,' she says.

'The elderflowers?'

She nods.

'Mind if I record our conversation?' I point to my hearing aids. 'So I'm accurate.'

'Sorry, yes. Fine.'

'Thanks.'

'You're hearing impaired?'

'I'm not impaired, no,' I say. 'I'm deaf.'

She thinks about that.

'I'm going to contact a lawyer,' she says.

'Why?' I say, imagining myself in the dock of a courtroom facing a libel case for some article.

'Harassment,' she says. 'Potentially. I don't know, that's why I'm calling my lawyer. The police have always been heavy-handed around Rose Farm because of the tragic history of the place. They were monstrous when Kurt's wife got arrested.'

'T-Bone has a wife?'

'*Had.*'

'Oh.'

'She died in prison. Medical complications.'

'Why was she in prison?'

'Because she almost put Kurt in a coma.'

'What?'

'They had an acrimonious relationship, let's say. He was perhaps not the ideal husband – in many ways I won't go into. But he probably didn't deserve the crack to the head with a cast-iron skillet.'

'Shit.'

'Quite.'

'He tried to get them to drop charges. But they would not. That's the Swedish law, apparently. She split his head open and received a two-year sentence. She died in prison.'

'Jesus.'

'Please don't take the Lord's name in this house, Tuva.'

'I apologise.'

'Accepted. This is sovereign land, you see. Sovereign to us, we paid for it, we farm it, we look after it. And the police have no jurisdiction here. We assert our rights as free citizens.'

'Most of my friends are happy the state's there to step in and help them, sort things out for them, provide a structure.'

'They're deluded,' she says.

'Well, I don't know…'

'I meant no offence. The western world is deluded. But we strive to live free here and bother nobody. We're almost completely self-sufficient in terms of power and food and water. We strive to live away from the system.'

'But you're not survivalists.'

'We prefer the term *farmers*.'

'It's a bit more than just farming, no?'

'Is it? Is it really? A hundred years ago most people lived like we do. Five-hundred years ago everyone lived like we do. We bother nobody and we expect to be treated that way in return.'

'Is your husband here, Therese?'

'Abraham is practising,' she says, quick as a flash.

'Practising?'

'His music.'

I raise my head to indicate I'm trying to hear him play and then I frown.

'He writes music,' she says, impatiently.

I nod.

A flurry of deep barks outside on the farm. One dog howling.

'Sounds like a wolf,' I say.

She bites her lip.

'When can I expect to read your first draft? Of the piece?'

'I'll have to talk to my—'

A knock on the door. Alarms flash on the kitchen wall and I notice a bottle of pepper spray on the splashbacks by the hob. I didn't see it before, but the walls are all lined with books. Not just bookcases, but in each room the external wall is lined with books, the copies all arranged cover out like in a fancy bookshop.

'Lots of books,' I say, stupidly.

'We're big readers. Excuse me a moment.'

She stands up to answer the door. Sounds like a dozen dogs just the other side of it.

Fists pound wood.

I dash across to see who it is, and why they're so insistent.

Two dogs. Andreas. A gaunt expression on his face.

He's two steps down, but he's still taller than Therese and me.

'Mrs Viklund,' he says. 'I've found her.'

14

Therese looks at me for an answer and then looks back to Andreas on the manor-house steps.

'Elsa?' she says to him. 'Is she hurt?'

Andreas looks at me and then he strokes the head of one of his dogs. He caresses the ear of the dog, running it between his fingers.

'I don't…' he says, not looking at us directly.

Therese frowns impatiently, and my guts start to pull tight inside myself.

'She's not alive,' he says.

'No,' says Therese. 'Can't be. Not Elsa. Where is she?'

'Down by the reed beds not far away from her car. She looks real peaceful. Tranquil. She don't even look hurt for the most part.'

Therese looks back at me.

'We should call the police,' I say.

'Yes,' she says. 'I'll call them. I'll do it.'

'Sheriff left,' he says. 'He's not here.'

She fumbles with her phone and drops it to the square tiles and the screen cracks but it does not shatter. She picks it up and looks at it and her breathing is fast. She dials.

One of the dogs strains to get inside the house and Andreas pulls tight on its choke-chain, to the point where the dog's eyes are bulging as it fights for its breath.

'It's Therese Viklund at Rose Farm, north of Visberg,' Therese gives the post code. 'My colleague has found Elsa Nyberg.' There's a pause and then she says, 'No, I don't think so.' There's another pause and then Therese says to Andreas, 'Did you check for a pulse?'

'I checked her neck but I couldn't find nothing; was already cold.'

'No pulse,' says Therese. 'Please come as soon as you can.'

'She is dead, she really is,' says Andreas. 'I wouldn't have left her there by the inlet if she was just hurt.'

'Police are on their way,' says Therese, turning to me. 'I think we should check her vitals one more time; we'll get to her before the police do.'

I step outside and the air has cooled. It is springtime evening air now: misty and chill and completely devoid of insects.

We walk fast, not jogging, that'd feel wrong somehow, in the direction we came from earlier.

The sun reflects off the wide, smooth waters of Snake River, causing it to light up like a creeping flow of liquid iron ore from some long-ago smelt.

The dogs bark and howl, excited.

We pass by the fish ponds and T-Bone's red barn and reach the perimeter fence. I'm out of breath but Therese and Andreas are not. Through the security gate and down to the mud flats by the riverside. Some physical memory of an oxbow lake now evaporated. The tracks from Sheriff Hansson's taxi cab visible in the dew-encrusted earth.

'She's over there in the alders,' says Andreas.

'Tie up your dogs,' says Therese. 'They shouldn't get close.'

He goes back to the gate and tethers his dogs.

Therese and I step closer to the water's edge, to where the land turns to marsh turns to reed beds turns to mud. There's a figure in the distance, part-obscured by foliage. Someone in a long coat. Standing up straight on the other side of the riverbank. Too far away to see properly.

Suddenly I feel cold. An unexpected chill around my neck.

'No, there,' shouts Andreas. 'Back there.'

We retrace our steps and see the clump of alder. Ten or fifteen individual plants growing in a cluster on these fertile plains. Tiny green leaves, these ones less vivid than the birches all around. Therese steps closer. She looks back at me, and she looks afraid.

'We could wait for the police,' says Andreas. 'I already checked her neck, I said I did.'

Therese looks at him and then looks at me and her eyes open wide and she steps through the spindly trunks into the cluster of alder trees.

A branch whips me in the neck.

A boot.

Her body, part-covered in leaves and dead branches.

Clothed.

I take a couple more steps and see her face. What happened? Her head rests on a pillow of coarse grass.

Therese bends down to take her pulse, but then hesitates.

The air is still and it is whisper quiet.

She puts her fingers to Elsa Nyberg's neck but I don't think either one of us truly thinks it necessary.

Therese's head slumps on her shoulders a little and she looks at me and shakes her head.

I try to swallow, but nothing.

Elsa has no bleeding that I can see. No wounds save for a red mark at her temple. It's an awful thing to say she looks peaceful in death, but that doesn't stop it from being true. She looks like she's resting.

Therese covers her eyes with her hands but she does not cry.

I take her arm and lead her gently out of the cluster of alder trees and I realise that trunks this thick would belong to trees roughly of Elsa's age. Twenty years or so. Old enough to be fully-established but young enough to still be vulnerable.

Andreas shakes his head at us and we shake our heads back at him. He takes off his hunt cap and holds it down by his hip.

'Who?' says Therese. 'What could have…?'

'When I find out, I'll—' says Andreas.

The sound of an engine.

Thord arrives in his police car and in the passenger seat is Magnus Falk, the temporary stand-in for Noora; no relation to Ragnar in Visberg.

They get out and usher us away.

Thord and Magnus step into the shade of the alders.

They come back out.

'This is Elsa Nyberg?' says Thord.

'Yes, it is,' says Therese.

'Yep,' says Andreas.

'Who's been up close to the body? Can you tell me who's touched or affected the scene in any way?'

'We all have,' says Therese. 'I just checked her for a pulse.'

'Same here,' says Andreas. 'Her skin was already cold when I found her.'

'Poor, poor girl,' says Therese.

'Can you make the calls?' Thord says to Magnus, and Magnus nods and returns to their police Volvo.

Thord approaches. He's a good ten centimetres shorter than Andreas.

'Police specialists will be arriving here soon, and they'll need to seal off the area to do some forensic work. Take Elsa away in a respectful manner, check the area. And I'll need to ask you all to visit Gavrik police station to give statements.'

'Of course,' says Therese.

'You should start off by talking to her daddy,' says Andreas. 'He's got a temper on him, that man.'

'Let's keep our minds open,' says Thord, thumbing his belt loops. 'You can let me know your thoughts in your statement, but last thing we need round here is people leaping to assumptions. You clear?'

Andreas nods.

'Them your dogs?'

Andreas nods again.

'Do me a favour and take them away while my colleagues work here. Two dogs like yours can be mighty distracting.'

'Our land. You don't get to tell me what to do with my own dogs.'

'Not telling you,' says Thord. 'Asking, is all.'

Andreas looks at Therese. She gives him the nod and then he says, 'I can do it.'

'Thank you. All three of you, if you can find your way down to the station this evening, please. I'll talk to the other Rose Farm residents tomorrow.'

'It's awful,' says Therese.

'It's a horrible thing. Truly heinous.'

'She never hurt anyone.'

'Sad state of affairs,' says Thord. 'Now, I need to take some official photographs. You mind moving away now, so I can do this before the light goes?'

We walk away.

It seems improper to break this trio after our shared experience. But Therese and Andreas walk back through their security gate and I walk alone to my Hilux, parked halfway to the public road. My joints feel old. The mass of my body is not how I usually feel it, like I'm weighed down with wet rope. I'm tired. Uneasy.

My truck starts and I drive slowly up the incline towards the road.

Mists are forming on the fields and my Hilux warning light pops on. Danger: low temperatures.

An unmarked Mercedes turns and drives past me, the driver wearing sunglasses.

I pull up on to the main road and head back to Visberg.

Before I start to accelerate, I see an older man with a ponytail crouched in the verge. His phone is gripped tight in his hand. He's rocking on his boots and he's wrapped his arms around himself and he is sobbing.

I recognise him from my research.

It's Elsa's father.

15

I leave him alone.

Seeing a grown man, a man in his fifties or sixties, sobbing on the side of the road, rocking in place, foetal, exposed to the elements, shakes me to my core. And then I begin to question the scene. My human instincts fade slightly and my journalistic instincts grow stronger. It's always this way. I see a car accident and like any other decent human I worry for the people involved. I see if I can help. But then, perhaps sooner than I'd be prepared to admit, I start to fashion the bare bones of that story inside my own head. How I'll portray this incident. How I'll spread the news to the people in surrounding villages and forests who depend on me to learn how their community is faring. How I'll take a relevant photo in a respectful manner. I assume Elsa's father is grieving. I assume he has heard the news. That's my human reaction. Bu what if it's not the sadness he can't handle? What if it's the guilt?

I call the station.

'Björn Andersson, Gavrik police.'

'Chief. It's Tuva.'

I hear him take a deep breath. A sigh.

'You on your way in, Moodyson? Sorry state.'

'I'm on my way in.'

He pauses and I hear him clear his throat.

'Not right. Twenty-year-old with her whole life ahead of her. Sorry you saw it after what you've been through of late.'

'I wanted to let you know I just passed Leif Nyberg on the side of the road, past the turning to where Thord is now. He was crying on the verge. In case you want to know his whereabouts.'

Another pause. This one longer.

'I appreciate that. Drive safe, now.'

He ends the call at the moment I drive past the curious snow mountain, the artificial glacier, standing proud in its field. The ice looks grey in the evening haze, and the birch buds offer it a reflected neon-green halo, like the snow is fringed. I look away and keep my eyes on the road.

I'll head to the station, give my statement, then go home. I'm exhausted.

Beside me on the passenger seat is a bag of unopened wine gums but I don't have the stomach for them right now. Not after seeing Elsa's face. Her pallid skin. Her cloudy, lifeless eyes fixed open.

They say the eyes are the windows to the soul and I hope to God they are incorrect. Noora's eyes went blank as soon as she was shot. There were no last words or looks exchanged. You can't exchange anything with someone who isn't there anymore. She was shot and she fell. The perpetrator left their gun on my own kitchen counter and walked away, calm as could be. Sat on the steps of my building waiting to be arrested. Later, police interviews would detail how Noora was the intended target, how the shooting was an act of revenge, their twisted imagining of a plan. They ended there and Noora ended there, and in a way, a very real way, I ended there as well.

I see a police van, some kind of forensic crime-scene team, and we exchange glances as the vehicles pass. The whites of their eyes. Their intent. Doing their job. Wondering what I'm doing all the way out here in a Toyota pick-up truck. Wondering what the hell that white snow mountain is doing in an isolated field in April.

People talk about death being the end, but it isn't that simple. We're connected through time, all of us, like myriad underground mitochondria, linking each tree in a forest. The connections exist on an infinite number of planes. Death is the least of it.

Elsa's gone. She is no more. Someone in this Kommun arranged to meet her by the river or else stalked her or else stumbled upon her by chance. They killed her and they hid her body. There's no way that was a suicide, not with prickly brambles and wet leaves dragged to part-conceal the body. Some monster ended a young woman's life before it even had a chance to get going. Left her here alone with the wild things. The very least I can do is to make efforts to work out who that person is. And to track them down. And to help gain some version of justice. I write stories but I also follow up for the victims and the victims' families. That doesn't happen as much as you think it might, not in these out-of-the-way parts. Not anywhere.

The twin chimneys of the liquorice factory rise in the distance like a threat. Two fingers. A *fuck you* to the world.

You think death is the worst of it until you learn otherwise. When I was fourteen and dad died suddenly in a car accident I thought that was the worst thing that could ever happen to a family. The seismic impact of it all. And then my mum went into some kind of stasis that she never recovered from. Dad went from living his life to not living it. But Mum and me, we endured year after year of her decaying, suffering, growing smaller with each passing day. I wanted Noora to live more than I've wanted anything in my entire life. And now I think maybe I yearned for the wrong thing. Finality can be kind, even though it seems like a perverse notion. Elsa's gone. Noora lives on but she doesn't really, not in any true sense of the word. Maybe I'll know what the answers are when I grow old. Maybe I'll never know.

The back route into Gavrik is blocked by a loader delivering a Volvo earth mover so I detour rather than wait for it to finish.

I drive between McDonalds and ICA Maxi, our trusty gateposts, and head on up Storgatan. The shops are closed and the people are gone. There is no window-shopping in a town like Gavrik, the windows aren't set up for it. You finish work and you go straight home and you lock your door and you heat up your frozen pizza and you watch your television. A man in a beaver-pelt cap walks into Ronnie's bar and then he walks right back out again.

I slow and put my Hilux in neutral. To my right is the office. To my left is Benny Björnmossen's hunt shop, the stuffed bear in the window holding onto some kind of shotgun with a polished walnut stock. Ahead of me is Gavrik police department, home to three officers and three cells. Behind it, to the right, is Hotel Gavrik, with its off-centre sign. And backdropping the entire town is the Gothic façade of the Grimberg Liquorice factory. I can't do it. I cannot go in and talk to the police, not right now. My stomach churns. I came here, to Noora's office, to brief Thord and the Chief five days after Noora was shot. I left her bedside to return to her flat to pick up things for her – personal items, toiletries, clothes – because she was going to wake up soon and need them all, right? That day is engraved onto my soul and it will never fade. The way Chief Björn and Thord waited for me outside on the street. The way Thord gave me a hug, tears in his eyes. The manner with which the Chief, a man who took years to even look me in the eye, patted me on the shoulder and could barely speak. Three grieving residents trying to make sense of a senseless act. Trying to find justice for the woman they all loved in their own ways. Trying to find a way through it.

I drive away, my tyres skidding on the asphalt.

When I arrive at my building I'm crying, not even bothering to wipe the tears with my sleeve. I reach my door and the door next to it opens and little Dan is there, wearing his Spiderman costume.

'*Hej*, Dan,' I say, smiling, wiping my eyes.

He steps to me and hugs me around my hips and I hug him back. He says, 'You're just tired like Mamma is. You should take a bubble bath with lots of bubbles. You need to sleep now. You take a nap like my mamma does.'

I crouch down and kiss him on the top of his head.

'Go back inside, Dan. I'll see you tomorrow night? Tacos, right?'

'Not too spicy, though. It prickles on my tongue.'

He sticks out his tongue.

'I'll remember.'

He closes his door and I unlock mine and step inside. I kick off my trainers and pull off my clothes and pull on my joggers and a shirt. I switch on the kettle but I have no tea bags. I have no coffee.

Why Elsa?

The kettle starts to make a noise.

Why did someone take her life today? Or yesterday? Who would do such a thing?

The kettle starts to boil and I think about Rose Farm. Ruby and Niklas at the spa. Linda Larsson and her organic café. T-Bone's barns and his paintings. Therese and her manor house with each and every wall lined with layers of hardback books.

The kettle boils and switches itself off.

I gather my thoughts and step to the sink and splash cold water on my face. Then I leave the building and drive away.

16

Chief Björn's sitting at the reception desk. I've never seen him sit out here before. He's got a bandage on his left hand and the lights inside the cop shop seem dimmer than usual. Subdued.

He unlocks the door for me.

You may not think a police station needs a locked front door on a Saturday night, but then maybe you've never been to an isolated town like Gavrik. With three police officers working shifts, it's not that uncommon to find the entrance locked and a prominent sign explaining how to call for an emergency, as if you didn't already know, and detailing the closest police precincts at Falun and Malung.

'Come in outta that cold, the night has a pinch to it this time of year.'

I walk in.

'You alright? Took your time getting down here.'

'I'm fine, Chief.'

'Fresh coffee inside, courtesy of my good wife. The real thing, strong and smooth, not instant. Let's go through.'

He unlocks the keycode door and takes me back to the main office. Four desks.

One of them has a police jacket hung on the back of the office chair. It has three photographs on the desk itself, all framed. One of the photographs is of me.

'Pray for her every night before bed,' says the Chief in a low voice. 'Give you my word, I do. Same with Mrs Andersson. She sends you her best.'

'Thank you.'

'Noora's a capable officer. Fine career ahead of her, you'll see.'

I swallow hard. The Chief is being extremely kind to me, I know that, but hopeful statements like these make me feel all the worse for knowing, deep down inside of myself, that Noora will never work here again.

'Sit,' says the Chief, pointing to the chair in front of his desk. He perches on the desk. 'You up to this?'

I nod.

'Okay, then.'

He pours us both coffee and opens a battered old Grimberg Liquorice Christmas variety-box tin. Inside are his wife's shortbread biscuits – each one as thin as a DVD – topped with demerara sugar and cinnamon. He moves behind his desk and sits down and picks up a biro and adjusts his papers, and then he looks up.

'Tell me about what happened today, if you could. From the moment you saw the Volkswagen earlier, down by Snake River.'

'Well,' I say. 'I walked back to Rose Farm with Therese.'

'Therese Viklund?'

'That's right. She took me to the private part of their farm and to the main house.'

'The pink house? Old place?'

I nod.

'What did you talk about with her?'

'About Elsa, mainly. A little about the other Rose Farm residents.'

He gestures for me to elaborate.

'The murder suicide back in the '80s.'

'A rotten thing,' says the Chief, narrowing his eyes. 'One of the worst scenes I ever did witness. Completely unnecessary carnage.'

'And about how T-Bone's wife died in prison.'

'Just to clarify, by T-Bone you mean Mr Kurt Holm, is that correct?'

'Correct.'

'Okay, then. Did Therese Viklund mention her husband?' he checks his notes. 'Mr Abraham Benjamin Jeremiah Viklund. She mention him?'

'Just that he was busy writing music.'

'So you didn't see Mr Viklund?'

'No.'

'Go on.'

'Andreas came to the house with his dogs. He said he'd found Elsa.'

'Andreas Olsson? Round what time was this?'

'Around two, I think.'

'And how did he seem?'

'Stressed, understandably.'

The Chief takes a sip of coffee from his mug. When he swallows he licks his lips and then he wipes his mouth across his knuckles.

'Go on.'

'We went with him to see Elsa.'

'You and Therese Viklund did?'

'Yes.'

'Walk or drive?'

'We walked there.'

He nods.

'She was there in a cluster of young alder trees. I saw her boot. And then her face. Therese took Elsa's pulse.'

'Neck? Wrist?'

'Neck.'

The Chief writes that down.

'There was no pulse. She looked like she'd been there for a while, part-covered in leaves and reeds.'

'Was there anything else that was strange about the scene? Anything that you noticed?'

'No, it was just like I described.'

'Was Elsa bleeding? Did you see any injuries?'

'No. Just a mark on her face. Is that what killed her?'

'We don't know about that yet. Won't know for a while more, the experts are doing their work. Who else was around when you were checking Elsa's body down by the river?'

'Just Therese, Andreas and me.'

He takes a bite of shortbread and it shatters over his paper and he looks agitated for a moment.

'And there was someone in the distance,' I say, recalling the figure. 'On the other side of the river. But he was a long way away.'

'He? You're sure it was a man? Can you describe him?'

I take a deep breath. 'Jeans, I think. Long coat, almost down to his ankles. Sorry, I can't describe him better. It was in the distance. I was focused on Elsa.'

'And then you say you saw Elsa's father close by?'

'As I was driving out.'

'I need to divulge something to you this evening and I'm going to need you to be real discreet about it, can I have your word on that?'

'What do you mean?'

'I mean I can go to Lena if I need to, but I reckon we can sort this out you and me.'

'I don't understand?'

He takes a deep breath. 'I'm going to share something with you that you can't share with another living soul. And I know you'll say that's fine, you can do it, because that's what every person says when they're offered in on something truly confidential. But I want your word.'

'Alright.'

He offers me a biscuit and I shake my head.

'There was a distinguishing feature on the body of young Elsa Nyberg. We're working to keep it out of the press, out of our police briefings, but I think letting you know might be beneficial to the investigation.'

'Okay.'

'Do I have your word?'

'Sure.'

He clenches his teeth and blows out of his nose and says, 'Elsa had an inking on the back of her neck.'

'An *inking*?'

'Well, I'm not sure what to call it exactly. Maybe it's paint or ink or some kind of unusual tattoo. Semi-permanent, we think. I've got a photograph here from the crime scene people. I'd like your view on it if you wouldn't mind.'

'Okay.'

He presses a few keys on his keyboard and then swivels his monitor to face me.

'You ever seen a symbol like that before in your life?'

The screen shows a neck, grey in pallor, with an ant, half in the shot. On the back of the neck, just beneath Elsa's hairline, is a cross.

'A cross?'

'But, one like that?'

The cross is upside-down. Like a crucifix upturned. It is white.

'I don't recognise it.'

'You and me both, Moodyson.'

'Was it a tattoo she had?'

'Her daddy says no, adamant he is, but sometimes people are good at hiding tattoos from their loved ones. We'll get more information from the autopsy; sample going down to the white coats at the national forensics centre in Linköping. But Thord reckons it's fresh, whatever it is. Like it's been done recently. Could be it was done real recently.'

'So I can't mention this when I speak to people around the story, when I interview Elsa's friends and family?'

'Correct.'

'So why tell me about it?'

'You and me don't do things the same way, let's be clear on that. But I see you can add value from time to time. You poke your nose into something, you do your best to root out right from wrong, I seen you operate enough years to know it. So if you find another symbol like this, a car sticker or backpack badge, or someone mentions it to you, or you even think you see a similar tattoo on someone's neck up in hill town, you bring it straight to me, day or night, you hear?'

'Sure, Chief.'

'That's a deal then.'

'That's not a deal.'

'Excuse me?'

'I'll work on the symbol. I'll keep an eye out for it. And I'll keep it out of my newspaper. So what do I get in return?'

'Young lady, I just included you in some strictly confidential police business, something I'll give to no other journalist.'

'I can't use it.'

He frowns and scratches at the bandage on his injured hand.

'Access,' I say.

'Access to what exactly?'

'The case.'

'I reckon Thord usually fills you in more than he's wise to do already.'

'Access to Rose Farm, then.'

He smiles and sits back in his chair. 'Do you even know those people? Really *know* them? I don't have any more control over the Rose Farm Minutemen than I do over Washington DC or Buckingham Palace.'

'*Minutemen?*'

'Figure of speech.'

'I understand I can't get in to see them, to talk to them, through your police ways. But maybe with the Sheriff? They seem to like him, or at least tolerate him.'

'Sheriff Hansson is a credit to his community, but as you well know he doesn't report to me in any way. He's a community-liaison neighbourhood-watch officer or some such. A good citizen is what he is.'

'He looks up to you, though. Treats you like his de facto boss?'

'Well, everyone's got a failing.'

'Talk to him. Ask him to let me ride with him when I need. Maybe put in a good word.'

'He already thinks you're sound as reporters go.'

'Was that a compliment?'

'I don't know, was it?'

'Can I go now, Chief? I want to research what you told me.'

'It's between you and me. You remember that, Moodyson. If someone breaks their word then they're dead to me. Dead.'

17

I head outside on to Storgatan, and the moon is almost full and the town is almost empty. The stars shine clear in the sky. All is not well.

'Moody,' yells a voice from my left, from the hill by St Olov's church ruin.

Tammy jogs down to me and I open my arms to her and we embrace. She's one of those rare people who can judge how the recipient of a hug is feeling just by the intensity of the squeeze, and adapt accordingly. Tammy gleans that I need this hug. That it is about all I have right now. I squeeze and she squeezes back, the pressure of her arms around my back.

'You had a shitty day. I heard. I'm real sorry.'

'Are you okay?' I ask.

She nods.

'I can take you back to your place.' She looks me over, sees my weariness, my fragile veneer of a functional life. 'Maybe I can sleep on your obscenely comfortable couch again, if you want me to stay? You have a very fancy couch; I mean it's the best, better than my bed even. If anything you'd be doing me a massive favour.'

I smile.

'I'll be fine. Thanks, though.'

'I sold out of crackers or I'd have brought you a greasy bag.'

'How did you know I'd be down here?'

'Customer told me,' she says. 'Sara from the health-food store. Nosy Cow. Said she saw you go inside with the Chief.'

'Small town, news travels fast.'

'Tell me about it.'

'Not sure I want to go home just yet, Tam.'

She looks at me and she understands. How my flat is still my sanctuary but not quite as much as before. How I moved out after Noora was shot, stayed at Tammy's and then in Lena's spare room-slash-art studio on an inflatable bed. They both took me in.

'Ronnie's for a quick nightcap?' she says. 'I can only handle one, early start tomorrow.'

She can handle more than one. She may or may not have an early start in the morning. But she is limiting the scope of our night for me. Tam is saving me and putting the burden on herself like she has done a hundred times before.

'Fuck it,' I say.

'That's the spirit.'

We walk, arms linked, to Ronnie's Bar. Takes all of a minute. The street is frosty, crystals forming on benches and mailboxes, a frozen sheen clinging to each parked truck.

The bar is gently humming.

It's not dead quiet because this is their peak time. And it's not buzzing because, well, because this is Toytown. Manage your expectations. Then manage them some more. The only time Ronnie's Bar is buzzing is for an hour or two on Christmas Eve *Eve*, the twenty-third, and then again for the first ten days each hunt season. That's what folks are waiting for. The autumn. The big cull. For those ten days the schools around Gavrik turn a blind eye to poor attendance. They let their students go free to satisfy a collective bloodlust that has existed here since well before the town's creation, well before the construction of St Olov's, even. The pulp mill shuts down for the period. When a group of external investors pumped in cash back in the '90s, they questioned whether the company could afford to arbitrarily shut down production for ten days each autumn. And they were told. The managers told them. The unions told them. The workers made their voices heard. Hunt season is hunt season. It's something that needs to be done, the annual tradition, the management of woodland for the benefit of all creatures and all men. So, they got the message. The mill closes for ten days and the workers receive unpaid leave for that period, just like they always have. After the hunt, deer strung up in beech trees and wolves slung over shoulders and elk harvested by accountants and street sweepers, a good number would congregate in Ronnie's Bar on account of it being the only bar in town. The cloakroom would heave with camouflage coats and bright orange caps. The hunt dogs would be tethered outside. The room would smell strongly of pine needles, gunpowder and blood, and Ronnie would have his best week of the whole year.

Leonard Cohen on the jukebox.

A flicker from a light above the pool table, the bulb about to expire.

We don't hang up our coats, we just stride up to the bar counter and take a stool each.

'Tuva, Tammy,' says Ronnie, a glass in one hand, a cloth in the other.

'Two rum and Cokes, please, Ron,' says Tammy.

'Doubles?'

She looks at me for a moment and then says, 'Better make them singles. Big day tomorrow.'

He nods and starts to fix us our drinks.

A group of four or five in the back of the room start laughing and jeering at a joke and then one of them yells, 'Screw this, I'm leaving.'

Ronnie keeps one eye on them while he pours rum measures into tall glasses. Small-town bar like this, he's the manager, proprietor, barman, cleaner, waiting staff, and he's also security. Most people respect him enough for him to do all jobs simultaneously without too much bother. And when someone does step out of line, which happens from time to time, the locals back him up. It's a rudimentary small-town system but it works.

'Ladies,' he says, placing down two paper coasters and then two drinks.

He walks away to the back of the room.

'What happened?' says Tam.

I take a sip and then I take a bigger sip.

'What happened at Rose Farm?'

'You know it's a kind of closed community? Close to Snake River.'

'They got some sort of part-time café? Free-range place? I've been. I told you I've been.'

'Sorry, you did. The café's open weekends only.'

'What happened?'

'Girl went missing a few days back. I say girl, she was twenty. Elsa Nyberg.'

'I heard about it.'

'Her body was found today on the outskirts of Rose Farm, down close to the waters of Snake River.'

'I heard rumours that was the case.'

'I was there when the police came. I saw her.'

Tammy places her hand on my hand. Mine feels cold under hers.

'I'm sorry. With all you've been through, I'm sorry you saw that.'

I withdraw my hand and scratch my neck. 'It's okay. She didn't look injured in any way. Was strange.'

'People say she had a swastika on her head someplace, some kind of branding? A burn?'

'Who told you that?'

'Customer heard it from a salesman out of Karlstad. Not true? She wasn't a Nazi?'

I'm not sure of the facts yet, but I feel I need to defend this woman. 'Not remotely true.'

'What then?'

I start to speak but then remember Chief Björn. His speech about keeping your word.

'I didn't see anything on her head, no marks,' which is the truth. The mark wasn't on her head. 'Bruise on her face is all, up by her eye. No brandings, for God's sake.'

'Gossip spreads,' she says.

'And it distorts and gets uglier with every stage of the spread.'

'That pointed at me?' she says.

'Of course it isn't.'

She gives me some side-eye.

'Any idea who is responsible?'

I shake my head.

'Well, when you do figure it out I'd appreciate you letting me know, Tuva Moody. On account of the fact that I still, despite everything, operate a fine dining take-out business from an isolated van on the dark side of a car park on the edge of shitsville. I'd appreciate a heads up.'

'The farm is a long way from here, Tam. It's a whole different world.'

'Isn't that different.'

'They're preppers, you know what that means?'

'Means they expect an alien invasion any minute, right? Means they have underground bunkers and listen out for Russian armies on the border.'

I smile. 'Actually, no. I've been researching the movement, and it seems most preppers are normal, hard-working people who prefer to be more self-reliant than the average. Store some extra food, water, mindful of door locks, that kind of thing.'

'If they're so normal why did one of them end up dead in a river?'

'Next to the river. And I'm not sure Elsa was a prepper. I need to get digging.'

'Anything else to drink?' asks Ronnie.

'We're good, thanks,' says Tam before I can speak.

'Thank you,' I say.

Tam waits for him to serve someone else and then she says, 'You interviewed the girl's dad yet?'

'Not yet. Why?'

'Another customer of mine, Kommun bureaucrat, mid-fifties, shifty eyes, always leaves a five-kronor tip, like that's doing me a favour, he reckons Elsa's dad was some kind of money lender in the area. That was his main job once upon a time. Reckons people all over Visberg and Gavrik owed that man money and he'd be heavy-handed collecting his repayments, plus interest. You know, mob style.'

'Mob style? In Värmland?'

'Every corner of the earth, Tuva. People need cash. Desperate, willing to pay anything, whatever rate of interest, whatever terms. You'll always find people willing to lend it, off the books, backed up by muscle. It's the way of the world.'

'You think that might be linked to the murder of his daughter?'

'I don't know. Could be. Money motivates man.'

'That biblical?'

'Saw it on a bumper sticker last summer.'

'Could still be biblical, though.'

'Could well be.'

'I'm tired,' I say.

She ignores that and says, 'Same guy, shifty eyes, Captain Micro-Tip, he reckons Elsa had a boyfriend. Older man.'

'Your customers sure do talk a lot.'

'Oh, you don't know the half of it.'

I finish my drink and look at her.

'Most of them call ahead, like you would, like any normal decent person. They don't speak, some of them grunt a bit and tap their card against my reader, but that's about it. Doing the decent Nordic thing and keeping themselves to themselves. But then there's the minority. Even in midwinter when it's twenty-seven below, dark most of the day, they'll turn up, having not placed an order, and they'll queue, and they'll stand there shivering, freezing their tiny brains, and then they'll peruse my options like I'm a fucking buffet car on a train. Eventually they'll order, and then while I'm preparing and garnishing and boxing up they talk to me. Actually they talk *at* me, most of them. Happy to be apart from their disappointed spouse for a half hour, disappointing me instead. You'd be surprised what I learn.'

'I am surprised.'

I see Ronnie's back straighten. His eyes open wide and in one swift move he jumps the bar, knocking Tammy to the floor.

I swivel on my stool and Kurt T-Bone Holm is standing in the doorway of the bar and he's carrying a machete.

18

'Now, wait a minute,' says Ronnie, his voice loud but calm.

T-Bone flares his nostrils and Ronnie approaches him slowly with his hands in the air.

'I don't mean innocents no harm,' says T-Bone. 'Of course I don't. I'm here for information. Someone knows who killed my Elsie and that someone had better speak up.'

'Alright,' says Ronnie. 'Let me hold that for you, Kurt. You can go round and talk to all these loyal patrons with my blessing, but this is my place, my name on the licence. You let me hold it for you, now.'

T-Bone doesn't hesitate. He hands over the machete.

I hear someone in the back of the room say, 'That's T-Bone.'

'I didn't mean to frighten nobody.'

'I believe you,' says Ronnie. And then he turns to the thirty or so people in the bar and says, 'Just a misunderstanding. No harm, no foul. Let's keep this between ourselves, what do you say?'

There is mumbling. Tam looks at me wide-eyed.

'Next drink's on the house. What do you say?'

Several men yell out, 'Fine with me.' And a woman near the pool table says, 'We talking doubles, or what?'

Ronnie locks the machete away in his office and starts making drinks, a single bead of sweat quivering on his brow.

'They killed my Elsie,' T-Bone says to Tam and me. 'Either of you know who might have been responsible?'

I say, 'I was there today, T-Bone. It's me, Tuva.'

'I know it's you,' he says, but he looks exhausted, older than before. 'You find out anything, you let me know. Eye for an eye, tooth for a tooth, the Old Testament.'

'I'm going to try to find out,' I say. 'But we don't have any information for you right now. I'm sorry about Elsa.'

'She just turned twenty years old. Never got to live her life past chapter one.'

'I'm sorry,' says Tammy.

He staggers past us towards the pool table. He's not intoxicated with drink, but rather with loss. I know it. I've seen it and I've lived it. I am still living it to this day.

I sit quietly at the bar sucking on ice cubes and I think about how this must look. An insect on the ceiling would see a man walk into a bar carrying a half-metre sharpened blade and yet here, today, he faces no consequences. Not a police officer called, not a sanction applied. That bug would have witnessed one of the good things about a small town. The way decent people can sometimes resolve a complex issue with a simple answer. The way a bar owner with a high-school education, barely that, can come to be considered an elder of sorts by way of his fair and even-handed treatment of people over the years. His word is *the* word, at least in here. The man at the bar recognised the man walking in as a broken soul, not a real threat, just as men behind bars have had to do for centuries. Longer, even. And what's the net result of all this? No harm done, and T-Bone might just collect valuable information. If he doesn't, he'll be offered a drink and a handshake or two and some kind words from some good-hearted locals. It's not much but it's a start.

I hug Tammy outside on Storgatan and she shows me an object in the window of Benny Björnmossen's store. It's some kind of pre-assembled pulley rope, to enable a hunter to string up a half-ton bull moose using nothing more than the inherent strength of an oak tree or beech. It's called the Bull Hydraulic 3500 and it costs more than a week's wages.

I head home.

The apartment building is silent, save for two cats fighting out the back. They sound like twisted demons; a pair of tortured souls transitioning from purgatory down into hell.

I sleep.

In the morning my pillow alarm shakes me awake and I make instant oatmeal from a packet that already has the maple syrup incorporated. I pull on some semi-clean clothes and I drive straight to work because there's coffee in the office.

The Lutheran church bells chime.

In the dark places, the shadows by bins and trucks, there's still snow on the ground from last night. The lightest of coverings. A reminder that the freeze can still come back at any time to kill our crops and end us in the middle of the night. A reminder that we're only ever a few months from permafrost, either looking back or looking forward. The winter looms like a curse in these vast northern stretches. It is not to be respected, it is to be feared.

I have a key but the door is already open.

'Lars?'

'*Hej, hej,*' he says, his elasticated trousers high on his waist, his Roxette sweatshirt a size too small.

'You're in early.'

'Working on my book,' he says.

I love this guy. The way he's been working on his autobiography for as long as I've known him, almost five years. Maybe he's been working on it longer than that. The autobiography of a man who's never really done anything. I respect his commitment. He comes in here on weekends and spends months on a particular year, consulting his journals, using the *Gavrik Posten* archives to spark his memory from the days back when he was the only full-time reporter here. It'll take him his whole life to finish it.

'You look good,' I say, pulling off my coat.

'I feel good,' he says.

'Coffee?'

'Fresh in the pot.'

I pour myself a cup and sit down at my desk.

'What are you doing, Lars?'

He's using a hole punch. Over and over again on the same piece of paper.

'It's a mathematical challenge,' he says.

'No,' I say. 'It looks more like insanity.'

He smiles and slowly turns his head to me and his smile intensifies and then he punches a hole and his smile collapses. He scrunches the paper and throws it into the paper recycling bin, to join ten or so other balled up pieces of crocheted paper.

'My friend and I had a challenge back in school.'

I raise my eyebrows.

'How many holes can you punch into a single piece of A4 paper before you make an error and two or more holes join to make a larger, irregular hole.'

'You did this in school?'

'My friend and I did.'

I frown.

'Four hundred and eighty-four, theoretically speaking,' says Lars.

'How many have you managed?'

'Four hundred and seventy-one,' he says.

'That's pretty good.'

What has happened to my life? What the hell is this?

'It's not good enough,' he says. 'My friend can do better. He did better last year.'

'He's still doing this shit?'

'He sent me the paper. Not the original, of course, that would have been reckless. A photocopy of the paper. It was impressive.'

'Lars,' I say, shaking myself back to my world. 'Rose Farm, north of Visberg. Tell me what you know. Tell me more.'

He puts down the paper. He puts down the hole punch. He looks up towards the ceiling and then he blinks as slowly as anyone has ever blinked. He blinks again. Then he swivels his head to face me, like an arthritic owl might pivot to look at a distant sparrow.

'Tragedy a few decades ago.'

'The murder suicide.'

'Yes. The Edlunds of Visberg town used to leave that patch of land for outsiders. They owned all the surrounding riverfront farmland, all the fishing rights and water sources, but they shunned the plot of Rose Farm. They have shunned it for half a millennium.'

'Any reason?'

'Old man Edlund once told my pappa it was *bad land*. That they had no use for bad land in the family.'

'What does that mean?'

'He never did elaborate.'

Lars picks up his hole punch.

'Before you start again with that, what do you know of the current owners. The Viklunds?'

'Not a great deal.'

'Anything?'

'Rumours of them being survivalist types.'

'I heard that already.'

'The farmer, Holm I think his name is. His wife was incarcerated for…'

'Thanks, I heard.'

'She died in the prison.'

'Very sad.'

'Maybe she shouldn't have attacked him with a saucepan.'

'Anything else, Lars?'

'Cast-iron, it was.'

I frown.

'Le Creuset. Heavy bottom. Enamelled cast-iron pans. Excellent for casseroles.'

'Lars.'

'Sorry. Just that the missing girl, Elsa Nyberg.'

'She's not missing anymore, Lars.'

'What do you mean?'

'She was found yesterday up at Rose Farm. Suspected homicide.'

Lars closes his eyes and he bows his head slightly and he says, 'May her soul rest in peace.' He looks up at me. 'I didn't know.'

'You were going to tell me something about her?'

He sighs. Then he says, 'Doesn't feel right to talk more, not under the circumstances, Tuva. Feels grubby. Disrespectful.'

'It might help us find who killed her, though? Nothing grubby about that.'

'I don't know if it will help...'

'Please, Lars.'

He takes a sip of coffee.

'There was word, I can't reveal sources on this because I can't recall the facts, truth be told. Rumours her pappa wasn't actually Leif Nyberg. In reality, Leif wasn't her biological father.'

I wait.

'Rumour was she was Kurt Holm's up at Rose Farm. People call him T-Bone.'

19

Lars heads home and I turn up the intensity of my research. Office door locked, coffee pot on my desk, hearing aids out, phone off.

Google images.

It's the fastest way to link apparently disconnected pieces of information. The eyes see things faster in image format than in text. I search 'Rose Farm Värmland' and there are photographs of the compound: some of the café, some of the spa, some aerial shots taken by a local drone enthusiast. Most of the photos are older, though: 1980s. Back then the farm was much less fortified. No steep ditches or fences. The photos are all linked to articles and think-pieces and police reports relating to the murder suicide. The horror discovered out in front of the Rose Farm manor house. Two murdered boys and a murdered wife and a dead killer. One newborn baby, spared.

I run a Google image search on each tab on my laptop. One on 'Andreas Olsson', one on 'Linda Larsson', one on 'Abraham and Therese Viklund', one on 'Kurt Holm', one on 'Ruby and Niklas Gunnarsson' and one on 'Leif Nyberg'.

Each tab contains hundreds of images, not all of them relevant. Facebook photos, newspaper snippets, school journals, old social-media sites, now defunct, business interviews, LinkedIn profiles.

Eventually I zone in on an image of a man in black wearing a balaclava. He's holding a shotgun in one hand and a crucifix in the other. The crucifix isn't upside-down like the white ink on the back of Elsa Nyberg's neck, but it's a connection nonetheless.

I dig deeper.

I drink more coffee.

False starts and dead ends. So many.

Eventually I find a forum run in Swedish, but it has an English-speaking sub-forum. The name of the forum is 'The Four Horsemen' and it's based right here in Värmland. The sub-groups within the forum are: 'food', 'water', 'security', 'medical', 'comms', 'bugging out' and 'intel'. There are several other groups but these are locked to non-members. So I apply to become a member. I use an anonymous email address out of Iceland. I set it up three years ago, for just this kind of research. Via a VPN, I apply for membership of 'Four Horsemen' in the name of 'Alex Texas'.

Five minutes later I receive my welcome email.

Five hours later I've learned a whole lot about how to survive an EMP attack or a grand solar minimum famine, but I'm no closer to learning who killed Elsa Nyberg.

I head over to the newsagent. It's closed, but through the window I can see the owner restocking his shelves. I knock on the window and make a face like I'm sorry but I haven't eaten for a week. He rolls his eyes and lets me in.

'I'm sorry. Is it okay? Just one minute?'

'It's no problem, Tuva. But I've already cashed up and shut down so you'll have to pay me tomorrow, okay?'

Perks of small-town life.

'I owe you,' I say.

'Literally,' he says.

I grab a sandwich from the counter and a bag of prawn cocktail crisps and an XL bar of Marabou chocolate, the kind with salty biscuit inside, and a four-pack of pot noodles.

'Paragon of health,' he says.

I grab an apple and add it next to the till.

He smiles and says, 'Have a good evening, Tuva. Don't work too late.'

'Look who's talking.'

Back in Storgatan, the sky has darkened and there are no people around. It's like a snow globe left in a dark room. Still life. A dilapidated flea circus with only one visible flea left alive.

More coffee.

I post seventeen separate notes on the forum once I understand the tone and the expectations of the group. I allude to the fact that I have some kind of tactical background, military or law enforcement maybe, without stating it outright. It's never the people who state things outright who have skills to offer. It's the quiet ones. And on Four Horsemen there is one person quieter than all the others. He's a 'platinum member' called 'Grey Man' and he is revered. I can tell by the way other members reply to his posts, the way they seek his advice. Grey Man has built up quite a reputation. I find out that he's not originally Swedish. That he is a father. That he is a businessman. That he thinks most preppers are just playing at it.

One pot noodle and a row of chocolate later and I'm in deep.

I never knew this much about alien communications or Area 51 or mass vaccination programmes or the imminent collapse of the global monetary system. The truth is I have very little interest. If the end of the world comes, I will not fight against it. Who wants to survive shivering in a cave with a personal water filter when everyone else has perished?

Within the 'security' group there are numerous dog threads. Which is better, a German shepherd or a Rottweiler? Should you socialise your dogs or leave them unsociable? Pros and cons of an all-meat diet, that kind of thing. The photo of the man in black with the shotgun leads back to this thread, even though there are no dogs in the picture. In the background of the image, enlarged 600 per cent, I can see something shining, and something else on the horizon. I download some free software that promises to clarify an image but all I get is a barrage of adverts. I download another piece of software and it does clean up the picture somewhat. The man in the photo is genuinely anonymous thanks to his balaclava. But the shiny object to the left is not metal or glass, as I had suspected. It is in fact water. It's a river. And the other object rising from the horizon is a chimney from a roof. I can't be completely sure but if I was a betting woman, and I'm not, I have enough vices as it is, then I'd put money down that the man with the shotgun is standing in front of Snake River and Rosebud Cottage.

This is where I make a decision.

A fork in the road.

The woman I love has been taken from me. My parents are dead. A young girl, Elsa Nyberg, is laid out right now on a cold, stainless-steel table. A pathologist is cutting through her skin, peeling back her face, examining her brain tissue. I can either choose to be a coward and follow due process, or else I can keep on digging. I can either play this safe or I can try to bring some closure, some justice, some peace to soothe the wounded soul of her father, whoever that happens to be. I can stop now. Or I can continue.

I don't have much to lose.

So I resolve to go on.

Grey Man is active right now, I can tell by the green icon next to his profile photo. The photo is the silhouette of a man chewing a toothpick.

I send him a private message. I say I'm based in Värmland and I'd like to talk to him. Either over the phone or in a public place. I say I'm not police or anything similar, and that I have discovered his true identity but I will not reveal it. I say I'm a fellow Grey Man, of sorts, and a believer in self-reliance. I explain that I try to read more than I write; I try to learn from people who have been there and done it. I say I'm not making a threat, that I won't expose his identity to the group if he doesn't want to meet with me, but rather I'd like to talk for fifteen minutes.

Three minutes later he says he'll meet me tonight, if I like. Just the two of us.

And that makes me nervous. Seems too easy.

This is the moment when I say no. Or I lie and take three friends along with me. But the image of Noora in my kitchen, collapsed, is engraved in my mind. The image of Elsa, down by the riverbank, is right there with it.

I say I'm based in northern Värmland and I appreciate his willingness to talk.

He says we should meet somewhere off a main road. Somewhere quiet.

Alarm bells. But, again, what do I have to lose.

I suggest the snowberg.

He suggests 9pm. No weapons, no other people.

I agree.

His profile icon turns from green to red.

20

My stomach is uneasy as I realise what I have set in motion. Meeting an anonymous man out in a deserted field, when there's a murderer on the loose. When you live in London or Mumbai or San Francisco and there's a murderer out there, which is most days if you think on it hard enough – all days, even – it doesn't carry the same weight. You're insulated from the mortal danger of it all, from the possibility of homicide, by probability. It's strength in numbers that affords you some modicum of reassurance. One in a million. One in ten million. Well, that same comfort does not apply in a small, isolated community. The statistics run against you. Having one murderer in a town of 8,000 is like having ten in a large town of 80,000, or 100 murderers in a city of 800,000. Imagine that. Or worse, imagine a city like London with 10,000 murderers. These are the odds I'm talking about. And if you look those odds square in the face, they're enough to make your heart miss a beat. Miss three beats.

I'm not an idiot. As much as it might feel like I have a death wish right now, no, not a death wish, more of a numbness to life, an ambivalence, in truth I want to keep writing the headlines rather than *be* the headlines. So I lock up the office and drive down to Tam's food van on the edge of the ICA Maxi car park.

'You're just in time,' she says, handing me a bag of crackers, some spicy, some white.

'Good day?'

'Made my budget,' she says. 'People are running scared but people still gotta eat. And when the news turns sour they tend to favour delicious fresh Thai cuisine over their homemade under-seasoned lamb mince wrapped in boiled cabbage leaves or whatever the hell they cook.'

'People are scared?'

She passes me a foil container containing four crispy spring rolls.'

'Parents of teenagers, mainly. People afraid of what's gone on before. We had all those months with nothing so much as a traffic incident or post-box theft. And then: boom. Lots of people round here knew the victim. Her old school friends, or people who talked to her when they visited the café or the spa on Rose Farm.'

'Tam, I'm going somewhere tonight.'

She looks up at me and frowns.

'I need to tell you where I'm going.'

'I don't like the sound of this already.'

'Wait,' I say. 'I'm going to meet a source out by the big snow pile north of Visberg. You know the one I mean?'

'If you mean the snowberg a few kilometres south of Rose Farm, then no you are bloody not.'

'It's work,' I say.

'Fuck work,' she says. 'You know how stupid you sound right now, Tuva Moody? *Oh, Tam, I'm gonna trek up in the middle of the night to a freakin' ice mountain in a field nowhere near anything. What could go wrong? Just wanted to let you know. Could you stick a target on my back to make it more convenient for the guy? Really appreciate it, Tam. See ya.*' She looks at me. 'No, Tuva.'

'I'm taking precautions.'

'Oh, really?'

'Trust me,' I say. 'I'm meeting them at nine. If I don't call you by ten, then let Thord know. Please.'

'You're absolutely serious.'

'Yeah.'

'I'm coming with you.'

'If you come he won't speak.'

She insists I download an app so she can track my phone and I agree. And then I drive out towards the road. As I pass McDonalds I spot Ruby Gunnarsson, the spa owner, walking from her car to the restaurant. She isn't walking very well at all. She's stumbling.

I have time. I park and follow her inside.

I stand in line. She's two ahead of me.

She orders and opts for table service. I order a Coke and take the paper cup and fill it up and I walk back past her table, when I say, 'Oh, sorry, Ruby? I didn't see you here.'

She looks up at me, her mascara blurred under her eyes and she says, 'What?'

'Mind if I sit?'

She waves her hands around and pulls the drawstring bag she has with her closer to her side.

'I'm not staying long,' she says. 'What's your name again? Sorry, I forgot.'

'Tuva,' I say, poking my straw into my cup. 'Tuva Moodyson.'

She nods. 'Fucked up day.' I nod and drink and she smiles and then she says, 'Fucked up town.'

'When did you move here?'

'Valentine's Day, 2016,' she breaks out laughing. 'Valentine's Day, you believe that?'

I smile.

'Cupid shot me with his arrow, right in the fucking head.'

'Tell me about it.'

'You don't wanna know.'

'No,' I say. 'You're probably right.'

'You eating?'

I shake my head.

'I find this handsome guy on the internet, right. Back when I was living in Cape Town, simple life, no complications. We get to talking, and then we meet in London one time. We flirt by email for months. Then he invites me to Sweden for Midsommar. So I come. Nice, real nice. Even Gavrik and Visberg look nice in June, you know? Didn't figure on the winters though, did I. Eight months of every goddam year.'

'Sometimes nine,' I say. 'They can suck.'

She grins and says, 'They *do* suck.'

'Niklas was all sweet. A gentleman, I guess. Until he got a ring on my finger, you know? How things change.'

I gesture for her to go on, and she says, 'I'm shooting my mouth off again. Ignore me. Save yourself and go sit at another table before I drag you into my own foul mood.'

'It's okay. I don't have too many friends in this town. Or in any town.'

'You and me both.'

'And I share your bad luck with men.'

'Most men are pigs.' She takes the tray from a young server and says to him, 'Not you, honey. Other men.'

'Oh, I know,' I say.

'Niklas tries to control me,' she says, unwrapping a hamburger. 'He tries to decide everything I do, but then he twists it all so it sounds like I decided for myself, you know? He has this way of making me feel like I'm crazy in the head.'

'Is there anyone on Rose Farm you can talk to, like a friend?'

'Not really. They've all got their own problems.'

'Linda seems okay.'

'Linda's a cold-hearted bitch, but I respect her for it, I really do. I wouldn't want to be in a fight with that woman, she reminds me of a few I knew back home, but she gets things done efficiently. You gotta respect it.'

'Therese, then.'

She laughs and spits out a little of her burger bun.

'Therese? No, Tuva. Just no, I'm not saying more, just no. Trust me. No, ma'am.'

She eats a fistful of fries. Her nails are acrylic and her hair is stripy, three or four distinct highlight shades.

'You know, I was a web developer before I moved here? I could still be coding but Niklas wanted me to set up the beauty business. So he always knows where I will be. So I never catch him.'

'Catch him?'

'You know what I'm talking about.'

I push my straw in and out of my Coke to break up the ice and reach the bottom.

'I was in St Olov's before, thinking, drinking some whisky T-Bone made over the winter. I was on a bench down by the Grimberg family graves, you know, in the corner, near the factory wall. There was a guy inside the ruined church. Nice guy, I thought. Thirty, thirty-five. And then a girl comes in, must have been close to Elsa's age, twenty or a little older, and they start making out in that church ruin, and all I'm thinking is why can't he find a woman his own age and why can't she see him for what he is. Why can't any of us see it until it's too late.'

'Never too late,' I say.

'Not for you, it is for me. I'm thirty-eight. Everything's in Niklas's name. I'm locked down with a struggling business I don't want, on a farm I don't like, with a man I don't respect.'

She starts to look queasy.

'Are you okay?'

She holds her hand to her mouth.

She stands up.

'Bathroom,' I say. 'Come on, I'll hold your hair.'

But she shakes her head and runs to the Ladies.

She vomits. I know because I can see it on the faces of my fellow diners. They hear her throw up. Sometimes it pays to be deaf. After a moment, everyone goes on eating their Filet-O-Fish and their Big Macs. While she's sorting herself out I pretend to knock something on to the seats opposite. I bend to pick it up and check what's inside her drawstring bag.

There's a set of syringes and needles.

A pipette of some sort.

And a bottle marked with a label.

'Semi-permanent Ink'.

21

The streets are empty. Moonlight comes and goes and clouds arrive over Toytown, and then they move on in haste.

Just because Ruby Gunnarsson had ink in her bag and appeared to be an emotional wreck does not mean she was involved in the murder of Elsa Nyberg. There is no motive that I can see. It's ink, is all.

As I drive past the Grimberg factory, the immense brick chimneys grow and the janitor raises his grit shovel at my Hilux by way of greeting. I wave and he gets on with putting salt down on the paths leading into the liquorice processors.

A lone woman reporter driving to a snowberg to meet an anonymous forum guru. If there is a heaven and Dad is up there, behind that moon, looking down, what would he think? But I am not afraid. I damn well should be but I am not. Last year, in the weeks before Noora getting shot, she asked me to move in with her. She was cool about the whole thing. Sweet. Generous. And I was pathetic. Even though in my bones I wanted nothing more than to wake up next to her every morning, to share secret quirks and frailties, to shop together in ICA, even though I wanted all of those things, I was too afraid to reach out and take them. I lived in a small toxic bubble with Mum after Dad died. I know what it's like to be trapped in a co-dependent cage with another human being. And I didn't want Noora to live that life. And, more importantly, I didn't want her to see me drink.

I should have all that to lose. That life. By rights, I should have Noora to lose. But I've already lost her. For the first few months I didn't understand. The doctors and nurses, and later on the carers, they all tried to let me figure it out for myself. I probably knew the truth deep down, but couldn't face it. And then, in early March, Noora's mother sat me down with fresh lemon cake. She had been a cardiologist back in Iraq and whereas some experienced doctors can lack a gentle bedside manner, Noora's mum is goodness and patience personified. She didn't talk down to me or instruct me. She asked me questions about how I thought Noora was doing. She held my hand and asked me how I was doing and she let me ask her how she was doing. And through those chats, with mugs of hot chocolate, while periodically going in to check feeding tubes and change bedsheets, I came to understand our reality. That this woman had lost her only daughter and I had lost my love. It breaks my heart all over again just to think about it. But heartbreak is the least of it. It makes me angry, too. Furious. Livid at the world, but also at Noora. If she hadn't been as brave or as diligent, maybe we could have grown old together after all.

A bird of prey glides ahead, it's plumage picked out by my headlights and by the moon, its muscular form lit as a prima ballerina in some futuristic amphitheatre.

Zero degrees.

I turn off left towards Rose Farm.

Why are you coming, Grey Man? Why did you accept my suggestion to meet at such short notice? What skin do you have in this shadowy game?

The snowberg is pale grey through the wispy birch trees, and, further ahead, close to Rose Farm itself, I see something else.

I slow and squint. Lights? Fireworks?

No sign of any other vehicle by the snowberg but it's not like there's a formal parking area. This is just a field that some faceless bureaucrat, some committee of bureaucrats, deemed suitable as repository for all the excess snow from Gavrik and Visberg, Toytown and hill town, shitsville one and shitsville two. Lars told me they used to leave it in church land off Eriksgatan but the spring thaw came fast one year and it flooded basements and caused property damage. You leave all that pent-up liquid in just one place and when it changes you'd better be ready.

Salt in the air from the ploughed snow. For months the Kommun workers pick it up with mechanical shovels and dump it into special trucks. The snowberg is white in places and grey in others, grit held for months in suspended animation.

No Grey Man.

I open my truck door and stand beside it, my engine still running. The exhaust fumes hang low in the heavy air and they drift forward to linger around my boots.

'Kill. Your. Engine.'

The voice is deep and calm and firm. Otherwise I wouldn't hear it.

'Where are you?' I say, squinting into the darkness next to my truck.

'I'm right here, Tuva.'

My heart starts beating harder in my chest. This was not the deal, this was supposed to be wholly anonymous. Is this even Grey Man? Or is this one of the guys from Rose Farm?

The faint howl of a wolf in the distance. Or else it's one of Andreas's guard dogs.

'You wanted to talk so I came all the way out here. Should I go home?' he says, and I recognise the voice, the hint of an accent.

'I still can't see you,' I say.

'Turn off your engine.'

I turn it off. The silence is complete. My headlights die and the scene is dark again, the only light reflected from the moon off the snow mountain.

'That's better,' he says.

A face comes into view. I hear branches move and then I can see his eyes.

'Luka?'

And now I can see his teeth.

'Let's walk.'

He sets off around the side of the snowberg, itself an acre or more in size and five metres high. I run to catch up.

'First of all,' he says. 'You never mention this to a living soul. I need you to guarantee me that.'

'Sure,' I say. 'But I can't talk if I can't see you. I need to read your lips as back-up. We can't have this conversation in the dark.'

He stops and steps closer to me. A torch illuminates his face. 'I take my privacy very seriously, Tuva. I'm just a pizza grill owner these days. Father and husband and amateur chess enthusiast. That is how I prefer to be known in this country. And I don't want any future story or casual conversation in Ronnie's bar to change that. Word travels fast around here.'

'I'm a journalist,' I say. 'I always protect my sources. Anything you say is off the record if that's what you want.'

'I'm not a source, I'm just a simple middle-aged man who wants a simple life.'

'And who happens to be looked upon as some kind of demi-God on the Four Horsemen forum.'

'Everyone needs a hobby.'

'I thought you played chess.'

'Chess is for me. The forum is to help others.'

'Help?'

He sniffs the cold air and says, 'Most people in the West have no real idea how they'd fare if their comforts were to suddenly stop for some reason. If some freak weather washed away their home or a currency crisis wiped out their savings. I do my best to help people mentally prepare for the unknown. Physically prepare. All in the hope that they will never need those skills.'

'Are you a prepper, Luka?'

I see his teeth again. 'No, I wouldn't say that. I'm just a man who's lived a hard life is all.'

'So you don't prep?'

'When you've lived through what I've lived through you never stop being ready. It's not that I'm prepped, it's that I'm always expecting it.'

'It?'

'Whatever. Could be anything.'

A wolf howls again a few kilometres away and others join in. But I do not fear the darkness with Luka Kodro by my side. If he'd wanted to hurt me he would have done it by now.

'Is that a wolf or a dog?' I ask.

'Dogs,' he says. 'And if a wolf was tracking you, hunting you, he'd not be howling. He'd be quiet. Waiting. Starving hungry. Stooped low against the frost and biding his time. Sensing where his pack is. Preparing to strike.'

'You seem to be a fan.'

'A wolf took my dog years ago. We weren't out hunting, just visiting friends on the Dalarna border, not far from here. My boy wasn't wearing his spiked collar or his armour. The wolf, it was a lone animal, desperate, killed him in seconds. I didn't even hear the kill. When I found him I sobbed, I won't deny it. I'd failed him. A dog is like the folks on the forum site. They might look like they're capable of things but most of them are not. Not because they are physically weak but because they don't have the necessary aggression. The instinct to commit without hesitation. Dogs get fed and wolves hunt, Tuva.'

'I see.'

'What do you want from me? You've shown me you're very clever, finding me through the Four Horsemen site. So, what are we doing here?'

'I didn't know it was you.'

'I know.'

'What do you mean?'

'Every word I write on that forum is considered. I would never allow myself to give up my identity.'

'But you took a risk coming here to meet with me?'

'I did no such thing.'

'Well, I could have been anyone.'

'I traced your IP address to the *Gavrik Posten* newspaper office on Storgatan.'

'No, I used a VPN.'

'You used a weak VPN. You probably didn't even notice when it dropped connection for a split-second but that was enough for me to find your location. Was it a free VPN service?'

'Yes.'

'If you value your anonymity then you must pay for the privilege.'

The wind picks up. I shiver.

'So you came because you knew it would be me?'

'I think you're a serious person,' he says. 'If you took the time to make all those banal comments and read over three-hundred threads in one day, then I assumed you'd have something important to discuss.'

'I do.'

He doesn't say anything.

We trek around the back of the snow mountain and back to my Hilux.

'Where are you parked?' I ask.

'It is of no consequence where I am parked.'

'Sorry, I just…'

'What is it, Tuva?'

'Why don't you look around you, into the darkness? Shouldn't you be on constant lookout with your military background?'

He sighs. 'I have been ambushed in a valley. In many valleys. I have been shot through the shoulder by a sniper hiding in a church bell-tower. The shot didn't hurt but the infection after almost killed me. I have had grenades thrown at me in my home village by a man who used to teach me woodwork. I don't need to show you I'm aware of my surroundings. I just am. You believe that or you don't.'

The smell of sulphur in the air.

'Something's burning on Rose Farm.'

'It is the asparagus,' says Luka.

'Asparagus?'

'There will be a sharp frost tonight. Already is. Maybe it'll drop to four below. They burn hay bales and dry wood. Make heat around the asparagus crop, otherwise it will perish and wither away. They are the asparagus fires.'

'I didn't know farmers did that.'

He says nothing.

'I need your help, Luka.'

'I know it already. What do you need?'

I lick my lips. They're dry in this cold, salty air.

'There's only one thing I can think of that will get me inside Rose Farm, into their confidences, so I can work out who killed Elsa Nyberg, or at least give something useful to the local police.'

'You don't think police know what they're doing?'

'They need help sometimes.'

He laughs.

'They need help most of the time,' he says.

'The one thing I can offer Rose Farm is you. Your knowledge.'

'Me?'

'I want to offer them some time with you. Asking you questions. You assessing their preparedness, their shelter plans, their first aid, all of it.'

'I am not the man for this.'

'You know more than they do. More than anyone on the Four Horsemen forum knows. They will listen to you because you've lived it and they haven't.'

'Lived it?'

'When the shit hits the fan.'

'Yes, I have lived that.'

'So?'

'What do I get in return? My restaurant is full. I don't need to advertise in your newspaper, so I can't want a discount on what I don't need. Only restaurant in Visberg, I keep it that way.'

'Elsa was twenty years old. You have a wife and two daughters. I will give you my word that I won't stop until the killer is brought to justice.'

'Okay, but I don't think you will stop whatever I decide to do, no?'

'That's fair. But getting deep inside their compound, meeting Abraham, talking to them, that will get me the valuable intel I need.'

'Intel? You know all the jargon, eh?'

'Three hundred threads,' I say.

'Most of it bullshit. Boys comparing their knives. You know some of the guys on the forum site have over a hundred combat knives. But they have no idea how to work a knife in a genuine fight. How bad that would be. How brutal. Most of them would run away long before a knife fight would ever be an option. And I could tell them they only need two knives: one and a backup. But I let them chat nonsense. Drives up ad revenue.'

'It's your forum?'

'It's my wife's business. She's an entrepreneur. I am just a pizza man.'

'The other thing I can offer is to keep you in the loop.'

'The loop?'

'To let you know if anything is happening that might be relevant to you and your family. Your interests. I have close ties to the police in Gavrik, to local Kommun and business leaders. Might be useful.'

Luka Kodro looks up into the sky and then sighs. 'I will require NDAs.'

'NDAs?

'Non-disclosure Agreements,' he says. 'Confidentiality agreements. My wife will draft them. No mention that I was ever on Rose
Farm. No mention of my identity on the night. I will be wearing a
mask when I visit. No photographs or videos. I will make myself
available for three hours of Q&A and I will require no food or
refreshments.'

'Coffee?'

'I bring my own coffee. Oh, and, Tuva.'

'Yeah.'

'It may one day seem opportune to break your word. Perhaps you
feel you must tell someone about me, about the forum, to further
a story next year, or in five years. But I think you are smart. You
can understand what I have done in my life. What I am able to
execute. I think that means more that the agreement written on
paper. I think you see exactly what I am capable of.'

22

I sleep a full ten hours, the longest since February. Back then I was still staying at Lena's place when I was in Gavrik, and in Noora's parents' place or the hospital when I was visiting. It's remarkable how much sleeplessness and despair a person can handle when hope is dangled in front of their face. Just out of reach. I thought the odds of Noora improving, even slowly, even just a little each year, would increase just by the sheer force of my wanting it. That hope, that willing with every cell of my body, I thought it would make a difference. It didn't help. Nothing like that helps. The universe doesn't care about what you wish for. Nature is ambivalent to your desires and dreams. That kind of wishing deceives your husk of a body into hanging in there for a little longer. Some base, biological trick. And then one day in late February when I woke up in the hospital to check Noora's breathing, to check her tracheostomy before the nurse came round, to make sure she was comfortable, I broke down. It was the hopelessness. The way this event has bent time to the extent where a week could feel as long as a month. It could start on a Monday, with terror as she suffered an epileptic fit as a result of the brain trauma. And then by Thursday she'd be settled and she would eat better. And then on Sunday she'd suffer some new swelling and the doctors would gather around again to discuss whether they need to put a drain in. The worry was constant. It took a toll on me and for that I felt guilty because in the next room was a teenage boy of nineteen who'd crashed his motorbike three years before. His parents never complained or looked like they could collapse from it all. They'd taken him home but every so often they needed to bring him back to the hospital for specialist care. I thought I could be like them, be strong for years on end, decades, pause my own life to hold Noora's hand and read to her and wash her hair. But I'm not as strong as them. I'm not as strong as I should be.

At the police station, three TV vans are parked outside. One has a fancy new logo on its side, the result of a merger of two Nordic media groups. But I can still see the old logo through the new paint.

The vertical strip-blinds flicker as I open the door and step inside.

'Morning, Tuvs,' says Thord, ticking me off his list and holding up a presser pass as if such things were even needed in this town. Who'd try to slip into this conference when everybody knows everybody else?

'Hi,' I say.

'Usual spot,' he says. 'Front and centre.'

'Appreciate it.'

He does this for me, reserves the best spot, partly because he's a friend but also he knows I'll have difficulty hearing or reading lips from the back of the room.

I go inside and Magnus Falk, the new temporary cop, Noora's replacement, is standing at the podium, his back as stiff as an ironing board.

He coughs as I step in. I ignore him and sit down.

The room smells the way it always does at this time of day. ICA Maxi shower gel, anti-dandruff shampoo, cheap deodorant, coffee breath, old carpet tiles and pine-scented air fresheners. The combination of all that in an airless room.

Chief Björn steps through the door behind the podium and Magnus clears his throat again. I dash up and place my Dictaphone by the microphones and Magnus ignores me and taps a mic and says, 'I would say good morning but I don't think that'd be appropriate.' Nowhere near appropriate, fool. The room cools to him and

I can tell that remark will add a year, a whole year, to him ever being halfway accepted in Gavrik. 'Chief Björn Andersson will address you all in a moment.'

The Chief walks up to Magnus and taps him on the shoulder and Magnus walks away and the Chief watches him like a flatmate might watch a one-night-stand walk out of a flat-share kitchen.

'I'd like to thank everyone for coming at short notice. As many of you will know, Ms Elsa Marie Elizabeth Nyberg was found, deceased, adjacent to the property of Rose Farm north of Visberg town three days ago. Ms Nyberg was twenty years old. On behalf of the police department I'd like to express my sympathies to the Nyberg family and the surrounding community. It's a sad day when we lose a local citizen but it's a tragedy with one so young.'

He takes a sip of water from his plastic cup.

'I can confirm that following extensive police work, we are treating this death as a homicide. The coroner has communicated to me that the victim was struck by some kind of object. Blunt-force trauma. One blow to the head around here.' The chief points to his temple. 'I think it's relevant to note that the coroner stated to me, over the telephone, that in his professional judgement, Ms Nyberg would not have felt any significant pain.'

A camera flash behind me lights up the Chief's face.

This is the kind of detail, the pain remark, that you won't find at a police presser in a large city. It's the Chief doing his best to start the healing process.

Three more flashes go off.

He looks tired. Like he's seen too much.

A woman next to me with an Alice band – when was the last time you saw one of those? – puts up her hand and the Chief says, 'I'll be inviting questions presently,' and he says that without even looking at her, and I think that's probably because she wrote a less than positive remark about him in the *Falun Enquirer* about four years ago.

It's exhausting trying to follow a press conference, turning back to look at the speaker's mouth, trying to fill in gaps. People mumble and talk over each other. I doubt I'll ever be comfortable in one of these.

'Can you all hear me?' he says, tapping the new mic that is not switched on.

We all say yes.

And then the mic does switch on and it squeaks feedback and squeals and the Chief looks over at Magnus Falk and says, 'Switch that off.'

'As I was saying, I'm obliged to you all for coming in this morning. We have a piece of closed-circuit television footage for you, taken from the property of Rose Farm on the day of the homicide, and I'd like to show you the clip now.'

He gestures for Magnus to turn on the projector and he does and an image appears on the wall. It's upside down.

The Chief grits his teeth and the muscles of his jaw bulge.

Magnus Falk fixes the problem.

'Now, this is low resolution because of the distance the camera was from the river. Lighting isn't optimal and we have no sound, but the forensics team out of Linköping have cleaned up the recording as much as they can. There, you see a figure on the far side of the river. There, you see him again: a heavy-set individual setting up his boat. There, one last time, looks like the person in the shot is wearing some sort of hunting cap or baseball-style cap. Long coat. I'd like to appeal to you and your readers and viewers for any information on this individual. It is vital that we speak to them so we can eliminate them from our investigations.'

The woman next to me puts her hand up again and the Chief just stares her down.

'Constable Falk will be handing out an A4 image of the person in the footage and there'll be further details posted on the Gavrik-police website later on today. I must remind you all that due to the ongoing nature of this investigation I may not be able to answer your questions at this point in time. Thank you.'

Hands go up all around me.

The Chief looks at them and then points at me.

'Chief, do you know what the time of death was, please?'

He takes a deep breath. 'Coroner's narrowed it down to a window of twelve hours. We'll be sharing that information shortly.'

A guy at the back of the room from a Stockholm outfit asks, 'Chief Andersson, do you have any persons of interest at this stage? Any suspects?'

'We're still conducting door-to-door enquiries and waiting on further forensic results, but, to answer your question, we are following up on several strong leads.'

He points to a woman behind me and says, 'Yes.'

'Chief Andersson, what can you tell us about the mark on Elsa Nyberg's neck?'

The Chief looks over at Magnus Falk and Magnus frowns.

'No comment at this time. Moodyson? Any more questions?'

'Chief, are there any motives you're aware of yet?'

'Well,' he says. 'Police work is a complex business. We have a whole web of leads and potential suspects to work on. And we hope to update you in the coming days.'

The woman next to me says, 'Where did Elsa live? Work? What did she do?'

The Chief does not appreciate being talked to without the mention of his rank, but he swallows that down.

'Ms Nyberg was an active resident of her local rural community. I'm told Ms Nyberg was a valued member of staff at both the Rose Farm organic café and at the farm itself. Now, if that's all, I'd like to thank…'

'Is this a ritualistic occult killing?' shouts a nasal voice from the back. 'Is this death linked to the murder suicide back in 1987? Does the presence of an upturned cross and a pentagram mean we have a Satanic killer loose in Värmland?'

A pentagram?

The Chief bites his lip.

'Okay, now listen up carefully. I'd like to remind you all that we all have professional responsibilities here. The facts need to be reported accurately so as not to scupper our investigations. I can confirm there was no pentagram-style emblem on the body of Ms Nyberg, and I can also state categorically that we are not currently investigating any potential links to devil-worshippers or Satanists or any suchlike organisations.'

And then the lights all go off.

23

We don't get many power cuts in Gavrik town, not like out in the villages and forest hamlets, but we do get some. Journalists curse and laugh, nervous voices, and then someone opens an emergency-exit door out on to the street and the sun pours into the room and lights up Chief Björn like he's some kind of angel.

A reporter from Malmö, nice woman, kind eyes, asks me to McDonalds. Says she'll buy me lunch if I fill her in on some of the community details. I say I would but I have a meeting. I apologise to her.

The drive east is quiet.

No music in the truck, no phone calls.

I don't listen to anything just before I interview a grieving family member. Out of respect for them but also to prepare myself for it. To *steel* myself. Every time you talk with a human being in that much pain you can't help but take some of their pain on to yourself. You absorb it as an involuntary charitable act, a kind of rebalancing of energies. They're hurting so bad you can't help but take some of it. You don't get a choice in that.

I drive towards Visberg, take a left, drive past the heap of snow. The fires that were lit last night on Rose Farm to protect the aspar-agus crop from frosts are smoking, glowing weakly beyond the fences and the ditches. When I pass by the turning for the track to the riverside alders, where Elsa Nyberg was killed, I feel a pull inside my throat. A tightening.

Leif Nyberg, Elsa's dad, lives in a strange place. In the '60s and '70s, the Swedish government embarked upon an ambitious housing project. The *Million Programme* aimed to build a stock of public housing to ensure that all Swedes had a safe, warm, dry, affordable home. They understood that homes are essential to wellbeing. But the project had mixed results. Some of the buildings are still celebrated: mixed-use housing and work spaces, green leisure areas, shopping. Those were featured in magazines and are still desirable places to live half a century later. Other building projects weren't so successful. Like the one Leif Nyberg lives in.

Away from other towns, other cities, other villages even, sits a monolith of brutalist architecture. A huge concrete box rising from marshland. Featureless and uniform, one box apartment after the other. A small convenience store. A dry cleaner with a key-cutting machine. A youth centre. This is what the locals call 'purgatory': home to seven-hundred souls lost out in the middle of nothing whatsoever.

I park and find apartment 93B.

A horizon of broken trees and low mist.

The name plate says Nyberg.

I buzz.

The door opens. Suit trousers, a pale blue shirt, a V-neck sweater, one black sock, one grey. His eyes are red and sunken and his nose looks sore.

'My Nyberg.'

'Are you the reporter?'

'I'm Tuva Moodyson. I'm so sorry for your loss.'

He nods his head as if my words are falling to the ground somewhere between us. As if they don't quite reach through his thick aura of grief.

'Come in, Tuva. Come inside.'

The apartment is warm. A parrot sits in a cage in the corner of the room pecking at a cuttlefish bone. The TV is on in the opposite corner, but it is muted.

'Can I get you a drink? I have water or I have a pot of coffee. Just instant.'

'Water, please.'

He hands me a glass and we sit down at his kitchen table. I see him take something from the third chair.

'You're sitting in my wife's seat, in Marie's seat.'

'Oh, I'm sorry,' I say starting to stand up.

'No, no. She passed three years ago. She used to sit there because she said it was closer to the stove, see. I was never much of a cook.'

'I'm the same, I'm afraid.'

I pull out my Dictaphone and he stares at it.

'Do you mind?' I say.

'You know what you're doing,' he says. 'I'm not so hot on technology. Elsa used to use the internet for me.' He smiles and he holds up the scarf he took from the third chair. It's a grey wool scarf with tassels at both ends. He wraps his hands up in the fabric.

'Can you tell me a little about your daughter? Just some details so I can do her justice in the *Gavrik Posten.*'

He pulls the scarf tighter through his hands and then he loosens it and strokes the wool with his thumb. The skin around his nail is cracked.

'I was a steeplejack until I was forty-seven,' he says, smiling. 'Best job I ever had. Loved it.'

I nod.

'Most of the towers round these parts, well, I've been up them. Most, if not all. Grimberg chimneys in Gavrik town? Yep, up both of them, more than one time. Pointing the bricks, they've got some good brickwork up there, even close to the top where nobody ever looks. And I replaced one of the lightning conductors, just before Elsa was born.' His smile fades and his eyes turn gloss. 'My wife would tell me, she'd say, Leif, if I go into labour and you're stuck up in the sky on that chimney I will never forgive you. But I got the job done in time. All finished the day before little Elsa arrived. She was my whole life, that girl. My whole everything.'

'She lived here with you?'

'That room over there,' he says, pointing to a door. 'I haven't been in there since it happened. I worry maybe I'll walk in her bedroom and I'll never make it out again. And that thought won't bother me too much after her burial, but it's not like I can shut down before I've made all the arrangements. I need to pull myself together. Think straight.'

'Is there a date for the funeral yet? Anything you'd like me to add in the newspaper?'

He takes a sip of his coffee and I see the draining board has a teaspoon leaning against another mug next to an open bag of granulated sugar.

'I'm not exactly sure, to be honest with you. It's a bit complicated, with all the police business. They need some time with her before we can make proper arrangements. Chief Björn gave me his word they'd be gentle with her.' He starts to sob and then he holds his daughter's grey scarf to his eyes and he buries his face in it, convulsing, the wool taking his grief, holding it.

I switch off the Dictaphone.

I pat his arm.

Leif takes away the scarf, and then he inhales and squeezes his eyes together and says, 'I worked on the Lutheran church, all the copper work. Of course, it was copper coloured back then but now it's all green. My Elsa was just a toddler when I did that. She came to see me on a Friday with her mum, came to bring me my sandwiches and my thermos. She was a wonderful girl. Good-hearted, no messing about. Her and her mother were just wonderful.' He sniffs and another tear rolls down his whiskery cheek and he says, 'I lived a blessed life, all in.'

I switch the Dictaphone back on and take a sip of water.

Occasionally I'll start talking a little if a grieving local is in too much pain. I'll mention my dad or my mum. What happened to them. The time it took for me to recover any sense of myself, or the time it's still taking. To offer some comfort. But Leif already knows what I know. We are two strangers united in a nightmarish understanding of life. Of *death*. We see how nothing matters a jot, and how everything matters.

'Who were her friends, Leif? Who did she hang around with?'

'Well, Elsa was a hard-working girl. Ever since she was about fourteen or fifteen she's been helping out up at Rose Farm, first with the boss lady, Therese her name is, helping with some kind of paperwork project, lots of filing and such. Then at the café for Linda Larsson and later on for the beauty parlour place. Nails and face scrubbing, that kind of thing, learning it all from Ruby. She likes it there. She liked Rose Farm.'

'This is a difficult question for me to ask you, but did Elsa have any enemies you know of?'

'No, I don't think so,' he says. 'Police asked the same thing.'

'Nobody? Nobody you thought acted strange around her?'

'How could a girl like Elsa have an enemy? You didn't meet her I know it, but she was as sweet as pie. Good-hearted just like her mother was. They were set from the same mould, that's what we used to say. She never looked much like me but she was the image of her mother, was Elsa.'

'Do you have any ideas about what happened to her down by the river?'

He grits his teeth. 'Whoever did it should be hanged, that's all I know. And I don't believe in the death penalty, even. Don't think it's civil. But killing a twenty-year-old girl like that?' He looks at me with such intense sadness that I have to look away. 'Leaving her there by Snake River. On her own, out in the night, in nature. What kind of a person would…?'

He stands up and his hands are in fists around the scarf. He leaves and comes back with a photograph in a pine frame.

'This was her school graduation day,' he says. 'Her mother was the one who helped her with her lessons, all the books and learning, but I was the one who got to see her graduate and receive her hat. As hard as it was that day for me, without my Marie by my side, I know it was a hundred times worse for Elsa. No mother on her graduation day. Looking out into the crowd and just seeing me, a scraggly old fool. I remember trying to make myself look bigger.' He pumps up his chest and sits up straight. 'In the hope she wouldn't see it as bad as it was.'

'She would have been so proud to have you there,' I say, my voice wavering a little. Cracking. 'My dad died when I was fourteen. Car accident. Mum didn't take it well. She didn't make it to my graduation ceremony and I didn't expect her to be there. Most days I could manage through okay, but not having family on a day like that was very tough. I'm glad Elsa had you in the crowd.'

He pats my arm the exact same way that I patted his ten minutes ago. The same place, the same action, the same lightness.

'I was working on the bee, you'll know it, the spinning bee on the top of the Hive self-storage in Visberg town. You know the one?'

'I know it.'

'Odd thing, anyway; it was my job to repair it and repaint it every few years, the black and yellow stripes. One time, Elsa came up after her school day, must have been about eight at the time, and she gave me a gold coin that she'd won at school, just a chocolate coin. She'd won it for a picture she'd painted and she wanted me to have the coin because she knew I liked chocolate, always did have a sweet tooth.'

I smile and take another drink of water.

He digs around in his pocket for something.

'Two weeks ago she did the exact same thing. Came home after work at the organic café with a gold coin. Says she got it for helping with painting, same as before. Gave it to me. Well, I expected it to be chocolate didn't I, but it wasn't. It was real gold, like treasure. Heavy in my hand. She told me it was a Kruggerand from the gold mines of South Africa. Told me she'd earned it and she wanted me to have it.'

'Did she tell you who at the farm gave it to her?'

'I asked her but she wouldn't say.'

'Is it here?'

'I got it someplace safe. She said it was valuable.'

I start talking, but then he says, 'I should have kept my Elsa someplace safe, should have protected my own daughter.' I see his hands tighten through the scarf again. 'I failed her.' And then he says it again. 'Father's job is to protect. And I failed her.'

24

On the drive back I try to call in at Rose Farm but I can't even drive into the public area. The fences are up, the gates are locked and the guard dogs are roaming around.

I drive on and call Therese Viklund.

No pick-up.

I pass the snowberg and call her again.

She picks up on my fourth attempt.

'Viklund.'

'Therese, hi. It's me, Tuva Moodyson. Sorry to bother you.'

'It's not that, Tuva. I'm just a little tied up with…'

'I need a few minutes for a chat,' I say, cutting her off before she cuts me off. 'Five minutes maximum.'

There's a pause. Dogs barking in the background.

'Can I call into the farm? I'm nearby.'

'No,' she says. 'I mean, I'm not home right now.'

'Just five minutes,' I say. 'We can do it over the phone but I'd rather tell you in person.'

'Tell me what? Have you found out something about Elsa? Do the police know who killed her?'

'Not that. I've found something that might be valuable to you and your Rose Farm neighbours, especially in light of recent events.'

'Valuable? What are you talking about?'

'I'll clear my schedule,' I say. In reality I don't *have* a schedule to clear. 'I can meet you in Gavrik or Visberg. I'll drive all the way to Karlstad if that suits you better.'

She takes a deep breath.

'I'll be in Visberg in about two hours. Need to retrieve a few items from our storage unit at The Hive. I could meet you at the pizza grill?'

'No,' I say. 'Somewhere more private. The square. By the statue and the apple trees. Just for five minutes.'

'Fine.'

We agree a time and I drive back to the office and park in my place. The concrete steps leading to the back entrance, the one we keep locked. I sat there with Lena back in November. Her a step higher than me. Trying to understand what had happened to Noora. Her trying to salvage my career as I was intent on quitting. Her being kind and patient and urging me to just press *pause* and not *stop*.

Storgatan has one or two cyclists. A garbage truck and the number 1 bus and a few tired dads on paternity leave pushing buggies.

I go into the copshop.

'You wanted to see me?' I say to Thord, who's stood by reception typing into a laptop.

'Let's go back there,' he says.

We walk through the keycode door and all three officers are in the station at once, a rare occurrence. Normally one's on traffic duty or did the night shift or is away on annual leave. Noora told me she'd often be here on her own. A singular cop in a town that no one knows about.

'Chief,' I say.

He grunts something and doesn't look up.

'Tuva,' says Magnus Falk, Noora's replacement.

'Hi,' I say.

I don't hate him. I don't even dislike him. It's just that I abhor the reason he is here in Gavrik town. He shouldn't need to be here. It should be Noora driving that police Volvo. It should be her doing the shitty night shifts and public holidays because the Chief always pulls rank. I don't have anything against Magnus personally, but I just wish he didn't exist here in Toytown.

'We're gonna have to do this in a cell,' says Thord, already making a joke apologetic face. 'Don't worry, you don't need your lawyer, it's just that the Chief has some important calls and we don't want to be overheard. Cross-contamination, isn't that what you called it, Magnum?'

Thord calls Magnus *Magnum*. It could be because Magnus Falk has actually shot his service weapon whereas, to my knowledge, neither Thord nor Chief Björn ever have. Or else it's because he looks a little like a young, clean-shaven version of Tom Selleck. All jaw and broad lips and strong eyebrows.

'I was talking about evidence,' says Magnus. 'The cross contamination of samples. Fibres, blood, that kind of thing.'

'Same principle, though,' says Thord. 'Someone overhears something they shouldn't, it's like cross-contamination. Same family, no?'

We walk into the cell and the door stays open. Next to us is another empty cell and next to that is the third.

Thord sits on the cot sticking out of the wall, and Magnus and I have a folded chair each.

'What else do you need to know?' I say.

'It isn't that,' says Thord, glancing at Magnus. 'We need more cooperation from you, Tuvs.'

'Do I ever not cooperate?'

'That's not what he means,' says Magnus. 'You have your expertise and we have ours. We need to pool knowledge on some areas.'

'Pool knowledge?' I say. 'If you want me to name sources I will not do it and you shouldn't even be asking.'

'We'll share some details,' says Thord. 'You'll be a privileged individual.'

'Privileged? Who's taught you all these fancy words?'

Thord looks over at Magnus.

'Thord,' I say. 'What do you want? Plain speaking.'

'We help you and you help us, except who you're really helping is Elsa Nyberg's family.'

'I'm listening.'

'Not to forget Gavrik Kommun and fighting for justice,' says Magnus.

I don't even acknowledge the comment. He might look like a TV star, but he needs to learn some humility.

'Look at these,' says Thord, passing me a stapled bundle of A4 papers. 'Elsa died from a blunt-force trauma to the head.'

'To the temporal lobe,' says Magnus.

'Her temple?' I say.

'Yeah,' says Thord. 'The perp hit her with a bat or a hammer, something of that nature.'

I flinch at the image in my head.

'There's a bone directly behind your temple,' says Magnus. 'A shard splintered and pierced the victim's middle meningeal artery, the major vessel that feeds the brain.'

I wince at the thought of it.

'It would have been a quick death, so says the forensic pathologist. Massive internal bleeding.'

'Would she have been unconscious the whole time?'

Magnus says, 'The pathologist said it would have been very quick.'

'But they don't know what weapon hit her?'

Thord says, 'We have a list, but it's long, Tuvs. Anything from the butt of a rifle to a Kubota self-defence tool to a small round-nose hammer used for metalwork. Something not sharp, but hard. Something struck Elsa with significant force.'

'We didn't find any such object in the vicinity,' says Magnus. 'Some garbage, very old, but nothing hard enough to cause this injury. We did find bow wax, though.'

I look at Thord.

'Wax to keep a bow string supple. A bow and arrow, you know?'
I nod.

'Poor Elsa,' I say.

'ID of the killer,' says Magnus. 'Whoever did this was cool about it, and killing at close range like that, in striking distance, hand-to-hand, killing a twenty-year-old girl, that takes real malice, it takes ice.'

Thord clears his throat and crosses his legs.

'After the killing,' he says. 'The white coats think immediately after, the white painted cross was applied to Elsa Nyberg's neck. The Chief already filled you in on that detail.'

'I haven't told anyone,' I say.

'Keep it that way,' says Magnus and I give him a look that says *don't push me.*

'What kind of ink? What kind of brush?' I ask.

'We don't know,' says Thord. 'Still running tests. Pigment analysis. Was a neat job, though. Carefully applied. The perpetrator did not rush it. They took their time.'

'May have done similar things before,' says Magnus. 'Or been practising.'

'Seriously?' I say.

'What we need from you,' says Thord. 'And I think the Chief might have mentioned it already. We need you to keep supplying us with information we can use. You did it with Medusa, with the Ferryman, with the Visberg case...'

'And look where that got me,' I say. 'Magnus wouldn't be here right now if I hadn't pursued that Visberg story.'

'You did the right thing and you know it,' says Thord, gesturing for Magnus to leave. Magnus leaves. 'What happened was a tragedy. Appalling. But the way I figure it we all need to use our God-given abilities the best way we can.'

'Nobody ever gave me an ability. I earned them all by myself.'

Thord smiles a half smile. 'Marginal town like this, you need to write your stories and I need to lock up the evil. Keep the streets safe for Tammy and the Chief's wife and my kid when she gets born in the autumn.'

'Your *what*?'

'Ah, crap.'

'Your wife is pregnant?'

'Fiancée.'

'Thord, I'm so happy for you.' I stand up. He stands up. We have an awkward pat-on-the-back-football-mates kind of hug and then we sit down again.

'I wasn't supposed to tell anyone yet; God, I'm such a bonehead. Please keep it to yourself for now.'

I mime zipping shut my mouth.

'We'll feed you what we can on the case,' he says. 'But if you can get any information from the residents of Rose Farm, that would be helpful. Observations, even if you're not sure they'd be relevant. They're a closed shop up there and they're suspicious of all branches of the government. You keep us up to date and, as far as possible, we'll keep you up to date so you can break stories before your colleagues.'

'They might complain about that,' I say.

'Let them try,' he says.

I drive east to Visberg and pass by Svenssons Saws & Axes. They have a three per cent discount offer on, according to the sign in the window. I guess people around here don't have anywhere else to buy their chainsaws from so a three per cent discount will suffice.

I start to climb the big hill and I feel queasy. It's not the altitude or the angle, it's the memories attached to this place. To the forests. Past the white bike, past the two crosses, over the train tracks. The town is a riot of blossom and the streets are as full as they ever are here in the daytime: a dozen or so people, some in winter coats and some in T-shirts. That's April for you.

The bee on top of the hive spins and the sunny side of the street is bathed in light.

I park and walk through tangles of gnarled apple trees, the scent from their flowers filling the air, yellow butterflies fluttering from tree to tree.

'Over here,' says a voice.

I sit down next to Therese. Her thick, glossy hair shines in the light and she holds on firmly to a snow globe containing a tiny scale model of Visberg, complete with hive and pizza grill and statue and apple trees and the hill. She hands me the snow globe and, instead of snow, it fills with pale pink sparkles.

'Spring blossom,' she says. 'It's for you, Tuva.'

'No, I couldn't accept it.'

'It's okay,' she says. 'We have a thousand more in storage. Don't worry, they're well-made, not cheap imports. You need to crack a walnut next Christmas and you can't find your pliers or your nut-crackers, you just use that Visberg paperweight.'

25

A gardener employed by the Kommun walks from tree to tree carrying a spiked stick. The idea is she can pick up garbage without straining her back. But this is Sweden. There is no garbage. An unknown killer on the loose, but no street grime whatsoever.

'You like it?' asks Therese, cracking her knuckles.

I look down at the snow globe. The miniature Hive is striped yellow and black and the statue is in the exact same place, except, to scale, it's the height of a grain of rice. The slope away from the town is forested. The shady side of the square even has the clock-maker's shop complete with a clock affixed to the wall. It's as if I could look closer, with some kind of eyeglass, and see myself on this bench sheltered by a cloud of fresh blossom. It's as if I could view my own day.

'What do you want, Tuva?'

I snap out of it. 'I have an idea.'

'I'm listening.'

'Some locals have told me a little about Rose Farm, about what you all do there.'

'We farm.'

'About the preparedness. The contingency plans.'

'Do you have insurance, Tuva?'

'Yes.'

'It's the same thing. People think preparedness is some exotic, outlaw behaviour. It's just insurance. We're not the doomsday preppers some make us out to be. We're farmers who keep ourselves to ourselves. I used to be a senior management consultant in Stockholm for goodness' sake – its's not like we're waiting for Armageddon to arrive.'

'No?'

'No.'

'Then I guess you wouldn't be interested.'

'In what?'

'I have a friend.'

She puts her snow globe inside her coat pocket.

'Go on.'

'He prefers to stay anonymous. All I can tell you is that he lived in a conflict zone for many years, first as a citizen, trying to survive with little food or water, being shot at, and later on as a soldier.'

'Is he Swedish?'

'He would rather stay completely anonymous.'

'Okay.'

'He is an expert in survival, although he would never describe himself in such a way. Not the glamorised version, where people hoard weapons. He understands herbal medicine, how to start smoke-less fires, how to barter effectively. The man has lived through hell.'

'This is not what I was expecting you to come to me with, Tuva.'

'Oh?'

'I thought you'd ask about Elsa. About the police interviewing us all.'

'Would you have told me anything?'

'There's not much to tell. Linda, Ruby, Niklas, me and T-Bone, we're all heartbroken to lose Elsa. Abraham is sick with the pain of it all. But we don't know anything that you don't. We've handed over all our CCTV footage and we hope the police catch whoever took Elsa away from us.'

'The man I'm talking about. He isn't some TV bushcraft expert. He doesn't give TED Talks. But he knows how to treat a gunshot wound with no tourniquets or chest packs. He knows how to suture an artery. The man knows how to travel to an underground market in the dead of the night to barter disposable lighters for bread.'

'What are you suggesting?'

'He travels to your farm to tell you his truth. His story. And you and your colleagues get to ask him whatever questions you have about life without rule of law, without currency, without retail supply, without clean water. You can grill him.'

'How much are we talking?'

'He wants no payment.'

She frowns.

'His only condition is that you allow me to be there when he analyses your preparedness and gives you advice.'

She shakes her head. 'Your friend is wise to be discreet but we are equally discreet. We don't want any trouble.'

'Everyone signs confidentiality agreements before the session begins. He's been flown to Colorado to do this for a tech company CEO, and he's been flown to Moscow to help an aluminium industrialist protect his assets for future generations.' These are lies. 'I'm making the offer of a lifetime.'

'I'm not sure.'

'He owes me a favour and he lives in a neighbouring region to Värmland.'

'He does?'

'You're maybe eighty per cent prepared on your own. He can get you to a hundred.'

'Look at them,' she says, gesturing at the women and men walking past the clock shop, past the old newspaper office of *Visberg Tidningen*. 'They walk around like lemmings, and none of them know how fast things could unravel.'

I look at an old man with a walking stick stop to smell the apple blossom. I watch a toddler fall on the grass and laugh and get back up again. And then I see the door of the dental surgery fling open and a short blonde woman runs out into the street with blood pouring down her chin, staining her white blouse. She stands in the street and a man approaches her and puts out his arm and she walks the other way. One of the dental staff emerges and then goes back inside and closes the door. The 'No Refunds' sign swings on its string behind the glass.

'I'm potentially interested,' Therese says. 'In your friend. But I'd need to see the confidentiality agreements in advance. And I can only say we'd listen and not talk until the point where we want to ask questions. It'd be a one-way information flow, as it were.'

'My dad was prepared to a certain extent,' I say.

'Was? He stopped?'

'He died.'

'Oh, I am sorry.'

'Ever since Chernobyl he kept tins of spam and corned beef in the bottom of a cupboard. We never even ate spam or corned beef.'

'I believe that most medicine should be preventative,' she says.

I frown. 'Like taking medicine to avoid a heart attack?'

'No, like exercising and eating well and meditating, to avoid ever needing to take heart medicine.'

'I'm not sure it's always that simple.'

'It can be.'

'I get ear infections because of my hearing aids. I wear hearing aids because of my deafness. I can't avoid them.'

'You probably could if you tried.'

My blood starts to boil.

'What would you know about it?'

The Sheriff turns up in his beige taxi cab with its rooflights and its lettering on the the doors. It says 'Sheriff' in large letters and 'Taxi' under it in smaller print. He walks into the dental surgery.

'Preparedness can prevent most emergencies ever happening,' says Therese.

'You think Linda and Ruby will want to hear what my friend has to say?'

She sniffs. 'They might. Kurt will be interested, and Andreas. My husband would probably like to meet a genuine war fighter, hear what he has to say.'

'You've all been interviewed in Gavrik?'

'We don't know anything, Tuva. It's Bengt Nyberg the police need to be interrogating, not us.'

'Elsa's relative? With the elkhound?'

'He tries to hunt wolves with his dog and his gun,' she says. 'And he was too fond of Elsa, ever since her poor mother died. Sickening.'

'The wolves hunted his dog,' I say. 'That's why he puts on a spiked collar and armour, I saw the injured dog last week.'

'He's dangerous,' says Therese. 'A quiet and polite psychopath. He tries to hunt wolves with his elkhound and his gun, hunts them deep into the forests and up by the river. Sometimes you see something that looks like prey but it turns out to be the predator. Sometimes nature spins on its head.'

'He seems normal.'

'They usually do. And...'

'Yes.'

'We'll listen to your friend. If he can come tonight I'll make sure we all attend. Abraham needs a break from his composition, he's been saying as much. Email me the confidentiality contracts this afternoon.' She hands me her card. 'If he agrees, come at nine and park by the main house, in the private zone. I'll have the gates open for you. Oh, and Tuva.'

'Yes.'

'Don't tell a soul you're coming.'

26

I spend three hours writing up stories, some of which happened almost a week ago, before the murder of Elsa Nyberg, before the community changed, before parents started bribing and pleading with their teenage daughters to stay home each night. Every culture has its bogeyman folklore. Pied pipers and charming werewolves and tall men of the forest who snatch adolescents from their beds. Trolls who swap their own offspring for human children. But right now, right here, we have something worse. Because our monster is real. And he, or she, is still at large.

Drafting headlines and copy is soothing, it always is. Hearing aids out, bag of wine gums open on my desk, Lars in the background, working on arranging and sorting all the photo entries for the *Posten*'s 'Scenic Spring' competition. We've extended it to Visberg of course, and we've had a record number of entries: twelve. Lars told me one year, before I arrived in shitsville, they had one entry. So, she won. This year we have relatively fierce competition and the prize is a meal for two at the Visberg Grill (no drinks included) and a kilo of Grimberg salted liquorice, which sounds to me like a guarantee for volcanic diarrhoea, but whatever floats your boat, baby.

My focus is Elsa's murder, but I still need to work on the peripheral stories. There's a local interest piece on the new weather vane for the Lutheran church. Well, I guess they're all local interest pieces by default. Some argument at the Kommun planning offices over a cycle-path extension by the gymnasium school. Another article on how the mild winter has affected tick populations in Utgard forest and beyond. Nice quote from a mother, who's boy was bitten by twenty-two ticks all in one day. Two good photos. All this seems irrelevant, almost ghoulish, in light of Elsa's story, but such is the reality of a small community newspaper. If I wrote every page on the murder then locals would be overwhelmed. They'd shun the paper and they'd talk to their neighbours and their colleagues and they'd agree that the paper has gone downhill since the deaf girl from Stockholm started almost five years ago, and they'll say they need positive news, not just negative, why does she try to talk the town down, why can't she write about the good things that make Gavrik so special?

Why indeed.

I check the Four Horsemen forum but Grey Man hasn't posted. Seventeen members have asked him questions, asked his advice, and most of them have asked in such a way that they communicate the fact that they're not newbies, they're pretty serious operators, they try to make that clear within their question, to validate themselves.

The door moves so I look up. By the time I've put my hearing aids back in, the bell above the door has stopped tinkling.

'I won't get in your hair, just come in to say hello as I'm passing...'

It's the owner of the now-defunct town stationery store. Rushed eyeliner, faux-leather handbag, coat so substantial it'd stop a bullet.

'How's your neighbour?' I ask. 'Still at it?'

'Never quits it, Tuva. Starts up with his damn nailgun or screwgun, whatever it is, at nine o'clock in the morning, even on Sundays, he does. Well. And it's not like a hammer, that'd be bad enough, it's a *gun*. Using a nail weapon right next to my bedstead on the other side of the partition wall. I said to my niece, I said every nail I hear explode out of that gun is attempted murder.'

'What's he doing?'

'Renovations. He's watched too many of them home-improvement shows. You know the ones, off the television. Reckons he can stick up a bit of floral wallpaper and a few bits of old tat, maybe a bookcase, and he'll sell it for more than he paid. Greedy little swine.'

I reach across to the filing cabinet and grab her a copy of the *Posten*, because the pile by the honesty biscuit-tin has run out.

'How much do I owe you?'

She wants me to say, *nothing, just take it, on the house*, but I say twenty kronor, as if she doesn't already know.

She takes out a ten-kronor coin from her purse, like it's a rare Asscher cut diamond extracted from the crown jewels of some alpine principality. And then she looks at me and she takes out another and she places them down on my desk. I jump up and place them both in the biscuit tin.

'Honesty box,' she says, looking at the tin. 'In this town?'

'It's worked for years,' I say.

'So did I, dear,' she says. 'So did I. You hear about the girl on Roseberry Farm?'

Rose Farm. 'Yes, I did. It's very sad.'

'The farmer up there, his name's Isaiah or Abel. Benjamin? Jacob, I think. One of those bible names. He comes from the Appalachia people, did you know that? He's one of them paediatricians.'

Abraham? I raise my eyebrows.

'I thought he was a composer?'

'He's got distasteful compulsions.'

'What do you mean?'

'She was a very young girl, is what I mean.'

'Elsa? Elsa was twenty.'

'I heard he talked to young girls. Maybe that was back in the Appalachia. Maybe he got reformed, they say it's possible in some cases.' She puts her index fingers to her temples and then she starts to shake. 'The electricity shock therapy. They say it'll zap the evil right out of you.'

'Do you mean *paedophile*?'

'It's wrong. In God's eyes and mine, both. Rotten.'

'I don't think anyone's arguing with you.'

'If they did I'd report them to Chief Björn. Not in my town, not anywhere near it.'

'I'd do the same. But be careful spreading that, unless you can back it up. It's a serious accusation.'

'I go to bowls on a Saturday, down at the leisure place on Eriksgatan. Friend of mine, Ingrid, her sister's landlord told her about Roseberry Farm last year, she did. All about it. You know they had a mass murder back in the '80s? Bodies all over the place. A blood-bath, it was. Wondering if the same man did it. Maybe they both liked the kiddies.'

The man who shot himself in 1987? 'If I hear about anything like that I'll investigate.'

'Just don't use the internet to do it,' she says. 'They'll think you're one of them.'

'Thanks for the tip. Have you ever been to Rose Farm?'

'Never. If I can't catch a bus there and back then it's too far out of town for me to feel safe. You couldn't pay me to get near that place. Now, I'm not being rude, but I got a glaucoma appointment with Doctor Stina down at the surgery. You can ask me more questions tomorrow if you like, I'll be back in.'

Oh, great.

She leaves and as I already have my aids in I save my unfinished work and call Thord.

'Gavrik police,' says Chief Björn.

'Hi, Chief. Is Thord there, please?'

Some rustling noises.

'Tuvs.'

'What's new?'

'Asking you the same question.'

'I'm working on something,' I say. 'If I dig up anything firm I'll let you know in the next day or two. I gave you my word.'

'Good.'

'What you got?'

'Honestly, I'm not the best to explain it. Wait a sec, I'll put Magnum on.'

'Hello,' says Magnus Falk.

'It's Tuva. Thord wants you to tell me something.'

'Hang on a beat.'

The sounds of a sleeve over the receiver as Magnus confirms this is the case.

'Metal,' he says. 'Lead.'

'Lead?'

'White coats haven't come back to us yet with paint analysis from that cross, but they found some trace elements on the skin of the victim.'

'Traces of lead?'

He clears his throat. 'You ever heard of comparative bullet-lead analysis?'

'No.'

'It's a way to help distinguish between types of ammunition, not conclusively, but it can help an investigation. The white coats use plasma-optical emission spectrometer...'

Now I understand why Thord asked Magnus to explain. In fact, I'm glad he did because Magnus enunciates and speaks slowly. If he spoke like Thord, I'd be unable to decipher all the jargon.

'...to identify tiny amounts of trace elements,' he says. 'They found lead remnants close to the head injury.'

'Like a lead weight or something?'

'Could be. Lead piping, lead from a roof, lead anything.'

'That would explain how much damage the blow did.'

'Yes, it would.'

'Not only that, but someone living close to the scene has reported river birds found dead near the area. So far we've collected two, and they're being analysed in the same lab. Working theory is they may have died from lead poisoning, and we hope, if that's the case, long shot, we might find something in their digestive tracts.'

'Good,' I say. 'Smart.'

'It's not all parking fines and speeding tickets, you know.'

'I wish that was all you were doing.'

'How's Constable Noora?'

This question takes the air from my lungs. Magnus Falk has never confronted the subject with me. And I appreciated that. Partly because I resented him for the longest time for taking her place, and partly because I find it the most difficult question to answer. How *is* she? Whenever someone asks a person that, they expect to hear, 'oh, on the mend,' or 'taking one day at a time.' But with Noora the truth is 'not good, no improvement, no signs of cognitive capacity, she'll probably pass away from an infection.' And just thinking that makes me want to hide under my duvet with a bottle of rum. So I say, 'No change yet.'

'Fingers crossed,' he says.

'Yeah.'

We end the call and I start packing up to go home for a shower and change before tonight's apocalypse lecture at Rose Farm.

A notification pops up on my screen.

It's a private message from a new user on the Four Horsemen forum.

It says, 'You will die in agony with your wrists bound in silk and your eyes pinned open.'

27

As I drive home I think about the private message. I've had trolls send me worse things, usually photos of themselves, and I just block, report and move on. I've grown up with this nonsense, we all have. But this one feels more personal. The threat was specific and it comes at a time when a woman only a few years younger than myself was murdered. Murdered and then left out in the bushes with a Satanic icon painted on her neck. What kind of person could bring themselves to do that?

I shower and change into fresh clothes. It's strange how you morph your appearance to suit the crowd you'll meet. No matter how strong your core image is, how unyielding you are to peer pressure or societal expectations, you always dress to be accepted or to shock or to impress. I see goths sometimes and I salute every one of them. Not so much when they're in a group, but when I see a lone goth in a gang of preppy, blond teenagers, the others all wholesome and tanned and clothed in polo shirts, I tip my cap. The one in black always gets my attention. And my admiration. Tonight I'm wearing jeans and a grey hoodie and some winter boots. I don't look military in any way, but it's the closest I can do.

Johnny Cash on the Hilux stereo all the way to the base of Visberg hill. A live performance from Folsom Prison back in 1968. Him whipping the inmates up into a frenzy and performing one of the best sets of his life.

The mound of snow stands resolute, despite the mild weather. It'll take more than a few days of sun to melt the thing. I'm reminded of the ice houses of old aristocratic properties outside London. I used to visit them when I studied there. Old castles and palaces with follies and boathouses and river frontages. Not that different from Rose Farm, really. But the English ones were made from pale stone, not wood. And they were much grander. And the ice houses were dug deep underground, and they were filled with ice, skimmed off the lake in midwinter to chill ice cream for the gentry.

The sky is pink.

When I reach Rose Farm the light is all but gone and the gates are locked. I show my face at the camera and the gates start to open. It looks tidy, like they want to impress their visitor. Not me, they couldn't care less about me, it's Grey Man they're excited about, someone who has actually lived through what they all term SHTF, someone who has bartered in the darkness of the night and evaded snipers as he returned to his derelict shelter with water taken from an open spring.

I'm relieved Luka agreed to do this. But I'm also aware I will be in his debt. Something tells me a man like Luka Kodro isn't so interested in the value of my intel. Something tells me he'll cash in this favour one day, in the next year or two, and it will cost me dearly.

Andreas has two dogs straining at their leashes, but his size means he can control them with ease. He points over at the red barn to my right and I wind down my window and say, 'Therese told me to park by the main house.'

He says, 'No.'

I park by the barn.

'Trespassing,' says a whisper behind me.

I turn on my heels and Linda Larsson's standing there with a plank of wood strapped across her chest, held in place by a length of blue rope around her neck. 'You going to see T-Bone? Me too.' She links her arm through mine, which feels strange as we hardly know each other. 'Asparagus,' she says.

'Come on, then,' says Kurt from the barn. 'We've got to get going if we're to be ready for GI Joe tonight.'

He walks away and Linda says, 'his nose is out of joint. Usually he's the one with the boots-on-the-ground experience, if you can call it that.'

'T-Bone served?'

'Just national service. And he spent most of that out of action with bunions so he's hardly a Navy Seal, is he?'

We pass through the barn and the air smells of horse manure and straw. Beyond, in the distance, are a dozen or more hay bales, large circular ones.

'Take this,' he says, handing us each lighters and a bag of white cotton wool. 'You show her how to do it, Linda.'

He walks off and Linda starts pushing cotton wool into each hay bale.

'That's all there is to it,' she says. 'Covered with petroleum jelly, it is. Same stuff as you rub on your lips. Sets a decent blaze.' She lights the cotton and eventually, with some blowing, the hay begins to catch.

I walk three bales along and take out cotton wool and press it in. It feels wrong on so many levels. The slimy cotton wool. The bone-dry hay. The wilful setting alight of something when the ground all around is dry enough for both the Swedish Meteorological and Hydrological Institute and the fire service to issue forest fire warnings.'

'Come on, Tuva,' yells T-Bone from the far end of the field. 'Linda's already done four.'

Getting the cotton wool to light isn't difficult, but getting the hay itself to catch is. I blow and cup my hands and blow some more and eventually the thing starts to crackle and the yellows and reds flare up into the dusk.

I ignite three of them.

When we meet again at the red barn the field is ablaze and the fragile, vertical asparagus spears – each one poking up from the sandy loam in contempt of the frost and flames – look like the withered fingers of some underground beast thrusting up from deep below.

'Over a hundred-thousand kronor, this harvest,' says T-Bone. 'Gotta keep an eye on it. Who's the man coming tonight, then? What does he know?'

Linda elbows me in the ribs, a little too hard.

'He's lived through more than we could imagine,' I say. 'Might have some tips.'

'We'll see,' says T-Bone. 'I always wait to judge a man on his handshake, on his voice.'

'And what about a woman?' I say.

'On her accuracy downrange at two-hundred yards,' says T-Bone, and Linda bursts out laughing; some kind of in-joke between the two of them.

I offer them a lift up the hill to the main house and they agree but they don't sit in the back seat of my truck, they jump in the flatbed instead.

Outside the house, two more dogs are posted, their choke collars linked to chains attached to a wing of the house.

Niklas and Ruby are standing there in full camo gear. Her, just trousers and a shirt, him with camo hat, some kind of knife sheath on his belt, and a gold cross swinging from his neck. I climb out of my truck.

'We'll wait out here for your friend to arrive,' says Therese, emerging from the main house.

'Will your husband be joining us?' I ask.

'Once your friend gets here.'

Andreas walks over scratching at his red beard.

'He late?' he says.

'No. We're all early,' says Therese.

'Same thing in my book,' says Andreas.

The sky glows from the asparagus fires. The air is smoky and the ground under our boots is slick with dew that promises to freeze any minute.

An alarm goes off inside one of the wings. Linda Larsson walks inside to turn it off, and then we see a motorbike on the horizon. One headlight. The engine buzzes, something small. The headlight slows and the bike pulls in off the road.

'Bang on time,' says Niklas.

I see everyone look at their phones. I can see Ruby's in her hand, an image from the front-gate camera. She swipes her phone and she sees a thermal image, and then a night-vision image. The gates open. Grey Man still has his helmet on.

He rides his bike up through the public area to the next locked gate. He's buzzed through.

The motorbike is old-looking. Something from the '70s.

Luka Kodro steps off the bike.

T-Bone moves closer to him.

Luka unzips his motorbike leathers. He's wearing ICA Maxi jeans and a ragged black sweater with moth holes.

'Welcome to Rose Farm,' says Therese, approaching with her hand out.

He takes off his motorbike helmet.

I look at his eyes.

This man is not Luka Kodro.

28

I take a step back and the man looks at me.

What's happened here? Is this an ambush? A trap? Where is Luka?

I start to shake my head, to panic, to ponder my next move when he says, in a deep, rough voice, 'Tuva Moodyson.'

Niklas looks nervous, like a schoolboy in army fatigues.

Who is this man?

Therese steps forward, 'Welcome to Rose Farm, I'm Therese Viklund.'

He says nothing, but moves to take off his motorbike helmet. There's a spider symbol above the visor, a spider on a web.

The man holds his helmet under his arm. He's wearing a balaclava. His eyes are chestnut brown, not blue. Is this Luka's brother? His cousin? I need to stay calm. Act like this is who I expected it to be.

'Tuva invited me. I am here to tell my story and answer your questions. Then I go home.'

'In there,' says T-Bone. 'That's my house, that is. We'll talk in there.'

'First we all sign these,' says Therese. 'The confidentiality agreements.'

The papers are signed roughly, on knees, and then I photograph them all on my phone and send them to Therese's email account.

'I'm thirsty,' says the man in black with the balaclava. One of his front teeth is missing.

'We've got *saft* inside,' says T-Bone. 'Make it from our own elderflowers.'

We file in. I have never been inside T-Bone's home before, just his barns. The house is small, everything on the ground floor, some kind of attic above. A simple, old-fashioned kitchen with wood-burning stove, a living room with TV, and a bedroom at the end, all visible from the entrance because there are no internal doors that I can see.

I feel uneasy. There is electricity in the air.

'I know we've signed the papers,' says T-Bone. 'But I'm not a paperwork man, truth be told. So let me make this clear. Nothing you see here, and I mean nothing, not a single detail, is to be shared with your drinking buddies in Falun or wherever you're from, get it?'

The man in black looks at me. 'They want me here or they don't?'

'We do,' says Linda. 'We're just private is all. Especially right now.'

'I help you because Tuva ask me to. That simple,' says the man. 'I do not tell anyone anything. But I don't have all the time in the night. Shall we start or shall I go home to my wife and sons?'

T-Bone mumbles and then he unlocks a thick steel door and climbs a staircase.

We follow him up.

The staircase is made out of bricks.

We ascend into an attic lined with whitewashed boards. The windows, one at each end, have been covered over. Spotlights illuminate the space and it measures about fifteen metres long by seven metres wide. On the walls are metal shelves and stacked on the shelves are jars and cans and tins and boxes and buckets. Organised in military fashion. There are five chairs up here in the centre of the room, all facing one chair set with a bottle of elderflower *saft* and a glass.

The man in the balaclava with the missing front tooth walks to the chair and sits down on it. The Rose Farm residents sit on their chairs and then Niklas says, 'Thanks, Tuva. You can see yourself out.'

'I'm staying,' I say.

'She stays here,' says the man. 'If I stay, she stays. Part of the deal.'

'What?' says Niklas.

'Part of the deal,' says Therese.

I stand at the back of the room as there is no chair for me.

The man drinks *saft* and looks around and says, 'This is all very good. Your stocks. How long have you been storing this food here?'

'You don't get to ask us questions,' says T-Bone, shifting in his chair. 'Tell us your credentials and then maybe we can have a friendly chat after.'

'Credentials?' says the man, smiling.

'Why do you get to come here like some exam inspector and tell us what we're doing right and wrong?'

'I don't care if you are right or if you are wrong,' says the man. 'Why would I care?'

'Please tell us about your experience,' says Linda. 'Therese told us you have some direct experience.'

'I have too much of it,' says the man. 'More than I ever wanted.'

Niklas rolls his eyes.

'Almost thirty years ago I was like one of you people. I was younger, though – younger than your giant here,' he points to Andreas. 'Sixteen years old. I was living in a nice town in a normal house. I had girlfriend from my schooldays. My father was an engineer and my mother took care of the house. Me and my sister. And then the world changed. Our sky fell on top of our heads.'

'The war?' says Andreas.

'What people don't understand is how quickly everything can fall apart. For years, or generations even, everything can be normal. You go to work, you pick up groceries on the way home, you eat on your balcony with your parents, you go to sleep in a warm room on a soft bed. Maybe there are some political changes, a leader who promises a lot, some skirmish in a town far away. The newspaper has statements from the government saying it's just a temporary problem and telling you to stay calm. So you do. There are rumours of tanks on the border of your region, but you still go to school and you still do your homework and play soccer with your friends. And then, one day, you see helicopters in the sky. A man returns to your neighbourhood. A man who used to be a popular boy in your school, he returns from another town and tells you of the dead bodies on the side of the road. He wears a pistol on his belt. You look into his eyes – eyes only a few years older than your own eyes – and you see only blackness. And then you realise that nothing will ever be the same again.'

Silence in the attic. Nobody moves a muscle.

'Our town was besieged on all sides for almost one year. We could not leave. My father had already gone off to fight, and I was left with my sister and my mother. On the hills outside the suburbs they positioned their artillery and their snipers. I used to play in those hills. They were our hills and our woods. My father and my uncle would hunt there and now there were men who hated us and they were hiding in the trees with sniper rifles and mortars. I left school, I had to. My girlfriend and I married one night. A mechanic married us. Me and my high-school sweetheart. My sister carried on studying. The school was at the end of our street, a five-minute walk, but it took her an hour because she had to pass through burnt-out buildings and sneak behind structures to avoid snipers. They would kill anyone they saw. Maybe they saw us as some kind of enemy, or maybe they were using our heads and our chests as target practice.' He takes another sip of his drink. 'You don't think you will ever get used to seeing grandmothers dead in the street but eventually you do. The bread that they may have exchanged for some silver jewellery or American dollars they'd hidden away, long since scavenged by hungry children willing to test the sniper, willing to get close to the dead old lady their mother once knew.'

He takes a break for a moment and everyone in the room is transfixed. There are no questions, no doubting this man.

'The siege felt like it lasted a lifetime. To get water we'd have to walk a great distance to a spring and queue with a container. It was very dangerous. So we'd harvest rainwater from the building roof. We boiled it on a small stove that my mother got in exchange for her wedding ring. After a while things felt almost normal. No glass in the windows because of the mortar fire. No food in the house. No heat. No medicines. Sometimes there would be food dropped by foreign planes but it'd be taken by the strongest or the richest. Women would have to offer themselves up to men in order to feed their children. It was a slow nightmare. One you do not wake up from. I consider myself to be a lucky man, living here now in this country, a survivor, but I wear my scars on the inside of my skin.'

The man scratches his head through his balaclava. I can see his arm is tattooed all the way to his wrist.

Linda Larsson frowns and chews her lip.

'The speed of change is not something you can prepare yourself for. To have comfort and justice and the law, and then go from that to chaos in days is not something you can ready yourself for. It just is not. One week you are going to the supermarket to buy your potatoes and your cod and the next week people are hungry, looting, fighting over the last tin of food, no staff in the buildings, fires raging, no police, the sound of gunfire growing ever closer. Men do things they didn't think they would ever have to do. They protect. They make awful decisions. Some form communities and gangs quickly. Gangs to protect their building, or the other kind: gangs to go out looting and raping. Those men, and they might not be the same men as you imagine in your heads, they relish the chaos. They are angry before the world goes to hell and then they reap their revenge. They thrive in the anarchy and they do much harm to the people all around them.'

He looks at Niklas in his camouflage clothes.

'We were not prepared like you people are. We did not have fancy army jackets or buckets of grains. We were just normal people getting by. But one thing I didn't expect in the first weeks was that the big houses, the people with security, with dogs, with gates, they got attacked before everyone else did.'

He pauses here. Ruby and Niklas look uncomfortable.

'The people in burnt-out shacks and flats could hide in plain sight. Hungry and dirty. But the people with defences showed the world that they had something worth protecting.'

'Did they defend themselves?' asks T-Bone.

The man swallows.

'They tried. They were armed. But it is not possible to fend off a large gang. You think you can do it, but you cannot. The gangs broke in eventually. They fought their way inside to take what they wanted. After six months, all of those big houses had been ransacked. The people who survived had taped-up boots and filthy skin. They had a gun on their person at all times. I kept mine by my pillow, not even underneath it. You think if you have a car, a generator, a big gun, you will be okay. But those things don't help you when the sky falls on your head. The car has no fuel, and if it does it is noisy and will draw attention to you. Someone will take it from you. Kill your family. A generator has no fuel, but if it does it is noisy. There is smoke. People see you and they take it and they kill your family. The only way to survive is to keep a low profile and stay smart. You must live in the shadows.'

The man crosses his leg the other way.

'Cigarettes were useful, they became like gold. Like currency. Some alcohol was useful. And ammunition, of course. Antibiotics were very important. Almost everything else is a luxury. I am not trying to scare you, I am just telling you my truth. Imagine walking into ICA Maxi and finding dead bodies in the bakery aisle. Blood on the walls. No police sirens. Nothing. You cannot imagine it. But it can happen. A few missed meals. The police have to stay home to protect their own children. Bad men take advantage. It can happen in a few days.'

'You said the siege ended after a year,' says Therese. 'What happened afterwards?'

The man takes a deep breath.

'By then I was old enough to fight. So I went and fought for my people. I left my mother and I went to fight.'

'Your sister?'

'She stayed with my mother. They were both very strong.'

'And you said you married your childhood sweetheart?'

'Alexia,' he says, smiling. 'She was five months pregnant with our child. She was a very special person, a very kind person. Walking back from collecting firewood on the other side of town after most of the trees had already been taken down. Passing by a narrow street. The sniper killed her. The sniper killed her and our baby.'

29

The mood in the attic changes.

Linda and Therese both move in their chairs and then Niklas starts to cough into his elbow. The silence is disturbing. But what is more disturbing is that the man is so featureless in his balaclava. He delivered the news of his partner's death with an even tone and now we cannot clearly see his eyes or his mouth, his humanity, we cannot draw upon those features for signs of how to react, how to go on.

T-Bone says, in a muted voice, 'Did you... did you get your revenge, somehow?'

The man turns to face the shelves of food cans and buckets of wheat. Then he turns back.

'Not so simple,' he says. 'Complicated.'

'I would have hunted him down,' says Niklas, patting the arm of Ruby. 'I would have ended him.'

The man removes a stick of gum from his pocket and then he unwraps it. He looks at it. He places it on his tongue, showing us all his missing front tooth. And then he chews.

'You do not know of what you speak,' he says. 'You don't know what you are talking about.'

'I know...'

'No. You *think* you know,' says the man. 'You all think you know how it could be but none of you do know. And that is not a criticism, far from it. If anything, it is a compliment. You have never lived as animals, as savages, done bad things, so you don't know. I am glad you don't know.'

'You've done bad things?' asks T-Bone. 'What did you do?'

'We all did terrible things to survive,' he says. 'You did the things or you died. We were seven in my group. Many days were quiet. It is a boring time, a war. Keeping watch and sleeping and cooking. We all did the bad things. There are no good men in that situation; we were all bad in our own ways.' He looks around the group. 'You have a bad person amongst you here, as well. The woman by the river. Tuva, what was her name?'

I'm slightly taken aback but I reply, 'Elsa Nyberg.'

'Now wait a minute,' says T-Bone. 'Elsie was one of us. A friend.'

'You have been misinformed,' says Therese, looking at me. 'We are just as keen to find Elsa's killer as everyone else is. We want justice for her.'

The man waits and then he says, 'Maybe.' And then he chews and watches us.

'What is this shit?' asks Niklas. 'Who is this guy? Take off your mask, man. Let me see your face.'

'How long will this food store last you?' asks the man.

'A year, maybe eighteen months if we ration,' says T-Bone. 'Plus, we keep food on the hoof, best way. Meat birds and egg layers. Rabbits, Andreas keeps them up with his dogs. Then we got bees and of course all the wild game we need. Fish in the ponds and in the river.'

'And how will you defend yourselves when the bad men come to take away your food and your women?'

'Maybe we are the bad men,' says Andreas.

'No,' says the man. 'You are not.'

'We have what we need to protect the farm,' says Linda Larsson. 'Self-defence is my department.'

'Show me, and I will tell you what you really need.'

'Who the hell does this guy think he is?' says Niklas. 'Hey, Batman. Watch your mouth. You're on our farm now.'

'Have you ever fired a bullet at a man?' he asks Niklas. 'Have you ever had a human face, human eyes, human forehead in your sights? Taken a breath, deciding whether or not to end that person's life? I can help you with your preparations. But I don't need to do it. It's up to you.'

'Whatever,' says Niklas.

'We keep the defensive stores in my attic,' says Linda. 'Over in the other wing.'

'Good,' says the man, and then he stands up.

Linda leads us down and over the courtyard and into her house. The ground floor is more comfortable than T-Bone's even though it's the exact same layout. There's country wallpaper and framed prints on the walls. Thin rugs dampen our footsteps. She unlocks a steel door and we head upstairs and I have never seen anything like it.

'Usually, everything's locked away in gun cabinets, ammunition boxes and so forth,' says Linda. 'I keep inventory, and I clean and lubricate the weapons on a rotation basis to ensure they're all ready. What you see here is the bulk of our protective resources, but we do have caches in several locations, which we have agreed, as a group, not to disclose at this time. Nothing personal, we just agreed that as a group is all.'

'I respect that,' says the man. 'May I ask how you prepared your caches?'

'I do it all with T-Bone,' says Linda. 'Two-man job. We service weapons and tools and then vacuum-pack in plastic. We add freeze-dried food rations, Mora knife, disposable lighter, batteries, ammo, that kind of thing. Everything vacuum-packed. Then sealed inside a thirty-centimetre drainage pipe. We glue the ends on with plumbing cement and we tape the outside. Then we bury them.'

'I could learn something from you,' he says to Linda.

Niklas picks up a rifle.

'Mauser,' says the man. 'Reliable.'

I count fourteen rifles in total, and six shotguns.

'All registered?' asks the man.

'Of course,' says Linda. 'Registered, licensed, maintained, stored correctly. Chief Björn is a stickler for gun safety.'

'They will confiscate your registered firearms,' says the man. 'They did it during hurricane Katrina. You must have some unregistered weapons, also.'

'No comment,' says Andreas.

The man looks up at Andreas and says, 'Okay. I understand.'

Linda says, 'We have compound bows and recurve bows, with razor-sharp broadhead hunting arrows; can penetrate body armour better than a round from a .22.'

'But do you train to use them?' asks the man. 'Are you accurate with these bows?'

'We all train,' says T-Bone. 'Spontaneous tests and planned schedules.'

'We never used these in our war,' says the man. 'Bows, I mean. I think it is good that you have, as a back up, but we never use these. What else?'

Therese says, 'We have slingshots for hunting game, we have spearfishing guns, we have air rifles.'

'Toys,' says Niklas.

'Not at all,' says the man. 'Sometimes a quiet air rifle will be a hundred times more useful than an AK47 Kalashnikov. You want to hunt a pigeon to feed yourself, but you don't want everyone in the town to hear the shot, you use an air rifle. And if it's powerful enough, and you use dieseling, you can use as back-up weapon. I have seen this done one time.'

'Dieseling?'

'Air rifle creates tremendous pressure behind pellet. Use heavy lead pellet, like a small slug, and put oil or lighter fluid in base of pellet. Bang, will be very powerful now. May blow out your seals and O-rings, may blow up your gun if you're unlucky, but might also save your life as last resort. What about perimeter defence?'

'Well, what do you suggest?' asks Linda.

'What do I suggest? Well, you have a different set-up here to us back in the war. We were in a town, small street, damaged building. We barricaded windows and wall gates with rubble and then we kept lookout at all times including people on roof, two in the street. You are on farm. Lots of ditches and fences. All pretty useless in my opinion.'

'Useless?' says Therese.

'You have big farm. Great for growing food but impossible to defend with just you guys. Even with fancy cameras and lasers. Best thing you have is your dogs, very good, they are excellent.'

Andreas nods.

'What do you know about a breakdown of law and order in Sweden?' asks Ruby. 'It'd be totally different to what you lived through.'

'Keep telling yourself that.'

'What?'

'Looks different when it happens in Somalia, in Venezuela, in New Orleans, in Chechnya. Always looks different. But always the same. People kill for resources. It is that simple. And, I have to say, you guys have a lot of resources. Lots of valuable preparations. Who do you think, from outside here, is responsible for hurting the girl?'

'Elsa?' Says Therese.

'Yes.'

'We still don't know,' says Linda. The police are dealing with it.'

I look at their faces when he drops these questions. Trying to gauge their expressions. Is there a person here protecting another person? Or are they all genuinely unaware of the identity of the killer? I know that setting all this up was foolish. It puts me at risk and it puts me in debt to a whole bunch of people. But I need to help bring the killer to justice. For her sake, for her father's sake. But also because I had no resolution process after Noora was shot. If I'd had an investigation, a hunt, a puzzle to solve, I could have diverted all my misery and grief into that endeavour. But the shooter just gave themselves up. No fight. No escape attempt. In some weird, fucked-up way I need to find Elsa's killer to placate my thirst for revenge. For balance. I need to help the police bring whoever is responsible to justice.

They talk more about DIY grenades and tripwire alarms and machetes. About making claymore mines from shotgun shells. About how Ruby went to a hand-gun club for years so she could get a pistol licence. How the weapons are all registered in their individual names, all linked to their hunting licences, or club memberships, and stored in their own individual gun lockers, but if the rule of law was ever to break down they'd have ample stocks.

'You have American dollars?' he says.

'We don't want to talk about that,' says Therese. 'If you don't mind.'

'Fair enough. Bartering, then. You have barter items?'

'In the stable block,' says Linda. 'Batteries, lighters, medication, cigarettes, snus tobacco.'

'How many cigarettes?'

'Enough.'

'How much alcohol?'

'Enough.'

'You do not have enough.'

'Yeah,' says T-Bone. 'If she says we have enough then we have enough.'

'During war, people drank ten times more than they drank before. Everyone smokes cigarettes. You need much more vodka. More tobacco. Lots of tampons and lighter fluid and condoms.'

'Condoms?' says T-Bone.'

'Lots of sex in a war,' says the man. 'You hold on to what humanity you have. Who is in charge of your medicines?'

Therese puts up her hand.

'Where is it?'

'In the main house.'

'And?'

'First-aid kits, of course. Tourniquets, bandages, alcohol wipes. Needles and thread. The usual.'

'Antibiotics?'

'Some, but not much. Difficult to find.'

'They are almost as important as your bullets.'

'We have some from going to the doctor but it's not easy in Sweden, they don't like to prescribe it.'

'Buy fish antibiotics on the internet.'

'Fish?'

'Fish.'

'For humans?'

'It is all the same stuff. And anyway you keep the human drugs for yourselves and you use the fish antibiotics for barter. Worth more than gold, more than a woman. Back in my town, two of my friends died from infected wounds. Three from bad water. The antibiotics are very special.'

'Okay,' says Therese.

'What is that?' asks the man, pointing up to the ceiling. 'Elephant gun or something?'

'Take a look,' says Andreas.

The man stretches up on his tiptoes to reach the weapon and he reveals a slice of skin between his black jeans and his black sweatshirt.

It's another tattoo.

A cross.

It's upside down.

30

The man's sweatshirt falls back into place as he removes the gun from the wall.

He looks over at Linda and says, 'Flame thrower?'

'Yes, sir. Built it with my own fair hands.'

'I have never seen one of these.'

Was that tattoo an upside-down cross or was that just my mind playing tricks on me? It could have been some other symbol, or the top half of an anchor, perhaps.

'What's wrong, Tuva?' says Ruby. 'You look like you've seen a ghost.'

I shake my head. 'Never seen a flame thrower before, that's all. Never seen half of these things before.'

'Hopefully,' says the man in the balaclava, 'you will never see again.'

He replaces the flame thrower on its wall brackets.

Did this man kill Elsa Nyberg in cold blood? He's the only one here who's known to have killed before. Did he actually say he's killed before, though? He said he'd done terrible things. Is he back to relive a heinous crime? He does seem to know his way around Rose Farm very well, considering he's never been here before. He seems right at home.

'Sanitation. Water. Who is in charge?'

Ruby puts up her hand.

'You gonna give me a grade?' she says.

Niklas snarls.

'What is your preparedness?'

'Well,' says Ruby. 'Back home water was a real concern, but here, in the wettest corner of planet earth, it ain't no big thing.'

He waits for her to speak on.

'We have Snake River right outside the window, first of all. Pipework diverting into two, underground storage tanks and then pumped by either hand-power or electric. Then we have three wells on the property, two of them good. Berkey water filtration in each residence, I service them myself, replace the inner filters. Keep all the spare parts in my section of the stable block along with water purification tablets – I shrink-wrap them by the hundred in Mylar bags and store them in plastic buckets, same as T-Bone does with his pinto beans and wheat berries.'

'Toilets,' says the man.

A sudden bang outside, like the house has been struck by a bullet.

Niklas picks up a bolt-action rifle and moves towards the window.

'It's frost,' says the man. 'Frost at night. The wood expands and contracts; relax, put down your tool.'

Niklas ignores him and walks outside to investigate.

The man waits until Niklas has gone and then he says, 'First smart thing he's done since I got here. Now, toilets.'

'We got eight water closets on property,' says Ruby, twisting her highlighted hair between her fingers. Most of them run to a septic but we have two, the ones in the big house, they can run out to a sewage-treatment reed pond, but we don't have it hooked up on account of the Kommun worrying about river spill-off. We got it in case we need it. And then compost toilets, five of them. Enough toilet paper to last a year or more, plus hand bidets, plus expanding towels.'

'What is expanding towels?' asks the man.

'They're real smart – like white discs, you put water on them and they expand and form moist towelettes. We got about half a million. Double as barter items.'

'The dogs,' says the man.

Andreas says, 'What about my dogs?'

'Are they trained?'

'Yes, they are.'

'Will they attack?'

'You want me to show you?'

'Most people,' says the man. 'Most socialise their dogs these days. Neuter and socialise. So you end up with a teddy bear rather than a useful dog. Do not socialise your pack. Keep them lean and hungry.'

'I already do it,' says Andreas.

'You're in charge of comms, as well?'

'Ham radio. I have my licence. Good aerial up on the hill. CB's and two-ways for all farm residents. Gear stashed in faraday chests in case of EMPs.'

'Sounds like you have it under control.'

'You think you'd come here to find us all standing around holding our dicks?' says Andreas. He turns to Linda, 'Sorry, you know what I mean.'

'Power?' asks the man.

'What do you mean?' says Andreas.

'Electrical power.'

'That's Niklas's domain; he's good with amps and volts and all that.'

The man looks out the window to see Niklas and the glow from the asparagus fires lights up one side of his face. Fire and ice.

'Do you have bullion?'

Therese clears her throat. 'That's my husband's domain.'

'And where is your husband?'

'He's working tonight, I'm afraid.'

Niklas walks back in, his cheeks flushed.

'Power,' says the man.

'Electric?' says Niklas.

The man doesn't say anything.

'Well, we have solar, you've seen that. Good set-up. New cells. Submarine batteries in three locations. Also we got a hydro turbine connected through the pipe from the river for when it isn't sunny enough. Generators, dual-fuel, but I don't rate them.'

'Night vision?' asks the man.

'Yep,' says Linda. 'Third generation.'

'We never had night vision,' he says. 'We were not prepared like you people.'

'Can I ask you a question?' says Linda.

He waits for the question.

'If there was a problem on the horizon. An invading force. Something you could see coming. What thing would you buy or how would you train in advance.'

'No,' says the man.

'No?'

'If it's a true situation coming your way you get out. You're standing on a train track and see a locomotive coming, you get off the train tracks. Leave this place. Go to England, to Norway, to Holland. Anywhere. Leave early. Do not decide it's better to stay and fight just because you have expensive night vision and good fences. They will mean nothing.'

'It'll mean something,' says Ruby.

'If there are more men outside than inside, and they want to get in, they will get in. You think you can hold them out but you cannot. The leaving is the most important decision you can make and that takes real leadership. So, let me ask you all. Who is the leader in this group?'

No one says anything.

Then a low, melodic voice floats out of a speaker on the wall.

'My name is Abraham, son of Jacob. It is time for you to leave our farm.'

31

We all look at the speaker.

The man turns to Therese and says, 'You want me here or don't you?'

'We're very grateful to you. We've learned a lot from this evening and we're thankful.'

'Abraham Viklund,' the man in the mask addresses the speaker on the wall. 'Who are you hiding from? Me or these people? Or yourself?'

No answer.

'I got to check on my fires now,' says T-Bone.

'And me on my dogs,' says Andreas.

'Alright,' says the man. 'I wish you people well. I wish you good fortune.'

We start to file out of the attic and I can't help think that this anticlimactic end to the evening reminds me of being at some lame church-hall nightclub, aged thirteen. The boys and girls weren't really mixing; they stayed to their sides of the hall. Fizzy cola bottles and salt liquorice and soda. No alcohol. An innocent evening. And then when it was time, our parents would file into the room and the lights would come up and all of the electricity, because there was electricity there that night, the potential of what might be, it fizzled into the ether and we all went home in back seats.

The night air is cold, maybe three below.

Ruby and Niklas argue about something in the courtyard. Therese starts to walk up to the main house. T-Bone heads towards his red barn. And then a scream. A deep and animal exclamation.

'Heads!'

The farm residents scatter, ducking for cover, running to buildings and trees.

'Heads?'

'Arrow!' yells T-Bone, and that's when I look up to the small hill and see Andreas, all two metres of him, bent up to the sky holding his bow like a mythical figure might be depicted on the ceiling of a faraway temple.

I'm struck so hard it feels like I've been hit by a car.

Down to the gravel.

Being dragged, my hand bleeding, my forearm scratched.

The masked man has knocked me to the ground and pulled me down, low, under the front end of a parked truck. We shuffle to be concealed by its bulk. I can see Linda's boots beneath the main branch of an oak tree that's shaped like a clawed hand, and I can see T-Bone cowering beneath a timber bench.

Silence apart from the spitting and crackling of burning hay bales.

Andreas maintains his upright cupid pose, his teeth visible in the light from the flames.

The arrow comes down in the centre of the courtyard, not ten metres from where I was just standing, and it shatters on impact.

We crawl out from under the truck.

'Engine block,' says Linda, approaching. 'Good spot. Excellent cover.'

'What the fuck was that?' I ask.

'Training,' says Linda. 'We all test each other. Constantly. If you expect a training exercise, then it's not authentic. It's no way to train.'

'I go now,' says the man.

'Thanks for...' I say, and then I notice a face in the upstairs window of the main house, backlit. It could be Therese but I think it's a man. I think I can make out a beard.

The balaclava man rides off on his motorbike and I drive away in my truck.

On the main road he speeds off and I'm left alone, doing fifty with my headlights on full beam and my heart pounding against my ribs. Who was that guy?

Two missed calls from Noora's dad. One from little Dan's mum. Home.

Five hours sleep.

Hot shower.

A knock on my front door.

'I'm really sorry,' says little Dan's mum. 'I know it's early. I did try to call before breakfast. I need to pop out, just twenty minutes, half hour tops. Is that okay?'

'Sure.'

She pushes little Dan into my apartment and closes the door. I attach the safety chain and lock the main lock and bolt the extra bolt I had fitted earlier this year. If I'm with someone in this place then it will be secure, I will make sure of it.

'Hungry?' I ask.

'I had a toast,' he says. 'Spiderman has three toasts but I had two because I'm Peter Parker. Peter Parker has six muscles on his tummy but I only have one.'

'Smoothie?' I ask. 'Might help with your Spidey senses.'

'You think it will do?' he asks. 'Spidey senses means I can see the future before it even happens. Like on the TV.'

I pour frozen berries into my blender, a Christmas gift from Tam, and add an old banana and some yoghurt and some honey.

'Is there lots of vitamins in there?' asks Dan.

'Hundreds,' I say.

Little Dan flexes his tiny noodle arms and I say, 'Look more like Hulk than Spiderman,' and he says, 'Spiderman is smaller but he's got web shooters.'

We drink from straws but our smoothies are too cold, so Dan wanders around telling me all about his school project on crocodiles.

And then he sees the photograph of Noora on my bedside table and he says, 'My granddad is dead.'

'I know, sweetie.'

'He is under the ground now.'

'He is.'

'I'll never see him again. He's dead.'

I walk over to my bed and sit down and say, 'He lived a good, long life, Dan. Everyone, everything, dies, but the magic thing, and this is a special secret, really, everything lives on forever.'

'Not Granddad. He's dead, Mamma says so. He's dead now.'

'But his body will help feed the soil and one day in a hundred years there might be a beautiful apple tree growing in that field and part of that apple tree will be made up from your granddad.'

He stares at me.

'So if I ate an apple from that tree...'

'No, I don't mean it like that. I mean things go on forever, they just look different.'

He stares at the photo of Noora again.

'My granddad is buried and there is no air down there.'

'I know, kiddo.'

'And Todd in my school, he's got a snow-racer and it has a steering wheel and a brake.'

I smile and say, 'Very, very cool.'

'Like a car on skis.'

'Like a car on skis.'

My phone rings.

'Morning,' I say.

'It's the crawfish man,' says Thord. 'The figure in the distance from the photo, the man from the CCTV on the other side of Snake River the day Elsa was killed.'

'Yes?'

'Local crawfisherman. We have an ID.'

32

I drive to McDonalds because Thord advises giving Chief Björn a wide berth: something about the fire chief and him disagreeing over who has responsibility for the upcoming Valborgsmässoafton celebrations to mark the beginning of spring. Thord tells me the Chief doesn't want anything to do with it this year, on account of the dead Nyberg girl and the fact that her killer, or killers, are still at large.

The town is attractive, relatively speaking. The Lutheran church roof shines green in the sun and I think about Leif Nyberg working up there years ago, repairing the copper, fixing the weathervane, looking out over the whole of Gavrik town day after day; all that time alone to think about life, to think about how lucky he was to have his wife and his daughter.

McDonalds is busy. It's always busy. Recession? Most people will still go to McDonalds from time to time. Laid off work? Most can still afford the golden arches. Want to be alone and eat to forget, like I do some nights, you come here.

I park and get out of my truck and then he walks to me.

'ID?' I say.

'Really?' says Thord. 'We're not even greeting each other anymore, Ms Moodyson.'

'Don't call me that.'

'What?'

'You said you'd identified the crawfisherman.'

He stops by the drive-thru menu and then he turns to me and he says, 'Bengt Gustav Nyberg.'

'Elsa's relative?'

'The very same.'

I think about the dog. Bronco.

'So Bengt was there, on the other side of Snake River, at the time of Elsa's murder?'

'Estimated time,' says Thord. 'Big difference. Even in this day and age, the white coats can't pinpoint time of death that accurately. But, yeah, he was there for a while with his buckets and his pots. So we're working on the assumption Bengt was there the time Elsa Nyberg, his relation, was killed and concealed.'

'She had what could be a Satanic sign painted on her neck. Bengt Nyberg doesn't seem the type, you know?'

'They never do, Tuvs. They never do.'

We walk inside and one of the twins who used to clean the canteen up at the factory is now working here. His brother's still on the Grimberg payroll. Some kind of feud. Thord and I chat with him for a while and then we both order coffee and donuts.

'Walking cliché,' Thord says holding up his coffee and his ringed donut.

'I should have had a McMuffin,' I say.

'A long life is littered with regrets and old lovers.'

'You make that up?'

'No,' he says, removing the lid from his coffee to let it cool. 'Some folk band from Torsby. Pretty good, actually. Heard them up at the reservoir a few years back.'

'You bringing Elsa's uncle in for questioning?'

'Already have. And he's not her uncle. Bengt and her dad are cousins.'

'And?'

He takes a drink. 'Straightforward. Says he was there on the river most of that day. Says he's heartbroken to lose her from the family.'

'You believe him?'

'Maybe. He did say he saw something on the Rose Farm bank of the river, though.'

I raise my eyebrows.

'A man not too close to the area where Elsa was found. Rather, near the terrace at the back of the big house. He says he saw a man there with a gun on a sling.'

'But Elsa wasn't shot. She was hit.'

'Magnum has a theory.'

'Does he, now.'

'Apparently, paintball guns are pretty harmless, I never played it myself. Toys, pretty much, fire little balls full of paint. But Magnum reckons they can be modified, reckons he saw something about it on YouTube one time when he was researching. Turn a normal paintball rifle into a serious weapon.'

'Firing paint?'

'Firing solid balls.'

'Would they do damage?'

'I don't know for sure, but you gotta reckon one might inflict injury, say from close range, say if it hit someone in the temple.'

I take a bite of donut and Thord starts to sneeze.

'Damn hayfever starts earlier every year, I swear it.'

'But the lead traces?'

'That's what I said. Magnum's back at the station right now, keeping out of the Chief's way, seeing if a paintball marker could be tuned strong enough to fire a lead ball of some kind. I have my doubts, personally, but he's checking with a ballistics expert outside Stockholm. Might talk to Benny Björnmossen as well; that man's a fount of information. Speaking of which, you got anything for me yet on all this?'

'Not really.'

'Not really?'

'I've been putting some plans into action. Getting deeper inside Rose Farm, trying to get them to accept me, or at least tolerate me.'

'And how are you doing that?'

'You don't want to know.'

He smiles and sneezes again.

'Be careful.'

'I am.'

'I mean it.'

'I know you do. Have you completed all your interviews?'

'Everything from Rose Farm. We have a timeline of sorts, pasted together from the farm's CCTV, the statements from Leif and Bengt Nyberg. But there isn't as much footage as I would like – never is out in the wilderness. If I was working in Malmö, I'd have a dozen eye witnesses, car-registration plates picked up on cameras, public CCTV, private CCTV, the whole lot. In the background of the images, I'd have the public, vehicles, all sorts of details. Whereas I'm lucky to find a grainy image with a crawfisherman in one corner lifting up river rocks. I live in the wrong spot, I surely do.'

'You and me both.'

'You hear they found a moose up past Utgard forest this past month with, I think I remember this right, over two-thousand ticks attached to it. Well, they found the skinny old moose on the side of the road, in a right sorry state she was. Must have been like that most of winter. Ticks all over her skin, most of her fur rubbed off out of sheer frustration. You see, this is what the Chief told me, anyhow, the more they gotta focus on grooming, the less time a moose has to find food. And God knows it's slim pickings here in wintertime. Chief told me each tick can expand to over six-hundred times its original size. Six hundred, can you imagine it? With pincer jaws and some kind of barbed thing to suck the living blood right out. Vet was called to the moose, and in all my years out here I never heard anything like it. You call a vet when your horse is sick or when your cow is ill. A moose is a wild thing. They get left alone or they get hunted, that's all there is to it. Well, the vet had to come put the moose down. Euthanise it. Had to put the moose out of its misery. And she did the whole thing what they call pro bono, means nobody got the bill for it, not even the Kommun. You don't think a tiny thing like a tick could bring down a half-ton moose but you'd be wrong. Sometimes the ones in the shadows, the ones nobody sees, they're the one's efficient at the killing. Out here in nature it can be the one you least expect.'

33

We leave McDonalds and Thord says, 'Walk me home?'

I punch him on the arm and he says, in a serious tone, 'Not when I'm in uniform, Tuvs. People gotta feel authority in the law.'

'You don't think they do?'

'They see you punching an officer in public, when I've got a gun on my belt, people won't know what to think. You know, I've been watching some documentaries on the TV, watched them over Easter when my in-laws were over. Thing I came to realise is that civilisation is fragile. Brittle. Not civilisation, exactly, but people acting civil to each other. You start to see folks out beating on police officers, even in jest, and you don't know what will happen next.'

We walk up towards Storgatan. The chimneys of the factory pierce the horizon.

'Hear much on Kurt McGee?' asks Thord.

I frown at him.

'Kurt T-Bone McGee, calls himself Holm these days.'

'Farmer,' I say. 'Heirloom seeds. Asparagus.'

'Heard about some kind of disturbance relating to paintings. Artwork and suchlike?'

'He paints. But I haven't heard anything like that. What happened?'

'Something Abraham Viklund mentioned.'

A bus drives by. The number 2. It's always one or the other.

'You spoke to Abraham? What's he like?'

'Pain in the rear end.'

'What do you mean?'

'That was unfair. I'd like to take it back. Not his fault he's got the agoraphobia. Man won't leave his house, so I had to go up there to interview him. He doesn't come into Gavrik. Calls it Babylon or some crap.' He looks around at the town. 'Well, if this is Babylon, then I want a goddam refund.'

'What did Abraham say?'

'You know that house? Nice house it is. Him and Therese bought it years back. They got all the books against the outside walls, covers sticking out. I never seen that before in my life. Was like walking into a bookstore.'

'What did Abraham say about the paintings?'

'Oh, I don't know, Tuvs. Some domestic between T-Bone McGee and his girlfriend.'

'His girlfriend?'

'Well, I don't know if that's the accurate term for their relationship, but, yeah, I'd say his girlfriend. Lady who works in the organic café.'

'Linda Larsson?'

'The one and same.'

'They date?'

'Not sure it's dating, exactly. They live opposite each other in the wings of the main house. Real convenient.'

'What does that have to do with paintings?'

We cross the street and keep on walking.

'T-Bone paints. Landscapes, the river, his big red barn, all that. Abraham says he and Linda had a full-blown argument the night before Elsa Nyberg was killed. Argument about the fact T-Bone wouldn't paint Linda. Not sure why she wants to be painted so bad, but that was the spark. Abraham said he could hear the argument way back on his terrace on the other side of the big house.'

'Does Abraham have an alibi for the time of the murder?'

Thord burps and then he apologises.

'Says he was bidding in an auction.'

'An auction?'

'Antiques auction over at Bukowski's, Stockholm.'

'He was in Stockholm?'

'No, Tuvs. Like I said, he's agnostic.'

'Agoraphobic.'

'Either way, he won't go outside,' says Thord. 'He was bidding on his iPad. Showed me how he did it. Online auction for old coins, he said. He's a collector.'

Two figures emerge from a side street and they are unmistakeable. Dark hats hiding rough, grey, home-cut hair. Alice on the left and Cornelia on the right. The wood-carving sisters of Utgard forest.

I wave at them and Cornelia winks at me. Alice does nothing. They yield not a millimetre, so we have to walk out into the street to avoid bumping into them. Cornelia is carrying a bucket and Alice is holding what I assume to be a carved pine troll, wrapped in blankets like a newborn. Thord says, 'Afternoon,' and Alice just hisses at him.

'Takes all sorts,' says Thord.

'Does in this town.'

'Listen, Tuvs. I don't want to say anything out of line, but step away from the story if you need to get down to Gothenburg for a day or two. To see Noora, I mean.'

'I will.'

'No, I mean it. Lena will understand, and I'll keep you posted if any major developments happen, I promise I will. Go see Noora.'

'I said I will.'

He stiffens his gait.

'Sorry,' I say. 'I will go see her soon. I'm not getting obsessed with the case, I just want some resolution, same as you do. It's different now visiting Noora. Before, when I'd stay for a week at a time, always by her bedside, falling asleep watching her, taking care of her, washing her face, there would be hope. And I wish I was the kind of person who could be hopeful forever. Or, if not hopeful, just sacrifice my life, the rest of it, to be with her.' The Sheriff passes by in his taxi. 'Maybe I thought I was that person but you don't know if you're that person or not until you walk a mile in those boots, you know? After months of no progress, of doctors saying not to expect any progress, Noora's mum told me it was okay if I wanted to return to Gavrik. She told me she was the mother and she would always look after Noora, but that I could leave if I wanted, come back from time to time to check on them. That kindness floored me, you know?' Thord nods. 'It released me, released all the pent-up pressure from hoping so much, and it permitted me to let go. Obviously I haven't let go completely, I don't mean that, but time passing does something: it allows you to adjust to a new normal. This is my new normal. Her new normal. It's grossly unfair. Her mum deserves a medal. And I will visit her again, Thord. Soon. Regularly. For the rest of her life I will love her and I will show her that love. But right now I need to help crack this story and get justice for Elsa and her family. I have to listen to my inner voice and that is what it's telling me.'

'I'm glad you guys found each other,' says Thord.

'Yeah,' I say. 'Me too.'

34

I go back to the office and I am pissed off. Furious. Because I know what's about to pass. I've seen it before, and I can't imagine why it would be different this time. It's the funeral, you see. Once Elsa's funeral happens, there's a watershed with any investigation. Good police still want to catch the killer, of course they do. The family still urge them to work harder on the case. But pretty soon, after the death notices in the *Posten* and the memorial and the funeral service, the general public move on. Some kind of primitive coping strategy. They'll mourn Elsa and they'll do their crying, but all that will fade faster than you think it might. And that makes me mad as hell.

Hearing aids out, 500ml of red Coca-Cola in.

I build a matrix on my laptop and add the new information from Thord. The rare coin auction at Bukowski's and the crawfisherman's eye-witness account. And then I think back to T-Bone and his paintings. The argument he had with Linda Larsson. I google 'Kurt McGee' but nothing much shows up. When I try 'Kurt Holm, Visberg' I get the usual personal information but no news stories. 'T-Bone Holm' yields nothing. But 'T-Bone McGee' brings me to some blog posts from the late '90s. Some tour information for a band Kurt was once in. Other posts about him preaching in a church. All of them come from the United States.

Lars offers me coffee and I give him the thumbs-up sign and he brings me a fresh cup. What a guy.

The blogs aren't written well, and I can tell that some of the details and comments have been deleted, but I make notes as I go through. T-Bone was a bass guitarist back then. The church where he used to preach and pray has closed down, or else merged with some other church. It was called the Evangelical Free Church of Samto Mountain. It was based in the Ozarks, close to the Missouri state boundary. I search the church and there isn't much on it. Seems to have been a small, rural congregation. Lutheran meets Episcopalian, with a local twist.

The blog-post author is now over seventy years old. I was not expecting that. Eventually, after digging deeper, I find her details online and call her.

Strange dial tone.

'Delores Williams.'

'Hello, Delores. My name is Tuva Moodyson. I'm a reporter calling you from Sweden.'

'From Sweden?'

'Can you talk for a minute?'

'Sweden, Alabama?'

'Sweden, Europe.'

'I ain't buying.'

'I'm not selling.'

'Well, good. What did you say your name was?'

'Tuva Moodyson.'

'Moodyson?'

'That's it.'

'Tuva Moodyson?'

'Yes. Delores, I'm calling about a man you may once have known. He lives here in Sweden now. His name is Kurt Holm.'

'Never heard of him.'

'You may know him as Kurt McGee. T-Bone.'

There's a pause.

'T-Bone?'

'Yeah.'

'Oh, yeah, I knew a T-Bone. Norwegian man.'

'Swedish.'

'Coulda been from Denmark?'

'Sweden,' I say.

'Nice boy. Used to preach a little, tried to at least. Never did have the tempo for it.'

'The tempo?'

'The rhythm of our Lord, Tuva. You speak to the people about the Almighty, you need to maintain a certain rhythm. A musicality. That way, the Father's message shines through you and on to the people.'

'Is the church still around?'

'Got shut down in '99.'

'Shut down?'

'I don't know all the details. I wasn't privy.'

'And then T-Bone left? What type of man was he?'

'Who? T-Bone? What kind of men are any of them, Tuva? Womaniser. Drinker. But he wasn't the worst.'

'He ever get in trouble?'

'What kind of trouble?'

'I don't know,' I say. 'With the law?'

I see Lars out of the corner of my eye, and I can tell he's simultaneously captivated by this conversation and also concerned about the cost of the long-distance call.

'T-Bone was a law unto himself most weeks. Now, let me think…'

I wait for a minute or more.

'Hello,' I say.

'I'm still thinking,' she says.

I wait some more.

'Some kinda trouble back when he was lay-preaching.' She coughs into the phone. 'Girl from Appalachia. Real nice girl, hard worker. Used to help him on the ranch he was working at. She either went missing or else wound up dead in a turnpike ditch, I can't remember which one it was.'

Can't remember?

'You remember her name?'

'Whose name?'

'The girl.'

'Tuva, I hardly remember to put my pants on the right way round these days, no I do not remember her name. Missing, she was, so I reckon. Course, she could have ended up in the ditch. One of 'em did. I'm sketchy on the details.'

'Can I give you my number?

'What for?'

'That way you can call me back if you remember anything else about T-Bone McGee.'

'You can give it.'

I tell her the number.

'Big number, used up half my pencil writing it all down.'

'Sweden,' I say.

'You sound like you're in the next county, line's as clear as a bell.'

'Anything else I need to know about T-Bone?'

'Reckon he still owes me fifty bucks. You think he's good for it?'

'Anything else?'

'I'll call you on the long number if I remember anything else. You know, come to think of it, I got a granddaddy from Sweden. Originally, I mean. I doubt I'll ever make it that far but it's been nice to talk with you, Tuva.'

'Nice to talk with you, Delores.'

We end the call.

I add the information to my matrix and then I call Bengt Nyberg. No answer. I leave a message for him to call me. And then I ring Thord.

'Gavrik police, Magnus Falk speaking.'

'Magnum, it's me, Tuva.'

'Magnus,' he says.

'Thord calls you Magnum.'

'I know he does.'

'Listen, the gold coin you guys found in Elsa's bedroom. Can you give me some more details about it? The name, year and so on.'

'No cigar.'

'What?'

'We tried it, Sherlock. It was a Kruggerand from South Africa. Gold one-ounce bullion coin. Ninety-one point six-seven.'

'Sorry?'

'Ninety-one point six-seven per cent pure gold. One troy ounce.'

'Anything else?'

'I researched it. There are millions of them in circulation. One of the most common investment-grade coins.'

'Anything else?'

'No.'

'Year minted?'

'Year *minted?*'

'Yeah.'

'Let me check.' He goes away. He comes back. '1996.'

'Thanks, Magnum.'

He starts to correct me and say *Magnus*, but I end the call before he can get the word out.

I google bullion dealers in Sweden. There are three large dealers, two of which are based in Stockholm. I call the first but it's a dead end. They sell mainly larger bars. I try the second.

'PPX bullion.'

'Hi, my name is Noora Ali. Gavrik police.'

'Good afternoon. How can I help you?'

'I'm working on a homicide case out of Gavrik, Värmland. We have a piece of evidence and I hoped you might give me some general background on an object.'

'I can try.'

'Kruggerand. One-ounce. Minted in 1996.'

'Okay.'

'How common is that coin.'

'Very common.'

'Numbers?'

'Don't know off the top of my head.'

'That year?'

'Just one moment.'

He holds his sleeve over the receiver and yells to someone in the room. Then he removes his sleeve and says, 'Actually, it's relatively rare.'

'You said it was common.'

'Kruggerands are common. But I'm telling you the 1996 mint is rare.'

'Have you ever dealt with a private buyer in Värmland called Abraham Viklund.'

'Privacy laws.'

'Homicide case.' I pause, giving it time for those two words to sink in. 'Twenty-year-old girl died from internal bleeding. Hidden in alder saplings by a river. She was hit by a blunt object at close range. Killer still very much on the loose.'

'I'm sorry, I really am. But I can't talk names. You know I can't.'

'Do you have a private client in Värmland? No names.'

A pause on the line.

'Yes.'

'How many?'

'One significant buyer.'

'Okay, I appreciate that. What does he buy usually?'

'Gold. Never platinum. Never silver. Prefers coins to bars.'

'Kruggerands?'

'Yes, but also Canadian Maples, American Eagles, Buffalos, Austrian Philharmonics, Australian Koalas, British Britannias. He's not fussy. Whatever is good quality and close to spot. And he—'

'Spot?'

'Market price for the metal itself. Most of my buyers want the current year of production. People like new things, shiny things. Which is unwise. Gold is gold, created in a star implosion a billion years ago, and it'll still be gold in a billion more years. But they like them shiny. They pay for the shiny new thing instead of the older version even though it's made from the exact same element.'

'The man in Värmland doesn't care about the shiny coins?'

'He buys old coins. Close to spot. He's wise.'

My mobile flashes and I say, 'Can I put you on hold for a second?'

'Sure.'

I pick up the other line.

'Tuva Moodyson.'

'Hello there. This is Bengt Nyberg. With the dog, remember? You asked me to call you back.'

'Yeah, I remember,' I say. 'Bengt, I want to talk to you about crawfish.'

35

The sky is split in two. The upper section is grey, the base white. Through my windscreen it looks like the heavens have been ripped in half.

I pull off the main road and drive on towards Bengt's cottage. Green-painted siding. A swing-seat out front. Some kind of half-finished construction project behind the main structure.

'Look who's come out to see you,' says Bengt, appearing on his front stoop with a leash in his hands. The elkhound pup surges at me.

'He's so cute!'

'Picked him up yesterday morning. Spent hours scared, wondering where he was, but then he found Bronco's old chew toys from when he was young, his old blanket, and ever since he's been right at home. Haven't thought up a name for him yet. You want a cup of coffee, Tuva? Something stronger?'

'Coffee, please.'

'Hot in the pot,' he says.

We sit out on his un-mowed front lawn. The pioneer shoots of bindweed and bramble are starting to push through the earth all around us. Vigorous barbs evolved over millennia to cling and exploit and climb. Green tendrils purpose-built to outperform the competition; to dominate and conquer.

'I was talking to Constable Thord earlier,' I say.

He pours coffee into his saucer for it to cool. My grandma used to do the same thing.

'Oh?'

'He mentioned you were out fishing on Snake River the day Elsa passed.'

'Nope.'

'No?'

'Not fishing,' he says. 'Crabbing.'

'Crabbing in a river?'

'Not so much *in* the river.' He slurps his coffee from the saucer. 'In the creeks off the river, mainly. In the slow-moving waters and under the rocks. By the riverbanks. There's an art to it and I got my places.'

'So you were close by when she was killed.'

'The police say it's possible. If only I'd have heard her scream I'd have come running. I'd have swum across Snake River if I'd heard that sweet voice. Keep thinking back. Seeing if I could have done something.'

'You didn't notice anything was awry?'

I take a sip of the coffee but he's poured milk into my cup already and it tastes a little off so I put it back down.

'Too hot?' he says.

'It'll be fine in a minute.'

He points to his old-fashioned saucer cooling-technique and I smile.

'Did you see anything around the river that day?'

'Have you ever been out crabbing for mudbugs, Tuva?'

'Mudbugs?'

'It's what I call them. Crayfish, crawdaddies, yabbies, crawfish, mudbugs, redneck lobsters, signal stunners. You ever collected them up in a ditch or a lake or someplace?'

'No.'

'It's like a blessed meditation.'

'How so?'

'Well, that sad day when Elsa was taken from our lives, the sun was still low in the sky. Springtime crabbing is one of my favourite things. Sure, I'll make decent money in the late summer selling to folks up the reservoir, the out-of-towners, folk with money, but my crabbing experience is best in April and May time. It's the light, see. You get shallow sun coming down and bouncing off the flat waters and it just does something to you, does to me anyhow. A kind of simple tranquility. Inner peace of a sort I struggle to find now, at my old age. I stand in the shallow waters looking down, sunbeams warming the back of my neck. And then I focus. Turning over rocks and reaching under the riverbank overhangs, you know it's carved right out in places; you could fit a whole person under the bank at some stretches of Snake River.'

'Did you see anyone that day?'

'I caught an even half-dozen that afternoon. Boots were keeping the water out. My vest was still holding the chill off my back. And I remember thinking, Bengt, what you're missing is that musical backdrop. I haven't ever been to an actual opera house but I reckon Sydney and Milan got nothing on us when Abraham Viklund's outside practising on his back terrace, surrounded by rosebushes in bud, and I'm at the water's edge picking out crawfish. The tunes carry across the water like he's playing just for me.'

'But not that day.'

'Nothing. Just the sound of the water and the fluttering of the first butterflies of the new season.'

'Was that strange, not to hear Abraham play?'

'I wouldn't say it was strange, but I'm used to hearing him nine times out of every ten. At first I found it odd, after all them years quiet by the river, but now I got used to it. Got to like it, even. He's a maestro, that's what they tell me.'

'Did you see him close to the alder trees? Close to the area Elsa was found?'

'I didn't, Tuva. If I'd have seen him there, I'd have told the police, or else I'd have gone hunting him down with Leif, my cousin. We'd have most likely shot him cold dead if we'd seen him in them alder trees.'

'You didn't see anyone?'

He turns to attend to his dog, whose leash is tangled around a pillar, so I pour my rancid coffee out on to the grass.

'I've been thinking back on it, on that day. Like I say, I'm real focused down at my boots, at the riverbed, the best positions, so I don't get to see much else. But I reckon I might have glimpsed a woman walking down from the big house towards that alder patch.'

'A woman?'

'Might have been a girl, I guess. Wasn't Elsa though, I'd have recognised our Elsa.'

'Linda? Therese? Was it Ruby from the spa? Someone else?'

He looks up at the sky.

'I wish I could tell you. It was just a split-second kind of a thing. A glance up, squinting into the light. Think I saw a woman is all.'

'You know what she was wearing?'

'I do not.'

'But you were on the opposite riverbank?'

'That's it. The Dalarna side, I call it.'

'How do you get across?'

'How do you think I get across? I use a boat.'

'Motorboat or row-boat.'

'The boat I got has both.'

'So you started out on the same side as Rose Farm, near the alder patch, and then you crossed over?'

'Not sure why you're so confused about how a river works? You write the newspaper; surely you understand you gotta cross from one side to the other.'

'Could you show me?'

'Could I show you what?'

'Your boat. The view from the other side, the Dalarna side. It would be useful for me to see the farm from that angle.'

'I got plans today,' he says, a guarded look in his eyes. 'Some other time, maybe.'

'Your pup looks like a smaller version of Bronco,' I say, crouching down to stroke his head. 'I wish it had turned out different for your dog, Bengt. But I'm glad I found you both that day. Glad I was able to get him to the vet before he suffered any more.'

'I think I know what you're saying,' he says, flaring his nostrils. 'You did a good deed. An eye for an eye.'

That phrase again. 'That sounds more like a threat than a deal.'

'You see it your way and I'll see it mine, I guess. I don't mean to sound disrespectful, I'm genuine grateful for what you did for Bronco. I just sometimes get a little tired of outsiders pulling apart our old way of life up here, staring at us all through some kind of scope as if we're living in a science experiment.'

'I live in Gavrik.' I say. 'Have done for years.'

'Gavrik's *outside* for us. Big-city folks.'

'Should we take my truck?'

'I may as well save my gas.'

We drive past the farm and slow for the exit to the alder patch, and Bengt crosses himself and then we drive to the next exit, a dirt track through long, dead grass.

'Park up there on them pebbles,' says Bengt.

We walk to the riverbank and the first mosquitos of the year are starting to feast.

'Just ignore 'em,' says Bengt. 'They can sense your fear; I saw it on a documentary one time.'

He points to a derelict-looking rowboat.

'You cross the river in that?'

'Since I was fourteen, I done it. Even though I never did learn to swim.'

'Daredevil.'

'I like mudbugs, I guess. I like them that much.'

He rows me across the river and the current drags us so he almost has to row upstream to get across.

'There she is. Rose Farm. Back end.'

The surface of the river ripples and shines. Insects cloud the banks and a buzzard hovers overhead waiting to select its quarry.

'Where did you see the woman that day?'

He points to the gates and fences closest to the alder patch.

'Folks say they call themselves a pack. Abraham, T-Bone, Linda and the others. A real wolf-pack. They say Abraham, the man with the violin, they say he's the alpha wolf.'

'You often see people walking around there?'

'I see Andre the Giant, that's what I call him. Andreas. Big lad walks around with his dogs and a plank of wood round his neck. Can spot him from a mile away.'

'It wasn't him that day you saw?'

'No. A woman, I reckon.'

Bengt rows me back over to the Rose Farm side of the river and I can see that the oars of his rowboat are decorated. Each one has a black motif.

'Beautiful oars,' I say.

He digs them deep down under the water and says, 'my cousin's work. He's the artisan.'

'Leif?'

'That's it. Elsa's dad carved these oars. Carved my knife handles, too.'

One oar has a serpent motif and the other some kind of eye icon atop a pyramid.

'You share this boat with Leif?'

'It's his boat officially in the eyes of the law but I'm the only one that uses it. Leif is allergic.'

'Allergic?'

'Crawfish. They make him suffocate to death. Closes down his pipes so he can't squeeze a breath out of himself. Drown in fresh air, he would.'

I drop Bengt back at his place but then feel a compulsion to return to Rose Farm. An irrational part of myself thinks if I go there enough times Abraham will present himself to me. I know he's integral to this case but I can't figure out how.

The public area is open and there's a car parked by the spa. Must be a 'by appointment' customer. I drive on through the scorched, smouldering bales of the asparagus field and park by the big red barn.

'Hello?' I say, as I walk into the cool shade.

The scent of manure and fresh straw.

'Anyone home? T-Bone?'

I walk around with a full smile the way I always do. It's a strategy I learned from Lena, one of many she's passed on. You have to stick your nose in as a journalist, you have to walk through doors into the unknown, to push through them. But always announce yourself. Vocally and visually, as someone who is no threat whatsoever.

'Kurt?' I say.

There's a rough timber staircase up to the barn attic.

I walk up.

Each step creaks.

The log walls are adorned with the pencil markings that a farmer or carpenter made perhaps a century ago. Numbers and sums. Arithmetic to ensure the angles were right and the red barn would stay upright through storms and hard Swedish winters.

I step out into the upper level.

Bales of hay scattered around.

Easels and framed canvasses.

Paintings drying, hanging from the rafters and the beams of the barn by bailing twine.

I shiver.

Because the paintings all depict one person.

Every single one of them.

Elsa Nyberg.

36

There are miniature paintings of Elsa when she was younger. Thirteen or fourteen years old. Framed paintings. Pencil sketches and delicate watercolours. And then there are vast compositions, four wood boards arranged in a grid, Elsa wearing a short white sundress with flowers in her hair.

A noise from down in the barn. I stop in my tracks, my heart pulsing against my ribs.

I estimate there are a hundred paintings of Elsa Nyberg up here. What does this mean? I photograph the room as quietly as I can, and the images look absurd on my phone screen. An agricultural barn full of original artwork.

Outside, a tractor passes by on the road.

And then I see it.

The track through the asparagus fields, cutting the crop in half, and the other track intersecting it.

The blackened ash marks either side of the dirt.

The whole area looks like a white crucifix. Inverted. Like the cross painted on to the back of Elsa's neck.

I start to sweat even though the air is cooling. I jog downstairs, taking two steps at a time and a bull presents itself to me as I pass by. Steam from its nostrils, each dripping hole joined with a loop of thick steel. The bull grunts and it starts to get agitated, starts to emit something. A pheromone, or just an impression. If it wasn't for the cage I would be running for my life.

'What are you doing here?' asks a slurred voice.

'T-Bone. Oh, hey, I came to see you.'

'Well, here I am, sunbeam.'

'I'm glad I caught you.'

'You caught me?'

'Can we talk a minute?'

Andreas passes by in the background with a plank of wood swinging across his chest, held in place by a camo harness.

'I gotta see to my irrigation,' he says.

'It'll just take a minute. It's about Elsa.'

'They got somebody in custody yet?'

He looks tired. Or maybe he's been drinking.

'Not yet.'

'If I ever get a chance to see that man, just me and him, by God, I'll…'

'I never knew you lived in America.'

He wipes his mouth on his sleeve.

'Oh, that.'

'That.'

'Who you been talking to?'

'I can't reveal my sources.'

'You can't reveal them?'

'Kurt McGee, eh?'

'T-Bone.'

'Why did you leave America?'

'Why did you leave London?'

'My mother was dying. I wanted to make peace with her before she passed.'

'Did you? Make peace, I mean.'

I can smell the alcohol on his breath.

'In a way.'

'Well then, I'm pleased to hear it, Tuva. I never got the chance with my own mamma, never got the chance to even know her properly. Not sure what she'd make of me now.'

'I heard you were in some sort of local church in the Ozarks.'

'Beautiful part of the world. Especially back then. Good, local people. Honest and hard-working. Simple life writ large, and God-fearing, every last one of them.'

'But the church didn't last?'

'Samto Mountain? No, we never had much luck when it came to pastors and so forth. Turned from a good, solid, outdoors kind of a deal – pews made from local timber, services by moonlight, everyone dressing up best they could afford, good music, and everyone got a chance to preach their bit – to something not right. There was a generosity to that little church, and then some money came their way and it all got corrupted. So, I left and came back to Sweden, but that was many years ago. A whole different life, you might say.'

'Some kind of misinterpretation over a local girl, as well?'

'Who you been talking to, was it Virginia-May Higgins, was it her?'

'Just been sent a local newspaper article from back then.'

'Was it in the newspapers?'

'Just a local paper.'

'No offence, Tuva, but I'm no fan of media types. Fancy hundred-dollar words and twisting the truth to fit their agendas. Abraham knows even more about it than I do.'

'Did they find the missing girl in your town, back in the day?'

'I wouldn't know about that. I hope they did.'

He looks mournful all of a sudden. Smaller than before.

'Did you paint her, too, T-Bone?'

'Did I what?'

'Did she sit for you, the girl in the Ozarks, so you could paint her picture?'

I'm too angry to be afraid now. That's the trouble when you have nothing much left to lose.

'Did you obsess about that girl like you did about Elsa Nyberg, T-Bone?'

He squints at me.

I hold his broken gaze.

'Linda tell you all that, did she. Whiny little... I should have known better. Linda Larsson is a... I don't want to say it. I shouldn't. Doesn't hold a candle to my late wife. Linda tell you I painted girls?'

I don't say a word. Don't show any emotion.

'You see a farmer and you think, well, that's an uncultured swine with hams for hands, he ain't got no art in his whole body. Well, you might just be wrong. I'm a working man, proud of it, but I paint, too; what of it? Ain't no rule against that. What did Linda tell you? She don't know. She's just mad pissed because I won't paint her, is all. She's been bothering me on it for years.'

'Linda wants to sit for you?'

'That's what I said. But I can't paint her as much as I can paint you or Andreas over there. It has to feel right; I have to *feel* something to paint well. Elsa was a subject, is all. I could paint her. I could bring her essence out through my brush strokes. Linda never did like that. She always bullied Elsa on account of it.'

'Bullied?'

'Not bullied, but didn't treat her right in the café, you know. Didn't give her the breaks she was due, share of the tips, that kind of thing. You take a woman like Linda – we're kind of together in an informal way, ain't no arrangement to it – and she sees young Elsie hanging around me, taking all my attention for the paintings, nothing more, nothing bad I swear on my life, and a woman like that can work her way into a cold frenzy. That's why we never lived in the same wing cottage of the manor, I couldn't cope with Linda's temper. Maybe you seen it already. Vicious temper. And when she gets jealous, believe you me that woman's capable of anything.'

37

I leave T-Bone to irrigate his early potatoes and let my Hilux amble down the dirt track through the scorched asparagus bales, towards the old stable block. Ruby and Niklas are sitting outside the spa, each one sipping on a blue cocktail, each one wearing full camo as usual. I park.

'You bothering T-Bone?' says Niklas. 'Old man likes to be left to himself.'

'I'm just working on a story.'

'Just working on a story,' says Niklas.

'Oh, is it,' says Ruby, pushing her sunglasses up into her hair. 'You ever think maybe it's time to leave all us to mourn Elsa and get on with our lives.'

She takes a sip of her blue cocktail. Ruby looks serene tonight, like she's at peace with the world, like she's on the last day of a two-week cruise. Maybe she's high.

'What are you drinking? Looks refreshing.'

'Blue Lagoons,' says Niklas. 'I used to be a bartender in a past life. Exclusive place with a guest list, table service, that kind of thing.'

'Shame we just this second run out or we'd offer you one,' says Ruby.

'That's okay. I'm here for Linda.'

'She's probably washing up her dishes as per usual,' says Ruby, her speech slurring. 'State of that woman's cuticles, I tell her to wear latex gloves, I spend half my life in them, but she won't listen.'

'See you later,' I say.

'Whatever,' says Ruby under her breath.

Linda Larsson is painting a board of what looks like plywood outside her café.

'Waterproofing?' I say.

She looks over, sweat on her brow, white marks on her wrists, and she says, 'writing my menu blackboard. This stays on longer than chalk. Weatherproof. Amazing what you can buy on the internet these days.'

'I've just been talking with Kurt.'

'Oh, no, you don't,' she says. 'I'd advise you to leave that fool well alone while he's got his supping boots on.'

'His *supping* boots?'

'He's been drinking. Drinking to forget or to remember, I'm not sure which.'

'He said something about you being annoyed at him?'

'Well, that's none of anybody's business, now, is it?'

'I guess not. Just that he was talking about painting portraits. How he'd paint a girl back when he lived in America. How you didn't approve.'

'I didn't even know him back then,' she says. 'But he paints hussies and, yes, truth be told, I think it's degrading the way he goes about it.'

'How so?'

She wipes her brow and rests her fine paintbrush on the lip of the tin.

'Doesn't matter.'

She waves her arm and I see Andreas walking towards us from the hill, a plank of wood across his chest, a plate carrier underneath. That reminds me, I need to talk to Luka Kodro about the guy he sent in his place. I need to find out what that was all about.

Linda gets back to painting and Andreas yells something at me but I can't make out the words. He yells louder and I have to say, 'Deaf, can't hear you.'

He comes closer.

'You wanna see something special?' he says.

'Don't fall for that line,' says Linda. 'When men say that it means just one thing.'

'Linda,' says Andreas, blushing.

'He's okay, really,' says Linda. 'Big old klutz.'

'What is it?' I ask.

'Come, see.'

We walk halfway up the hill and Andreas stops to stare at something down in a dry ditch. It's a magpie, half eaten by something. Midges and bluebottles dance around its corpse.

'Not funny,' I say.

'Not that,' he says, walking on. 'Over here.'

Mists start to roll in off the waters of the river and some kind of pump starts up and it sounds like the two-stroke engine of a small boat.

'Over by the range,' he says.

We pass the claw-shaped oak tree and walk through a mowed area, the ground scalped by a sharp blade. There's a trench with targets on the other side.

'There,' he says, pointing to a flattened thistle.

'A thistle?'

'Look closer,' he says. 'Look.'

There is a papery, almost translucent membrane balancing on the thistle. Andreas takes a small twig, which looks absurd in his enormous hands, and he picks up a shed snakeskin.

'From a slow-worm,' he says. 'You can see the scales. The holes for the mouth and the eyes. This was its skin.'

He holds it up to the shallow light and I see Kurt's red barn through the membrane.

'Not a snakeskin,' he says, as if reading my mind. 'More like a legless lizard.'

'It is beautiful,' I say.

'Linda and T-Bone are falling out,' he says, still inspecting the skin, holding it up to the sky. 'I don't like it when people argue. I hate it. I don't like conflicts of any kind. They're going to break up.'

I did not expect this from a giant like Andreas.

'They'll work it out,' I say.

'The problem with a tight group is it stays tight by tension, like the skin of a bass drum. One connection snaps, and the whole thing comes tumbling down. I need them to stay together.'

'Why are they not getting on?'

'I can't talk about it.'

'Fine.'

'But he was in a different group before, in America. Told me about them. Eighteen strong. And they fell out eventually. Collapsed. If the same thing happens here I don't know what I'll do. This is my home. I don't want to live anyplace else. I just want everyone to get along.'

'Couples quarrel, man. It'll pass.'

I see Niklas walking up the hill towards us.

His boots kick up dust from the track and he swats away midges as he passes by the dead magpie in the ditch.

'Just when you think something's good,' says Andreas. 'Stable. You got in a solid routine. Something else always happens to ruin it all. The devil's work is clear to see.'

'You have to roll with the punches, I guess.'

'I've been doing that ever since I was a newborn,' says Andreas.

Niklas is still sipping from his Blue Lagoon cocktail. It clashes hideously with his desert army fatigues.

'Andre,' he shouts to Andreas. 'We're locking down the compound in ten minutes, Abraham's words. You ready?'

As he finishes his sentence there's a change in the air.

A stillness.

Niklas stiffens, gasps, and then he opens his hand slowly and drops his glass and it smashes on the hard, dry earth coating the creeping buttercup below with blue liquid.

He's bleeding.

There's an arrowhead pointing at me right through the centre of his chest and blood is starting to trickle from the corner of his mouth.

He falls.

38

The scene unfolds in slow motion.

I panic. I can't catch my breath.

Niklas on the ground, the arrow sticking up out of his chest, his eyes rolling back in their sockets.

'Pull the arrow out!' yells Andreas, hovering over me, flapping his arms. 'He's going to die.'

'No,' shouts Therese, sprinting up from the main house carrying a military-style first-aid kit. 'Leave the arrow where it is.' She holds Niklas's hand and speaks loudly. 'Hang in there, Niklas. Don't go to sleep. Stay with us.'

Therese steps away and says, 'Keep talking to him,' and then she calls the police and an ambulance. She requests an ambulance helicopter, if one is available. She urges them to hurry as she can't do much for him.

'Help's on its way,' she says. 'Stay with us, Niklas. Help is coming.'

I stare at the delicate feathers forming the fins of the arrow. The black-and-white stripes plucked from some bird or another to make this medieval device fly straight and true to its target. As I adjust focus I see Ruby down the hill, walking calmly towards us, her compound bow loose in her hand, a quiver by her hip, six or seven more arrows resting there.

'You need to restrain her,' Therese says to Andreas in a low tone.

But Andreas rubs his forehead and starts to mumble, starts to falter.

'Drop the bow,' says Linda, approaching from her café with a shotgun by her hip. 'Bow on the ground, now, Ruby. Lie down, hands behind your back. Nice and easy.'

Ruby just keeps on walking. Her red lipstick is stained blue at the corners of her mouth from her cocktail.

'Drop it or I drop you,' says Linda. 'Got witnesses to testify it was self-defence. You got three seconds.'

Linda lifts the shotgun from her hip to her shoulder.

Ruby says, 'I'll drop my bow, but I'm not lying on the ground for nobody.'

She places down her bow and puts her hands in the air.

'Andre,' says Linda. 'Get yourself over here.'

Andreas runs over and takes two cable ties from Linda's back pocket and tightens them around Ruby's wrists. He pushes her gently to the ground and she sits cross-legged with a peaceful expression on her face.

'He dead, is he?' Ruby asks.

'Don't talk,' says Andreas.

Ruby lifts her chin to see better and then she says directly to Niklas, 'What did she give you that I couldn't, eh? What did she have?'

'Faint pulse,' Therese says to T-Bone. 'He's weak.'

'You killed them both?' Linda asks Ruby, her mouth open in shock. 'Elsa and Niklas?'

'Those two deserved each other,' says Ruby.

Everyone else looks up to the sky so I look up as well. I can't see anything. Then, from behind the treeline, an ambulance helicopter comes into view and hovers overhead. T-Bone directs them to the asparagus fields and they land and two men run towards us carrying a stretcher.

The police arrive. Thord and Magnum.

The paramedics strap something around the arrow to make sure it doesn't move around and cause more internal damage, and then they run back to the helicopter, its rotors still turning, its engines still blowing, its noise filling Rose Farm. They take another arrow from the quiver, I'm not sure why, and then they fly away over the waters of Snake River.

Ruby does not resist arrest.

Thord removes the cable tie and places her in handcuffs. She goes willingly.

'Oh,' says Therese, looking down at her stained hands. 'Bloody hell.'

I've never heard her swear before.

We gather closer.

'Niklas never asked for that,' says Andreas. 'I don't care what he did. What Elsa did. They never asked for all that.'

'Hell hath no fury,' says T-Bone. 'Like a crazy drunk woman scorned.'

'She should have slapped him and be done with it,' says Linda. She managed to store away her shotgun before the police arrived, I guess. 'Smack upside the head, not an arrow to the torso. How bad is it, Therese?'

Therese just shakes her head.

'Heart and lung shot,' says T-Bone. 'Ruby's one of the best bow hunters I ever seen in my life. Forty-yard shot and she hit the jackpot. Poor old Niklas.'

Linda hugs T-Bone and T-Bone crosses himself and then hugs her back.

'Broadhead,' says Therese. 'Designed to inflict massive internal injuries. Barbed. Sunk all its power into his chest.'

Magnus says, 'You all need to move back now, back to the stable area. I need to seal off this scene. All of you need to move back.'

Everyone stays exactly where they are.

'I knew he was seeing Elsa,' says T-Bone. 'I knew it in my guts but I never had no proof.'

'Ruby killed them both dead,' says Linda.

'Move back,' says Magnus again. 'I'll need to take your statements, one by one.'

We start to move away from the scene. There isn't much blood on the ground, most of it's on Therese's hands, but the first-aid kit lies open and unused, gauze and shears and tourniquets and sutures and chest packs all pristine and absolutely useless. This was a medieval weapon used with medieval results.

I didn't photograph Niklas lying there but I did get shots of the helicopter taking off from Rose Farm, and I did get shots of Thord's marked Volvo driving away with Ruby in the back seat, and her compound bow, before it was bagged and stored securely in the boot.

'Weird thing is,' says Linda. 'I reckon that spot where Niklas was shot was the exact place, give or take a few metres, where the murder-suicide went down back in the '80s. That's the point where the old man killed his wife and children on the picnic blanket.' She blows air between her teeth. 'I guess sometimes history repeats.'

39

I spend two hours in the office writing up the story and filling Lars, Nils and Lena in on all the details. I'm still shaken from it. Rifle wounds I've seen – and they're horrific enough – but at least you never see the bullet, just the result. There's something nightmarish about looking at an arrow sticking out of someone's chest. Imagining the tip of it ripping through ribs and lung tissue, depositing itself deep within the heart muscle.

The police have my statement. They've called in support from Karlstad Homicide to help with managing the crime scene and evidence-processing and taking multiple statements. Magnus Falk found a paintball marker in the home of Ruby and Niklas. It was hidden under their marital bed, loaded with glass marbles, air tank in place. It was some kind of MilSim tactical paintball gun, not the kind with a huge air tank. It looked exactly like an AR15. And, according to Thord and Benny Björnmossen, it's conceivable it could have been used to fire a lead ball, albeit only at very close range. Point blank. They're sending the marker off for testing.

Lena opens her door.

'Anything on Elsa Nyberg yet? Confession? Any link?'

I shake my head and pick up my phone and she goes back into her office.

'Thord, it's me.'

'Too busy,' he says, and ends the call.

'I've seen it too many times before,' says Lars.

'Seen what?'

He stands up from his desk and loosens his belt one notch. It takes a full minute. Then he says, 'Marital affairs resulting in violence.'

'When have you seen anything like this?'

'Not a bow and arrow, of course, I don't mean that. But a fight. Interviewed a man once back in the '90s who'd been stabbed by his wife when she caught him with another woman. Stabbed in the abdomen.'

'Did Ruby kill Elsa Nyberg, though?'

'I hope so.'

'What?'

'Otherwise you have Robin Hood over there,' he gestures towards the police station. 'Plus another killer in Gavrik town. I'd say the odds of that are slim to none, wouldn't you?'

'Maybe.'

The bell above the door opens and Benny Björnmossen's standing there with a Marlboro hanging from his lips and a brown suede jacket and a pair of blue Levi's.

'No smoking,' says Lars. 'It's the law, not my rules.'

'I ain't indoors,' says Benny. Then he looks over at me, still out on the street. 'Can I have a word?'

I step over to the door and slide on my outdoor shoes.

'She's still in there.'

'Ruby?'

'Yeah, Ruby.'

'Niklas might live yet,' I say.

'He might,' says Benny.

'What do you want to talk about?'

'It's delicate.'

'Okay.'

'As you know, or you might know, I'm a man who built a small community business on the back of hard graft. Opened the store, it was just fishing back then, different location, not so much footfall, just off Eriksgatan, back in ninety-four.'

'Okay,' I say again.

'It ain't so easy as you think competing with all the internet mail-order places and the big out-of-town stores down the E16. They got their bulk discounts and their convenient customer parking right near a hot dog stall. What do I got?'

'Personal service,' I say.

He takes a puff of his cigarette.

'The local touch?' I say.

'Yeah, I got that.'

'What are you saying, Benny?'

'What I'm saying is that when news gets out that I sold Ruby Gunnarsson her compound bow, sixty-two-pound draw weight, broad-head arrows, bow wax, Luminova sights, the whole caboodle, and she went and hunted down her own damn husband, well, it might make some of my gentlemen customers think twice, you understanding me straight?'

'I think so.'

'Good. So we have an understanding.'

'A what?'

'You'll keep that detail out of your newspaper.'

'Where she bought the bow from?'

'Yeah. Where she bought it from.'

I think for a second. I hesitate. I had no intention of including this detail because it has very little to do with the story. But I don't need to tell him that now, do I?

'We can come to an arrangement.'

'What kind?'

'If I need your help in future you'll give it.'

'I ever not help you in the past, Tuva?'

'I'll keep it out of the paper if you help me going forwards. With whatever I need.'

'Okay, then.'

He walks off in a cloud of smoke.

I scroll through Twitter before I go back into the office, and the news of Ruby being charged with double murder is beginning to break. I run over the road to the cop shop.

'Hello, Tuva.'

'Sheriff? What are you doing here in Gavrik?'

'Just filling in,' he says, and his facial expression tells me he's genuinely over the freaking moon to be allowed to get out of his taxi and sit behind reception for a half hour. 'How can I help you?'

'Thord in?'

'Bit tied up.'

'Check for me?'

I'm guessing he doesn't have the keycode because he dials through and then nods and says a few words and looks up at me and then says, 'Wait just a minute, will you.'

Thord comes through almost immediately.

'I can't talk.'

'Charged with double murder? The news knows but I don't know and I'm right over the other side of the street.'

'Not charged with anything, Tuvs. She won't speak.'

'Won't speak?'

'Waiting for some expensive Stockholm lawyer to get here. Abraham Viklund arranged it all for her. Until then, I doubt there will be much change. Why don't you go break the story that there is no damn story, at least not pertaining to any official charges.'

'I could, Thord. But people don't care about that kind of story. Anything on the paintball marker they found under the marital bed?'

'No comment. Watch your volume, I got people back there.'

'He gonna make it?' I ask.

'Niklas? What, do I look like a doctor? I'm sorry. I just have a lot on my plate.'

'You think Ruby did them both?'

'I got to get back to work.'

He leaves and the Sheriff stands up behind the counter and looks right over my head.

'Tuva,' he says. 'Looks like you got Luka Kodro outside to see you.'

40

The sun hits me in the face as I walk outside, and I have to raise my forearm to shield the rays.

'I didn't mean to drag you out,' says Luka. It's difficult to read his lips in this harsh light so I move us to the shade.

'It's fine. I've been trying to get hold of you.'

'You want to talk over lunch?'

'At the hotel? McDonalds?'

'Well, we could,' he says. 'The hotel has some meatballs we could eat, I guess. Or what do you say I treat you to a pizza back at base, eh? I drive you there and back. Like a fancy chauffeur in a magazine.'

I think about saying I don't really have time for that, but Luka Kodro is not the kind of man to propose a lunch if he doesn't think it's important.

'I could do that.'

'Okay, we go.'

We get into his Volvo and the thing is spotlessly clean. It's not new; I'd say it's about ten years old, but it still has that new-car smell, either genuine or from some sort of bottle.

On the journey out of Toytown and along the straight, featureless road towards Visberg Hill we talk about the spring and the upcoming Valborgsmässoafton celebrations and the way wild garlic is coming into season and how he's adding it to his pizza menu. But every time I try to swing the conversation to Rose Farm he changes the subject. Eventually, I get the message that for some unknown reason he doesn't want to discuss that in the car. That chat's a sit-down pizza kind of chat.

Up the hill, past the bike, over the abandoned train tracks and we summit in the little town that time forgot. The bee spins on the roof of the Hive self-storage building and the apple blossom twinkles in the light.

'Take an hour break,' Luka says to his chef.

The restaurant is empty. It's closed at this post-lunch pre-dinner time. This is the period where things are cleaned and prepped and pizza toppings are chopped and stored in their boxes and the dough is proved and left to rest.

The chef leaves still wearing his whites, but with a black biker jacket over the top.

'What do you fancy? I cook it all. Ten minutes.'

'Just a margherita, I think.'

'A purist. I admire it. Me, myself, I can't resist the crayfish with garlic butter drizzle. I'm a rebel, maybe.'

He makes the pizzas and I take the place in. Gingham-chequered disposable paper tablecloths, huge plastic udders of ketchup and mayo and French's American mustard hanging up by the hot dog take-out hatch on the far side of the kitchen. It's a good place to have in a town.

Luka serves the pizzas and I take a bite and then I say, 'Who was your friend?'

He frowns and a dribble of garlic butter runs down his freshly-shaved chin.

'The prepping professor the other night on the motorbike.'

'What did you think?' he says. 'Did he know his stuff, or?'

'I have no idea.'

'What did the Rose Farmers think of him?'

'They were impressed.'

'Good. Very good.'

'Your cousin? A friend from your military days?'

'No,' he says. 'He was me, Tuva. I am him. Alternative realities.'
I frown at him.

'It is who I could have become, maybe, if I hadn't met my wife.
Or if I'd have met her and then we would have divorced when
troubles came knocking. He is a reminder to myself to work hard
and keep things straightforward.'

'The stomach? Eyes? The missing tooth? You screw that thing in
and out?'

He takes out a Polaroid from his pocket and slides it across the
table.

'My wife was a make-up artist in the theatre. She is a wizard at
these things. Contact lenses and a little padding under my clothes.
The tooth is just some kind of black enamel you paint on in layers
and, poof, like a magic trick, the tooth looks like a hole. It is semi-permanent. The eye sees what it wants to see. What makes sense. You
saw paint but what you think you saw was a hole.'

'With the dentists in this town, I wouldn't be surprised if you did
have a hole.'

He smiles and picks up a crayfish tail with his fingers. 'Very
good.'

Luka looks out of the window.

'You see that pollen?' he asks.

'No.'

'The green film on the windows. Not easy to keep a restaurant
like this looking respectable with all the birch pollen and the apple
blossom staining the glass. Full-time job just to keep this place
looking not derelict.'

'The tattoos?'

'Transfers. Good transfers. My wife had to shave my wrists and
my hands and that I did not like, but she said it was important to
make the special transfers look real. Rubbed cream into my skin
and then set the tattoos. I've never had a real tattoo in my life,
Tuva.'

'The motorbike?'

'That is mine. I keep it in the Hive. Work on it a little through winter, just a pastime. Basically rebuilt it from rust. Was fun to ride it all the way out there.'

'And what's your opinion of the farm? Of the people?'

'I didn't foresee Ruby killing her husband, if that's what you mean. I did not see that coming.'

'He's not dead, thank goodness. But no, none of us expected it.'

He says something I can't make out so I ask him to repeat.

'Takes a lot to pull a bow string and shoot someone you know well.'

I doubt he's ever shot an arrow at anybody, but I can see from his pained expression that he may have shot someone he knew. A neighbour. An old schoolteacher. An acquaintance.

'Ruby killed the young woman as well? Is it a fact?'

'It seems the most likely explanation, as Niklas and Elsa may have been in a relationship. But no proof as of yet.'

'I understand killing over an affair but I do not condone it. You need to dig deeper than your animal instinct, your first instinct. Sometimes to wait and breathe is to be the stronger person.'

'You taught that group a lot,' I say.

'Me?'

'They seemed impressed.'

'They are better prepared than I have ever been or will ever be. I've never seen stores like theirs. And yet the thing they should be most afraid of, the person they should be protecting themselves from, was living all the time within their fences and ditches and walls.'

'Yes, she was.'

'No. I am talking about Abraham Viklund.'

'How do you figure he is dangerous?'

'Because I have seen those faces before. The faces of a group who follow a charismatic leader and will do whatever he asks of them. Not cults, I've never seen cults. But in some ways a platoon of a militia or a gang or a ravaged army can be like a cult. The most effective teams are those led by brutal and charming animals. The kind of men who don't do the fighting but for some reason they possess the skill of charisma. Abraham is one of these.'

'What about the others?'

'Linda is the only one of the group I would want on my side. She is organised and collected. She has the skills and I can see in her demeanour that she has a cool head. A strong person.'

'Therese?'

'I don't know her type. She seems like a bureaucrat, more than anything. I don't know bureaucrats.'

'Andreas.'

'He is an interesting giant.'

'Go on.'

Luka pushes a length of pizza crust through a pool of garlic butter and eats it.

'On Four Horsemen, people have spoken of the giant man. That he has a secret assault-training course on the edge of Rose Farm. Scrambles and walls and rope climbs, that sort of thing. Some extremely challenging tests. And, for a fee, in the dead of night, he'll let local boys train there in secret. It's probably against the rules of the group but maybe he makes money on the side.'

'I was wondering how he made his money.'

'His course is very brutal. Psychological training as well as physical. I heard it was more gruelling than anything they'd seen before.'

'Okay.'

'This is not all.'

'What?'

'The talk on Four Horsemen, from reasonable men, men who I think are serious, is that Andreas is linked to that farm.'

'Well, he does live there.'

'More than that,' says Luka, biting into another crayfish tail. 'The talk is that Andreas's father went crazy. Killed the whole family there, his mother and his brothers and then himself. Left Andreas to live. And then, years later, the baby grew into a giant and returned to his home.'

41

The journey back to Gavrik with Luka Kodro is a time for me to piece things together. We don't chat much. I have to blink and look twice as bright-green haze clouds blow horizontal from birch trees, the breeze assisting them to spread and survive on.

Luka tunes his radio to some regional country station that combines old Billy Ray Cyrus songs with Swedish folk from the '70s. It's quite a thing.

'How sure are you that Andreas is the newborn from the murder-suicide?'

'The ages fit,' says Luka. 'And the person from Four Horsemen is someone I trust. Served in the Swedish military back when there was one.'

I crack my window open a little.

'Imagine going back to that place to live when you're all grown up. The psychology of it.'

'You ever do something that hurt, and then you did it again to make *sure* it hurt?'

I look at him.

'I mean, you ever relive the pain. The sensation.'

'Maybe.'

'I don't know,' he says. 'Whatever that man's mentality, I feel for him. Growing up an orphan, with that black cloud hanging over you, people talking behind your back, the way that could form a mentality.'

'You must have seen similar orphans in the Balkans,' I say.

He just looks forward and keeps on driving.

We don't talk for ten minutes. Three songs on the radio. And then he says, 'If you grow up without parents you grow up knowing you're the only one there is. You look out for yourself.'

'I guess.'

'There's not so much softness as there is with other people. Maybe there is if you get new parents, and they're kind-hearted. But for many the fit is never perfect. And for those orphans, maybe they grow up with a toughness that isn't completely healthy for a child.'

'Or an adult.'

'Adults should be tough. Most grown-ups collapse in a heap if their Wi-Fi slows down.'

'I know I do.'

He smiles.

'Yeah, me too, if I'm honest,' he says. 'Kodro is going soft in his old age. Splash that on your front page, I dare you.'

'I thought you were Grey Man, operating in the shadows.'

He wags his finger at me and grins.

A Johnny Cash tune comes on and he increases the volume.

I like Luka. He's different to everyone else I've met. Because I know something of his story, but also because there's a rock-solid moral compass deep within the man. His morality may not be that of a church or a government, but it is his, and he seems to adhere to it with no exceptions.

'Folsom Prison,' he says. 'You seen the music video?'

'I'm not sure,' I lie. I watched it just a few days ago.

'You haven't seen it? You see it tonight. When you get back to your house. Johnny looks at the prisoners and they look back at him. And, Tuva, they are brothers. They understand one another. The guards are there, of course, and they may as well be another species, they may as well be octopi or dumb vultures watching on as an artist reaches out with his voice and touches a group of untouchable men.

They communicate. I don't have the words to explain it, but there's an energy transference at that moment. The men have no hope and he gives them hope through solidarity, you know? Because he spoke the truth in that time. He performed with truth, from his heart. And they could see he was genuine. He was a man just like all of them. He gave them back the humanity that was withheld from each and every one of them on a daily basis. The monsters watch on, and Johnny Cash and his audience, they were synchronised for that time. For that night. I hope his music kept those men sane for a few more months.'

The song changes but I keep on thinking about what Luka said. About the group and the outsiders. The hope. And I relate it to Rose Farm. The insiders and the outsiders. The hopes and the fears. And also me and Noora. Her family. The insiders and the outsiders. The hope and the never-ending sensation of dread I carry around with me in my belly like a lead weight.

The twin chimneys approach and the clouds start moving on. Outside the Kommun offices, a stand is being erected for tomorrow's Valborgsmässoafton celebrations. You might see this kind of thing in any Swedish town: a bandstand and some seating and security ropes to keep the thousands of bystanders in the right place. Only here, in Toytown, it's on a miniature scale. Two pieces of rope and twenty folding chairs and a stand for a choir that looks like it might hold thirty. If you have low expectations, you have less risk of them getting dashed, I guess. This place is set up to be underwhelming.

Luka drops me off outside my office and drives on towards McDonalds.

I do two hours work and then Tam calls.

'What you doing?' she says.

'Working?'

'Get down here.'

'Already?'

'I'm bored. This fucking town.'

'Alright, I'm coming.'

'You better.'

I'm there in four minutes flat. Small town, no traffic.

She reaches through her serving hatch and gives me the kind of tight hug I need these days. She does not let go. I kiss her cheek and she unlatches.

'They caught the killer, so now you need to relax, Tuva Moody. Have some of my food, on the house, the good stuff, menu option six.'

I look at the food, and then I look at her.

'Pad Thai but I'm adding more lime now the weather's improving, don't ask me why. More peanuts. I'm being generous, basically. I'm being very fucking generous. You want some or don't you?'

'What do you think?'

She winks and fills a plastic container and then tops it with peanuts and stabs a pair of disposable chopsticks into the hot, steaming noodles and passes it to me.

'Tell me what you think. Be honest, now. Don't give me any of that Tripadvisor bullshit. Be brutal. Go.'

I eat. It's incredible. Oily, flat noodles speckled with toasted sesame seeds and flecks of red chili. The crunch of slices of fresh spring onion. Handfuls of coriander. Sweet shrimps cooked to perfection.

'Four out of ten,' I say.

'Watch your mouth.'

'It's amazing. Sublime. Best food I've had in months.'

'Closer to the truth.'

I eat on and let her serve two customers. Then she comes out and stands with me facing out to the fields and the forest beyond, our backs to ICA Maxi and the sporadic shoppers wheeling carts to their trucks.

'Valborg tomorrow,' I say.

'Who gives a shit.'

I laugh.

'Bunch of old dudes singing lame-ass songs wearing their grad-uation hats. People celebrating spring. Hello? Spring started like a month ago. Whereas the next day, May first, international workers day, for that I shut down my van and I celebrate. That's something to mark on the calendar, I'd say.'

'She killed the woman her lover loved. And then she went for her lover.'

'Shakespeare?'

'Ruby Gunnarsson from Rose Farm. She killed the girl her partner was having an affair with. Elsa. Lead weight to the skull or something like that. Up close and personal. And then she took her bow and set up an arrow and pulled the string and sent a broadhead through the man's heart.'

'He dead though?'

'Coma, I think. I need to get details for the story.'

'People kill for love and they kill for money.'

'I know.'

'Shakespeare,' she says again.

'Knew his shit.'

'Yes, he did. Bill was ahead of his time. You feel a sense of relief though, now the case is closed?'

'It's not closed yet, Tam.'

'She's in custody.'

'She's in custody but the story is just beginning. Now I need to understand her background, what made her act in this way. I need to learn more about Elsa, do her justice even though she only lived for twenty years. When young people die, the obituaries and stories are always so thin. Academic results and something about sports or how they were a good friend. But that's never enough. I need to talk to Elsa's family some more and write about her. Niklas, as well. Do them both justice.'

'You want a Coke?'

'Bottle of water, please.'

She gives me a water and then my phone rings.

'Lena, I just left the office.'

'Have you heard?' she asks.

'What?'

'Ruby Gunnarsson. She's confessed to the attempted murder of her husband, Niklas.'

'That's hardly news,' I say. 'I saw her fire the arrow.'

'But listen. She's insisting, or rather her lawyer from Stockholm is insisting, that she was not connected to the murder of Elsa Nyberg, Niklas's lover. She maintains she found out about the affair after Elsa's death. Tuva, I think we may still have a killer on the loose.'

42

I walk into my apartment and I am exhausted. If you have a family or a partner or a pet waiting to greet you, then that can take the edge off a bad day. If Noora was here, cooking pasta or watching a movie, I'd look forward to opening my front door. I'd be able to moan a little. Accept a hug. Share a bag of Doritos. But today, nothing. A dark apartment and half-empty fridge. I never knew I needed human touch so much until it was ripped away from me.

Change clothes. Make hot chocolate, the good, frothy kind with a sprinkle of cinnamon on top. Go to bed to research.

When I'm building a multi-page lead story like the murder of Elsa Nyberg and the attempted murder of Niklas Gunarsson, I have to build a structure so I can organise all my information, all my interviews, all my sources. You see similar things in movies: cops with whiteboards or genius private detectives with photos pinned to a wall; red twine connecting each one. For me it's multiple Word documents. Simple, but effective. Sebastian tried to get me to convert to Excel before he left, but I made my feelings very clear about spreadsheet journalism.

I research deeper into the murder-suicide in the '80s. It's not easy to trace Andreas through his childhood addresses, but using Facebook connections and other sites I can see that he doesn't resemble either one of his registered parents. He's a good thirty centimetres taller than them for a start. Which doesn't mean he was adopted but it might be a clue.

Ruby Gunnarsson ran a beauty place back in South Africa. She ran it with her sister. I can't find much on her past or her family, but I can see that her father was a keen hunter.

Four Horsemen is buzzing with the news of Niklas's injury. People suggesting that if he'd had better 'situational awareness' then he'd have been able to avoid the arrow. One anonymous fool saying he probably ran away in a straight line and how that's a common, amateur mistake. How common a mistake can it be in this day and age? He says Niklas should have run in a zigzag formation to evade the arrow. It's amazing to me how strong the opinions are, from people with no basic grasp of the reality of the situation. This kind of forum can help me get inside stories sometimes, but my God they tend to be populated by heretics and fantasists.

I hear Dan yelling from next door. A yell of delight, not like the yells I used to hear when his dad still lived there. I listen to him squealing and then I check the time. Past eight thirty.

It's wrong to knock on their door but I do it anyway.

'*Hej*, Tuva,' says little Dan's mum.

'I'm sorry to knock so late.'

'It's cool.'

'I wondered if I could read Dan a quick story before he goes to bed? Just a quick one?'

She looks puzzled. And then she remembers that I babysit him a couple of times a week for no money, so she smiles and says, 'Sure, come in. He's brushing his teeth.'

When I walk into his room he's sat on his big armchair and there are white marks around his lips. He jumps up and runs over in his Fireman Sam pyjamas and he flings his arms around my waist.

'Hello, young dude,' I say.

He just squeezes harder. So hard I start to lose my balance.

'Your mamma says I can read you a quick story, but only if it's an exciting one.'

'Yay!'

'Boring is banned, got it.'

'I got it.'

He pulls out some kind of space adventure book I've never seen before. He sits next to me and pulls his blanket up to his neck.

'Don't skip the pages,' he says.

'Like I would.'

And the world resets. Not completely, but in some sense. Being here in this apartment building, the scent of Dan's kid shampoo, the gentle pressure of him next to me, the glow-in-the-dark stars stuck to the ceiling. It resets. And I feel like my heart is easing a little. It was a tight fist earlier today and it's loosening.

I finish reading and he says, 'I'm going to fly to Mars when I'm all grown up. It will take a long time but Mamma says I'm good with journeys. I'll float in space and I want to do a real spacewalk with a helmet. It's black out there. Space is a vacuum.'

'I bet you'll go one day.'

'Oh,' he says. 'I know I will. You, too, maybe? If you're not too old?'

I smile.

He climbs into his bed and I kiss the palm of my hand and place it on his forehead.

'Why you kiss your hand then on my face?' he says.

'Because my pappa did that for me every night.'

'My pappa is in Norway now.'

'I know, sweetie. I have to go now. Sweet dreams. Shall I ask your mamma to come in?'

He nods and then he whispers, 'Goodnight, Tuva.'

'Night, kiddo.'

I close the door a little and walk into his mum's kitchen, which is identical in every regard to my kitchen.

'You alright?' she says. 'You look knackered. You look like you need a drink.'

'Busy at work, that's all.'

'I always read your articles. Never used to read them before, if I'm honest with you; I'm more of a phone person, news from Facebook, but now I know they're from you I always read them.'

I smile at her and pat her shoulder. 'Night.'

'Night.'

'Mamma!' shouts Dan. 'Story!'

I leave and go back inside my apartment and sit on the sofa. The respite has faded now that I'm alone again. It was short-lived. People say springtime is the most hopeful period of the whole year. You can't be depressed in the spring, it's impossible, look at the light, at the blossom, at the green shoots. But spring *is* difficult for some. I'm fortunate; I don't really get seriously depressed, not like Mum did. But I've written pieces on the phenomenon. I know some people here use their SAD lamps just as much in April as they do in January. Because their mood doesn't match the weather. There's a lag. And the disconnect makes their feelings all the more complex to understand. They know they should be happy and light and yet inside their heads it's still bleak midwinter.

Email from Thord. I call him straight back.

'I'm home,' he says. 'Long day. Nothing urgent so I emailed you. It can wait for the morning.'

'Tell me.'

I hear the unmistakeable noise of a cork being extracted from a wine bottle.

'Prosecutor has charged Ruby Gunnarsson with attempted murder. Nothing decided yet on Elsa Nyberg.'

'What else?'

'Well, just so happens we found three books on the occult and black magic in the living-space loft above Ruby's spa on Rose Farm.'

'Shit.'

'You got that right.'

'With the inverted cross on her neck. Is that enough to make the Elsa case stick?'

'Not my job,' says Thord, taking a sip of the wine. 'Prosecutor has to untangle that sorry mess.'

'What does Ruby say?'

'Fancy lawyer. Drove up in a Bentley, you believe that? An actual Bentley. First one in Gavrik I should imagine. He should try driving that thing round here in February, I can tell you.'

'She's not talking?' I say.

'She talked some. But she's guarded, you know. Says the books were just a gift.'

'Who gives devil-worship books as a gift?'

'Linda Larsson does, apparently,' he says.

'Linda Larsson who owns a sweet organic café?'

'The one and same. Ruby says she's the de-facto chief of the entire farm, she called her the "alpha wolf" if you can believe it, reckons Abraham and Therese Viklund are just two stooges she installed in the main house to draw attention away from herself. Keep a low profile.'

I think about the Grey Man concept of avoiding and diverting attention.

'You think that's true?'

'True or not, it ain't really any of my business who's in charge of that farm.'

'Is Ruby saying Linda asked her to kill Niklas?'

'No, no. Niklas was a revenge attack, Ruby admits to that. She says she found out about the affair with Elsa because their timelines were investigated after Elsa's body was discovered. She checked his phone. Niklas had to come clean, apologised, something about a midlife crisis. But Ruby says she couldn't forgive him.'

'Could Niklas have killed Elsa?'

'It's a working theory we got. One of about a dozen. Tuva, I got a call on the other line, let me ring you back in the morning.'

'Ring me back tonight.'

He ends the call.

I work a little on my files, trying to get the story together for the next issue, and then I do what I sometimes do this time of night. I scroll through old photos of Noora on my iPad. Her on this very bed, eating breakfast cake on her birthday with wrapped gifts and freshly-squeezed orange juice. Her down by the reservoir, trying and failing to fly the kite I bought her, because we built the thing wrong. Her and me having coffee outside a café in Karlstad last year. In some ways, the images are more real to me than she is. My brain still can't match up all these Nooras. Can't make sense of the change.

My phone rings.

'It's me,' says Thord.

'Yeah.'

'We got two murder cases. Niklas Gunnarsson just died in hospital from his injuries.'

43

I wake up from a flat, dreamless sleep, and I'm confronted by the pointlessness of my own life. The only thing that is constant, apart from my friends, is my work routine. Work on a story, deliver the story, publish the story.

Breakfast is milky coffee and a slice of frozen supermarket chocolate cake with squirty can cream. It's pretty good.

Outside in the town, people are in festive mood. The bonfire in the parkland behind my building, on the lovers walk that Noora and I used to watch from my balcony, is almost ready to set alight. The daffodils are still in bloom here and blue swathes of scilla act as counterpoint. Later tonight they'll ignite the thing and welcome the arrival of springtime.

I drive in a state of numbness, almost on autopilot, and I think about what it might feel like to walk into the abyss with Noora one of these days. To face oblivion with her, just the two of us. I'd need to make sure her parents wouldn't find us too quickly, and I'd need to square the concept with my own conscience. But honestly, for both of us, it might just be a blessed relief.

Out east towards Visberg, right turn, past the snowberg, which is shrinking with every sunny day, and on towards the farm.

Barbed wire.

Ditches

Fencing.

I drive into the entrance of Rose Farm, and everything looks tranquil at first glance. The fields of green shoots. The sounds of songbirds in the alder trees, back where Elsa Nyberg was found with her temple caved in. The pink Rose Farm manor house up on the hill backdropped by the river vista. A beautiful place for a group of people to plot how they'd navigate the end of the world. A scenic location for survivalists to turn on each other.

The gates are open to the private part of the compound, the inner sanctum of the main house and Andreas's yellow cottage. I park and walk towards the dog kennels.

Barking and growling and cameras pivoting on their brackets to track my movements.

There's violin music in the background. Abraham playing some piece he's written, shielded from the world by his layers and layers of vegetation.

'We're through talking,' says Andreas, shaking his head. 'We're all through. Therese didn't tell you already?'

'Haven't seen her.'

'We're on a war footing now.'

'A war footing.'

'A state of readiness. We've lost two of our own. *Two.*'

He measures kibble from an aluminium dustbin and feeds his dogs in stainless-steel bowls. They eat and he watches them eat.

'A pack,' he says, and then he looks at me. 'There's real strength in a pack. A *unit.* You think you can survive as a lone wolf, but in reality you cannot.'

'Is that aimed at me?'

'I ain't aiming.'

'Source came forward to the newspaper about you.'

'Did they now.'

'About your true family.'

'My *true* family?'

'How you were born here.'

'Well, I was born here.'

'So you're not denying it.'

'What in the name of the Almighty are you rabbiting on about?'

'You were born here at Rose Farm. Your father killed your family but let you go.'

He looks at me and then he wipes his nose on his sleeve.

'Someone came forward and told you this, did they? And who was that?'

'Doesn't matter who.'

'Doesn't matter to you maybe.'

'A local. Is it true, Andreas?'

'I ain't got time for this. I need to go check on the gates.'

I walk after him and he's faster than me, due to his extraordinarily long legs.

'Wait.'

'You're lucky I don't turn you out on the road and keep your truck as compensation.'

'Compensation for what?'

'For wasting my time.'

'He inspects the fencing and the gates and then he scopes the land around the farm with a pair of binoculars. His plank of wood is not on his chest today.

'No two by four.'

'Therese know you're here?'

'I don't know.'

'I got my full pack on today. Seventeen-kilo ruck and a level-three plate carrier. You have to train every week or you won't have the muscle memory. You think you'll be able to bug out but you'll get stuck in the doorway or you won't make it out further than the next village. You got to train to know.'

'Ruby sure had trained with her bow and arrow.'

'I wasn't close to Niklas,' says Andreas. 'But he didn't deserve to die that way. Ruby went way too far.'

'I think the judge will agree with you. She maintains she didn't have anything to do with Elsa's death, though. What do you think about that?'

Andreas unlocks a wooden shack and checks how much electricity is coming in off the solar panels into the batteries.

'I think we may never find out what happened to her,' he says. 'Could have been Niklas covering his tracks. Or could have been Ruby in a fit of rage. She has a whirlwind temper, that one.'

We walk over towards a series of ditches and pipes and bridges and ropes well inside the compound, away from the houses and the road.

'What is this place? A shooting range?'

'Partly. This is my training course.'

'For you guys?'

'Like I said, if you don't train and repeat, you won't know what you're doing. Tell you the truth most preppers are hoarders. Amateurs. They buy all the Paracord they can off eBay and they hoard cheap knives and they fantasise about conspiracy theories and living alone up a tree someplace. Clueless fools. Most of them never practise, get their hands dirty. You gotta do the tough things to know if you're capable of doing the tough things.'

'Like killing someone in a combat situation.'

'If it ever came to that you have to be able to protect yourself.'

'But do you need to kill first to see if you're capable of it? Because that's kind of what you said.'

He bites his bottom lip.

'Don't screw with my words, Tuva.'

'Did Elsa ever train here?'

'On my course? No, she did not.'

'But you've done it.'

'Yeah, we all do it regularly.'

'Even Abraham?'

'No comment.'

'Oh, come on.'

He shakes his head.

I wait.

'Okay, if you must know, Abraham holds the record for the casket. He's not a public guy but he's more capable than the motorbike Yugoslav you brought here last week.'

'He is?'

'Yeah, he is.'

'What's the casket?'

He points to a shallow, rectangular hole in the earth and then an identical rectangular hole five or ten metres away.

'That, Tuva, is the casket.'

'Okay. But what is it?'

'What is it? Closest thing to hell imaginable is what it is.'

'Are you adopted, Andreas? You can tell me off the record if you like. Did your father live here? Were you the newborn baby that was spared?'

He looks back to the casket on the assault course.

'You really wanna know?'

'Yes, off the record if necessary. I'm desperate to make progress on this story. To get justice for Elsa and her family.'

'You complete the casket, you'll get your answer.'

I look down at the course.

'But what is it?'

'I already told you,' he says. 'It's hell on earth.'

44

'How about I write a good story in the paper on dog training, and feature you, full-colour photograph, Q&A. Would that work?'

'That doesn't interest me in the slightest,' he says. 'Seeing you, a city person, make it through the course I designed. Now that interests me.'

'The whole course?'

'No, you wouldn't be able to do it. Just the casket.'

'I won't die or anything?'

'You'll feel like you might die. But nobody's died doing the casket. So far.'

'You've done it?'

'I've done a similar one.'

'But not this one?'

'Tuva, look at me. I'm over two metres tall. I'd get stuck down there and I'd perish. If you get lodged underground just here you are dead.'

'Okay, then, I'll pass.'

'Wise move.'

'Were you born here?'

'No deal.'

I take a closer look at the casket. It comes after some scramble nets and a corrugated pipe, semi-buried, that gets tighter the further you crawl along it.

'I could do the pipe?'

'That's not the deal.'

The casket looks like a casket. It's coffin-shaped. A rectangular hole about thirty centimetres deep, one-metre-ninety long, a metre wide. It's basically a neat hole the size and shape and depth of five doors stacked on top of each other. At one end is a dark slot. I guess that's where you crawl underground.

'What's through there?' I ask.

'You'll see if you do it.'

'How do I move?'

'You wriggle. The maximum depth is about forty centimetres but it varies along the length. The bottom isn't even. You lie down on your back with your nose closest to the ceiling of the shallow cave. Then you start to wriggle head first, your eyes up.'

'Head up? Why not just crawl.'

'You won't make it through,' he says. 'Not enough space to move your shoulders that way. And sometimes, not today I don't think, it can fill up with water.'

'Water?'

'So you keep your mouth and nose up to breathe.'

'No water today, though, right?'

'A fine sky.'

'Don't leave me down there.'

'Would I do that?'

Tentatively, I lie down in the rectangular hole and angle my neck back to look into the mailbox slit of a hole, and then I stand right back up again.

'No way.'

'I knew you wouldn't. No woman has completed this. I don't really blame you.'

No *woman?* I look over the structure again. Must be at least five metres long, five metres of wriggling on your back, your nose scraping the ceiling.

'What the hell is this?'

'This?'

'The assault course.'

'People think preparing is about storing food up to the roof. Canning eggs and all that.'

'Isn't it?'

'That's the easy part. We let T-Bone manage all the can rotations. The real preparedness is up here.' He taps his forehead. 'Mental toughness. You make it through the casket and you're ready to face some very bad experiences.'

'You think?'

'It hardens you. It prepares you so you can face what's to come.'

I think about what's to come in my life.

'Okay, I'll do it.'

'No, you won't. You keep saying you'll do it but you won't go through with it, I've seen it a dozen times before. Macho guys. They start, but then they wriggle out the way they came, screaming for their mammas.'

'What if I get stuck?'

'What if you get stuck?'

'You'll pull me out?'

'How would I do that? Listen, Tuva. This isn't Disney World. You go down there on your own and you come back up on your own. The casket is made from five metres of reinforced concrete. If you got stuck in the middle we'd not be able to dig you out in time even if we had pneumatic drills and earth movers.'

'Do you have those things?'

'No.'

'How long does it take to get through?'

'How long's a hellhole?'

'What?'

'Ten minutes to an hour. I don't recommend taking an hour, it'll feel like a day.'

'And you'll tell me about your family. The truth. You'll talk to me?'

'Listen, if you manage to do this, I'll tell you anything you want to know.'

'Hold my phone.'

'You sure you don't want it down there with you? Call your Bosnian friend if you get stuck? Use the torch function? Take a selfie?'

'Most people take their phone down there with them?'

'I'm just kidding,' he says. 'There's no space to move your arms like that. They'll be down by your sides. You need to use your shoulders, your back, your hips, your heels. Slither like a python that got flipped over on its back.'

I take a deep breath.

'Take a few more of those.'

I pass him my phone and lie down in the shallow rectangular pit and look up at him. His enormous bulk. Like a mountain staring back down at me, clouds passing behind his head.

'I'm going in.'

'So you said.'

I close my eyes for a minute. Lena will kill me if I manage to survive. But I must do this. I have to do it for myself.

'I'm going in,' I say again.

'Yeah, sure.'

I dig my heels into the dirt and push myself headfirst into the slot. My nose scrapes the cool, wet-concrete lid and within thirty seconds the upper half of my body is underground. My knees and feet are still in the light but the rest of me is entombed. This is what it must feel like to be encased within a stone sarcophagus.

My knees can bend a little. I push myself deeper and deeper into the casket but I'm only ever about half a metre underground. Horizontal. A lid on top of my face.

No air down here.

No noise, either.

Just the rhythm of my heartbeat in my head, in my ears.

Darkness swallows me whole.

I can wiggle my legs but the tips of my boots drag across the roof if I'm not careful and that sensation, being sandwiched, makes me start to breathe too quickly.

I swallow.

Fuck all of this. I can get to the end. Only a few metres to go.

I shunt myself along and my nose scrapes the roof again and it breaks my skin. Am I bleeding? I want to look. I want to sit up. To stand up. But I can't move. The casket is narrowing around me. My shoulders touch both sides and I start to pant. To breathe in the mouldy, damp air and the carbon dioxide that comes out of my mouth and hits the concrete-slab roof and then falls back down again.

Can I suffocate? There is no breeze, no obvious airflow.

I get brief urges to sit upright, to force the rock above me to move. To burst up through the earth. But I slow my breathing and continue. A panic attack now would finish me off. Two metres through, and I'd die from a heart attack, from pure terror.

A noise from outside. Maybe Andreas is shouting to me, but I can't hear him. The acoustics are impossible down here. My hearing aids don't help me at all.

I'm hot. The concrete all around is cold but I am sweating and I'm growing tired. The caterpillar movements are difficult. I'm moving, but it is slow work and I feel like there's a paving slab resting on my chest and one underneath me and a wall pushing each shoulder. I'm locked in a box that nobody has the key for.

I scoot along and the roof comes down lower so I have to turn my head to the side.

My breathing quickens.

Fuck this.

My hearing aid grazes along the stone floor of this hellhole, and then it comes loose.

I scream.

I shouldn't, it makes things worse, my chest starts to convulse, my breathing too fast, my ribs hitting the ceiling and then retreating. Hitting and retreating.

Sweat in my eyes.

One hearing aid gone. The urge to stand is unbearable. I want to get up and walk. I want to spread my arms

Blackness.

The smell of moss and wet earth.

And then the worst thing in the world.

My head hits a wall. The flat tunnel closes in and I realise there is no other end. This is a one-way journey.

45

Complete darkness.

The tang of iron in my mouth.

I purse my lips and try to breathe more slowly. In, out. Calm down, Tuva.

What is this thing? A trap? I feel like I'm stuck in one end of a crayfish pot and the current won't allow me to go out the other way.

I am tired.

Stale, damp air.

My body is cold and my muscles are aching – muscles I've never used before, muscles nobody has ever needed before.

I try to reposition so I can head back out the flat tunnel, boots first, but it's not as easy as that. My shoulders are scraping the sides and my nose is scraping the roof. This is worse than a coffin. This is lying in a coffin that's already half full with soil and then getting buried six feet under.

No.

I can't move the other way.

Part of me starts to give up, I feel it. The acceptance of my fate. Fresh air is only half a metre or so above me, but I am sandwiched underground on this survivalist commune of a farm, a giant dog-trainer watching on calmly, wondering if I'll make it back out of the hole I went in through.

I push my head and feel something.

An opening.

If I skew my shivering body and use the caterpillar action to scoot, I can push on. The wall is only half as wide as the flat hellhole. It's a kink. A bend along the route. But where does it lead? I keep going. I have no choice.

My shoulders ripple and my hips push and my back is starting to hurt. The ground is uneven: sharp stones and the nubs of branches or roots.

But I am moving.

I am shuffling, perhaps ten centimetres per minute. I am making progress.

Or is this a wrong turn? A test? A diversion to an underground dead end? A cave system?

I pause.

My heart is deafening inside my chest. I still have one hearing aid in.

Blackness.

Is this what it's like for you, Noora? Trapped and unable to move? Unable to assert yourself? Or is this not as bad as what you are living through? I've been doing this for maybe ten minutes, and you've been trapped for more than half a year already. The scans show no signs of brain activity. The doctors say you won't know what's going on. And I hope to God they are right.

Something scuttles past my neck.

My body stiffens and jerks away from the insect and my face hits the roof of the shallow cave and I scream.

The noise echoes all around my head. Imagine panicking from inside a concrete tomb. No way out. No opportunity to sit up or take a break from it all.

Steady, Tuva. Slow is smooth, smooth is fast. Steady as she goes. All things my father once said to me. I breathe but the air is rank with rot.

Breathe in. Hold it. Breathe out.

My heart slows a little.

I push on.

I'm getting through now. I visualise what this must look like to some omniscient god. A creature on her back wriggling through a slot in the earth, face up, halfway between one entrance hole and one exit hole. A man watching the scene. A river flowing nearby, as it's done for a thousand years before.

Somehow I sync my breathing to my shuffling and I make some progress. But it's different. I've moved through the kink in the route, through the bend, but it feels as though the flat, shallow tunnel is sinking deeper. On a steady, albeit gradual, decline. Deeper and deeper into the earth.

The blood starts to pool in my head.

Pulse rattling in my temple, just like it once did for Elsa Nyberg.

Keep going.

I cannot move my head to look at what is ahead of me. Sweat runs off my neck and I shiver. I could be moving towards an abyss, a grey wolf in its den, a sharp metal spike. I am propelling myself towards an uncertain destiny and I am doing it slowly.

More noises.

A thread of cobweb drags across my nose.

I keep wriggling and I keep moving. Not deeper anymore. On the level. My hands are filthy and my fingers are numb from the cold down here.

Something runs past my ear.

But it's not a centipede or a mouse. It's liquid.

Water.

A constant dribble.

Some of it enters my ear and I scream again. I swear. I sob in this hellhole and the water comes faster now, flowing down my neck and into my clothes, soaking my back.

I wriggle and twist, but now I am moving through mud and the mud is gathering in front of my head like a snowplough might collect fresh snow.

I am stuck.

46

A cramp in my leg.

I want nothing more than to sit up. To burst out of this shallow trap. I want to stretch, to stand, to move my arms, to walk away.

I scoot along, water chilling my neck.

But then the ceiling I am scraping against starts to light up.

I spit saliva from my mouth and the light comes stronger. I move. Faster and faster, my hips and shoulders working like some absurd, prehistoric amphibian, slithering on its back towards hope, towards answers.

More light.

My head emerges from the lip of the hole on the other side and I break out crying and smiling, and I work my arms free and pull myself, exhausted, out into the shallow hole. On to the grass. Sobbing. Gasping for air.

'You're a lunatic,' says Andreas, smiling.

I can't speak. I look back through my tears at the giant man and at the shallow grave I just crawled through. Six metres. Maybe seven. One of the worst experiences of my entire life.

'I fucking did it,' I say.

'You sure did.'

I get to my knees and then I stand, unsteadily, and brush the mud and the dust from my clothes.

'I earned answers,' I say.

'You earned yourself more than that,' he says. 'You want a water? A beer? I can get you a beer.'

'Who killed Elsa Nyberg?' I say, my words falling out of my mouth.

'I never said I knew that.'

I hate doing this with one aid missing, grit and mud down my neck. I have to focus on his lips.

'Who killed her, damn it?'

'Let me get you something to clean up, first. A drink.'

'Andreas, were you born here? Were you the newborn? You have to answer me.'

He shakes his head.

'You gave me your word. After what I've just been through.'

'Oh, I'll tell you,' he says. 'It's only fair. I only seen three people outside our pack complete this thing and you're the only one with no military background.'

'Were you the surviving newborn, Andreas?'

'No.'

'No?'

'We don't know for sure,' he says, walking closer to me, glancing around, lowering his voice. 'Because he doesn't share much. But Linda believes it was Abraham that was born on this land. And that Abraham is the last of his family to survive here.'

I see T-Bone walking up from his big red barn carrying a tray. He's dressed in white shorts and a white shirt. Arranged on his tray are bottles, and a vase full of red flowers.

'Here he comes,' says Andreas. 'T-Bone wants to celebrate you.'

'Celebrate what?'

'You passing the hellhole.'

'I don't want to celebrate it.'

T-Bone walks up the hill, careful not to drop the tray and then he yells, 'I hear somebody completed the course. Well, that calls for a festive Valborgsmässoafton drink, I'd say.' He walks closer and I can see his teeth, his grin is so broad. 'You really did it, didn't you?'

'How did you even know?'

T-Bone places the tray down on the grass and then he straightens his back and points over at a CCTV camera bolted to a birch tree.

'Been watching you the whole time. More exciting than the football world cup, that was. I didn't fully expect you to go down there, truth be told. I wouldn't countenance the idea, not at my age. Of course, as a younger man...'

'Linda's coming over to see you,' Andreas tells me.

She walks from her café and she's wearing white, too: white jeans and a white sweater. Flowers in her hair. Something swinging from her neck.

'She was more excited than I was,' says T-Bone. 'We was talking about you on the CB the whole time.'

'You're a brave one,' says Linda, walking closer, climbing the hill to the assault course. She has her high-school graduation hat in her hand. 'I didn't expect it of you. I guess I underestimated you, Tuva. You're more like one of us than I'd figured on.'

'One of you?'

'You want a refreshment?' asks T-Bone. The flowers in the vase are roses, long-stemmed, with their flowers still tight buds. 'We got the cardamom beer. I brew it myself, up in the gallery over the barn. It packs a pretty punch.'

'Try some,' says Linda. The item swinging from her neck is a rifle scope.

'You were watching me through that?' I ask.

'And on the TV,' she says. 'Once somebody goes down that hole we never know what to expect. One gentleman, he went down in the night-time, so we had to use the infra-red cameras, the ones that show body heat, them and night vision, well, he threw up as soon as he came out the other end, didn't he, Andre?'

Andreas nods.

'You fared better,' says Linda, nudging me with her wrist. 'You got through it in good time.'

'Here,' says T-Bone pushing a bottle of cardamom beer into my shoulder. 'Take one. You've earned it.'

'I need to drive back,' I say. 'I shouldn't.'

'You just passed the test, Tuva,' says Linda. 'Don't need to worry about no home-brew beer. Enjoy it.'

'Can I have my bag now, Andreas.'

He frowns and hands me my bag.

'After the drink we'll go down to the river,' says T-Bone. 'Abraham's putting on a special show for us.'

'He is?' I say.

'Every Valborgsmässoafton he does it. It's important to celebrate the old traditions, keep them alive. A beautiful rendition it'll be. Totally private.'

'I'm invited?'

T-Bone looks at me like I'm being silly. 'Well, you passed the hellhole, Tuva. The casket. That means you can stay now.'

There are three missed calls on my phone. One from Lena and two from Thord.

'I need to make a quick call,' I say.

'Can't right now,' says T-Bone. 'They're working on the mast. Back up in...' he checks his watch. 'About forty minutes. That's life out in the sticks I'm afraid.'

'Have you got a landline I can borrow? I'll pay.'

Andreas chuckles and says something.

'I didn't catch that. Lost one of my hearing aids down there. What did you say?'

'I said, landline, so the New World Order can listen in on us, you mean? No, we do not have a landline. You know what off-grid means, right?'

My truck is a three-minute sprint away from this hillock. But to make a dash for it would be an error of judgement. I'll play it cool. And I'll pick my moment. I need to see Abraham for myself.

'Maybe I will have one of those beers,' I say.

Andreas hands me one off T-Bone's tray.

It's fragrant. I take a small sip. Spicy. Hoppy.

'Really good,' I say.

'It's the Snake River water,' says T-Bone. 'I don't filter it. I reckon the microbes and the algae add a certain *je ne sais quoi*, so I leave them all in.'

I swallow awkwardly.

'Let's walk down,' says Linda.

The four of us amble away from the road, past Andreas's dogs and his yellow house, and on towards the riverbank. We're halfway between the main house and the alders, where Elsa Nyberg was found.

On the river is a boat. More like a pontoon. It's anchored either to a stump or to an underwater rock. The boat is covered with a pyramid of dry reeds and pine branches.

'God bless us all,' says Linda. 'May the Father shield us from the world outside and deliver us from all the evil within.'

'Amen,' says T-Bone. 'This here is a blessed refuge from Babylon. Flanked by a good river and three sides of ditches. We lost two of our own but now we're making up the numbers. We're as good as impenetrable here, Tuva. You're safe with us now, we're a pack, a family, there's no need for worry.'

I take a glance at my phone and they're telling the truth. No reception at all.

The boat goes up in flames. A searing firestorm rising into the early dusk: oranges and yellows splitting the pale blue sky. The night isn't yet here, but this flaming pontoon has changed the feeling in the air. Sulphur and expectation.

Andreas starts mumbling something under his breath, his tone deep and gravelly. Linda and T-Bone join him. Sounds like old Swedish. Some kind of Viking dialect mixed with Old Testament preaching.

And then the violin starts up.

Linda leaves us, so now it's just me and T-Bone and Andreas looking through the midges at the burning boat. The air is full of crackling pine needles burning at three hundred degrees, and the haunting melodies of a maplewood violin. Horsehair sliding against cat gut string.

'Therese coming to join us?' I ask.

'She and Abraham will join us presently. They'll enter the waters, as is our Rose Farm tradition.'

I know I should stay for that, to witness it, but I need to check my messages. Thord doesn't call me twice for no good reason.

'I'll be back in five minutes,' I say. 'I left something in my truck.'

They both look at me like I just suggested we sacrifice Linda on the pontoon.

I walk briskly up the hill, the cardamom and the bitterness of the homebrew still coating my tongue.

Their chanting intensifies.

My phone's still not working.

When I'm out of sight I start to jog towards the road.

But before I'm halfway, I hear a 'pssst' from behind an old oak tree, the one shaped like a clawed hand.

I look around it and Therese is there in the shadow of the oak and she looks worried.

'I'm going to my truck now,' I say.

She gestures for me to come closer.

'Look,' she says, pointing to my Hilux, to the entrance gates. 'Linda's locking you inside here.'

How did she get back there so quickly? Quad bike?

Linda Larsson is closing the gates to stop vehicles crossing between the private and the public areas of Rose Farm.

'I need to go, she can't stop me.'

'Check your phone,' says Therese.

I hold it up. 'No reception. The tower's out.'

'The tower is not out,' says Therese. 'Look.'
She shows me her phone. It's working fine.
'They jammed your phone, Tuva.'
'What?'
'I need to get you out of here right now.'

47

The sound of dogs barking.

'We have to go,' Therese says. 'They're locking us down.'

'Us?'

'Abraham and I have separated, Tuva. He's not... he's not what he seems.'

'What? How do we leave?'

She looks around the farm as if with fresh eyes. As a prisoner rather than a prepper. She nods to herself and says, 'Two options. Neither is perfect but they'll buy us time to get to the police. One, we head to the bunker under the main house.' She seems to doubt herself.

'What is it?'

'They may know ways to shut off the air, but apart from that we'd be safe. It's a fairly large space. We can probably wait it out.'

'Wait what out?'

'Whatever comes. Whatever he proclaims.'

'Abraham?'

'Or we make our way to Rosebud Cottage.' She points downriver to the dilapidated, clapboard shack that seemingly floats on the water. Some kind of hut on a rock built in the marshes and reed beds, elevated above the flood level.

'Is there a road?'

'Just the river.'

'Well, I can't swim that far, Therese. Can you?'

'There's a kayak,' she whispers. 'Flat-bottomed boat. It's not great, wouldn't survive the rough water further downriver, but it'll get us as far as the hut.' Clouds of smoke drift over from the burning Valborgsmässoafton pontoon. 'We have to make a choice. Commit. The journey to the cottage is riskier. It'll take longer. We might be seen. But we can call the police from there. The signal jam won't reach that far. Or we try the bunker. We can be locked inside within five minutes. What do you want to do?'

'What do *I* want to do?'

'What's best?'

I look her in the eyes and I see fear. Her doubting herself. I've never seen that before. 'The cottage? Rosebud Cottage?'

She takes a deep breath. 'Follow me.'

Therese leads me by the hand, crouching low, moving towards the alder trees, where Elsa was found. She tells me to be quieter. She guides me over a tripwire I never noticed before and along towards the locked gate. We have to skirt close to a pine-clad hut to avoid a CCTV camera, backs to the wall, until the panning lens moves on.

'When we reach the gate,' she says. 'We'll be seen. We must move quickly. Into the boat and off up the river as quick as we can row.'

'We can't run round to the public entrance? To my truck?'

'That's exactly what Linda wants you to do,' says Therese. 'She's a tactician, and we have well-rehearsed strategies. We'll get there and they'll take you. Take us both… to him. We must get to Rosebud Cottage. It looks abandoned but we have provisions there. We can phone for help. Can you make it?'

The cottage looks like it's a kilometre downriver, maybe two. I'm exhausted from the casket, but I nod and tell her we should go.

'Keep your head down and do exactly as I say.'

We run to the gate and she enters a code and it opens and the camera swivels on its mount and we sprint towards the alder trees. It takes Therese a minute or so to locate the old kayak, hidden in brambles and cut branches.

'Help me drag it out,' she says.

It looks like a death trap. Old, sheet metal and rust. A plastic cup to empty the inevitable water that seeps in to sink us.

We push it into the water and we step in.

The kayak is chronically unstable. Poorly designed.

We begin to paddle and then we hear screaming and yelling and dogs barking behind us on Rose Farm.

'Don't look back,' says Therese. 'They'll do whatever he commands of them. Keep paddling. Paddle harder.'

Desperation in her eyes.

The river bends slightly, and the setting sun melts into the calm waters. On either side of the river is thick undergrowth. Overgrown and wild.

Something makes the sound of a wolf howl behind us and that howl reverberates all around the river valley.

'Don't slow down. Keep on pushing.'

We paddle and then the cottage grows closer. Pink-painted boards to match the main house and the wings. Corrugated-iron roof, full of moss and weeds and grasses. The hut is built on large, granite stones, themselves resting on a large, granitic rock deposited from a glacier long ago.

Therese jumps into the water and it's only knee deep just here so I follow her in. Ice-cold. Deeper water all around us. We drag the boat up and she ties it loosely to the shore and then we climb up on to a rotting jetty, itself floating on polystyrene boards, and she unlocks the door of the cottage and we step inside.

'Your phone working now?' she says, fumbling with her pockets. I check it.

'Yes.'

'Thank God. Call the cops.'

I call the station but nobody picks up so I call 112 and tell them to come immediately to Rosebud Cottage on Snake River.

'Are they coming?' asks Therese, keeping watch out of the pollen-crusted window. 'What did they say?'

'They're coming.'

'Take this,' she says, handing me a long kitchen knife.

'Why?'

'The guns are back on the farm. Linda's in charge of all the fire-arms. But we store some basic gear here. I'll see what we have.'

'A new message from the police,' I say. 'A voicemail.'

She watches me call the number.

It's Thord.

'He says they analysed the ink found on the neck of Elsa Nyberg,' I tell Therese.

The semi-permanent tattoo.

'He says the forensic specialists have identified it as white black-board ink.'

48

Therese looks at me.

'But what does that mean? Blackboard ink?'

'Linda uses blackboard ink,' I say. 'For the organic-café menus.'

'That doesn't mean she...'

'And I've been told she was jealous of Elsa. Jealous of the hold she had over T-Bone. That Linda hated the fact that he would paint Elsa but never painted her.'

'Pull the blinds,' says Therese.

I look at her and then I pull the blinds.

She starts hand-pumping water into a large clear tank in the corner of the room.

'River water?' I ask.

'We have enough filters, enough purification tablets. LifeStraws for both of us.'

'You don't think Linda painted the cross on Elsa Nyberg's neck?'

She keeps pumping and says, 'I'm not saying that. She may have done. But it would have been on Abraham's orders, be clear on that. Linda was his second in command. She was never in charge.'

'I thought you were his second in command?'

She shakes her head. 'Linda was.'

'*Was?*'

'It's all gone to shit, Tuva.'

She finishes pumping.

'What happened?'

'Don't worry,' she says. 'We have enough food here for three or four weeks.'

I look to the far corner of the shack and there's a mountain of large tin cans and freeze-dried meals.

'*Three weeks or four weeks?*'

'We're prepared.'

'For what? The police will be here within the hour.'

'It's not the police I'm concerned about,' she says. 'It's whether Abraham will let the police come to our aid.'

'*Let them?*'

She smiles but her smile collapses. 'Abraham's wolf pack is better armed than Gavrik police, Tuva. By a factor of ten to one.'

'Wolf pack?'

'That's what we call ourselves. What *they* call themselves.'

'I don't…'

'You've seen some of their armaments, the legal ones. But there are more. Booby traps and diversions. Man traps. They're a family group and Abraham is their alpha. I'm not sure if Chief Björn knows the full extent to which he is outgunned, but he's better connected than you think he is. I reckon he knows to keep his distance. He'll be negotiating with Abraham, not with us. And truth be told, I don't know what that will look like.'

'I'm going to call the police again.'

'Tell them to send back-up from Falun if they can. We'll need all the help we can get. Tell them to send a helicopter. Or a police boat.'

I call Thord.

'Are you safe, Tuva? Are you being threatened?'

'No,' I say. 'Not threatened. I'm okay, in Rosebud Cottage, but you need to get here quickly. The Rose Farm group may come for us. Or for you.'

'Stay hidden if you can, we're on our way.'

'They're on their way,' I say to Therese.

'You didn't ask for a helicopter.'

'Thord knows what to do.'

'I bloody hope he does.'

Therese is constantly busy, constantly doing something. She checks on the alcohol stoves, and then she lifts a plate-carrier off the wall and says, 'Here, you might need this.'

'Body armour?'

'Better safe than sorry.'

'Have you got one?'

'There's only one here, Tuva. Level-three body armour is expensive.'

'What about you?'

'I've got something almost as good.'

She hangs the plate-carrier over my shoulders and it weighs me down. Must be a third of my bodyweight.

'Jesus, this thing's heavy.'

'Do not take the Lord's name in vain, Tuva. Not even in extremis.'

'What do you have?'

'This.'

She pulls down an almost identical plate-carrier vest.

'Looks the same.'

'Homemade,' she says. 'Airsoft vest with plates made from Kevlar fire blankets wrapped around ceramic bathroom tiles. Duct tape. Won't stop a direct hit but it'll slow one down. Now, I have to release our pontoon.'

'But, how will the police get to us?'

'Swim or wade.'

Therese takes a rifle from a locked cabinet and chambers a round. Then she wears the long gun around her neck on a sling, just like Andreas has been doing in training with his plank of wood. She says, 'I'll be a minute, and then she opens the steel door.'

I lift an edge of blackout blind to see what's coming.

There's nothing coming.

No wolf-pack military speedboats. Nothing. But Therese untethers the floating pontoon from the shack and she pushes it into the open water and she lets the current move it downriver. If I felt isolated before in this hut, I feel more isolated now.

She comes back in and locks the door and takes off her rifle.

'Nobody's coming yet.'

'That's good, right?'

She shakes her head and I have to focus hard on her mouth to understand her. 'They'll be taking their instructions from Abraham in his practice room. He and Linda will be firming up a strategy, arming, defining the rules of engagement.'

'The rules of engagement? This isn't a warzone, Therese.'

She looks at me. 'It is to them.'

I sit down on a stool. The shack is clapboard on the outside but it is corrugated iron inside. The floor is rough pine boards, the kind you'll see in a harbour. Therese passes me a bucket of river water and a blue straw. I frown.

'The straw is a filter. You can drink the river water by sucking it through the straw. See?'

She sucks up the river water through her straw.

'I'll pass, thanks.'

'You need to stay hydrated. You need to watch my back, Tuva. I'm relying on you.'

'I don't recommend you do that. I'm not good at protecting. I'm a loner. I'm not like you.'

'We watch each other's back until we're safe, got it?'

I nod at her.

She slumps on her stool and then she says, 'We need to shutter the windows.'

'How will we see what's coming?'

'We have peepholes and gun slats.'

She covers the three windows with metal shutters.

'Is this place built on stilts?' I ask.

'On a boulder. Solid granite.'

I push on a wall.

'And it's clapboard and corrugated iron. Made of scraps. No offence.'

'None taken. In fact, it's a compliment. Rosebud Cottage is designed to look like a derelict fishing hut. It's clad in garbage, but in the centre of these walls are three levels of steel plate. It's as good as a solid brick wall. Better than a brick wall.'

'So what happened here?'

'What happened here?'

'Elsa Nyberg.'

'You want to know for your newspaper or for yourself?'

'Both.'

There's a first-aid kit attached by Velcro to her plate-carrier. She pulls it off and checks the contents and then reattaches it.

'It's a long story,' she says.

'Well, we have three weeks of food.'

She sticks her tongue in her cheek and shakes her head. 'Abraham is a special person. He'd operate better as a lone wolf, you know? A thinking man. He's not really a soldier or a farmer or a boss. He wouldn't make a good general or admiral. He's more like a philosopher. A true artist.'

I nod for her to continue.

'Lots of the good things at Rose Farm are thanks to his planning. His foresight. He's a visionary man. But he rules through obscuration. He conceals as much as he reveals to be true. He hides his lies between truths.'

'What do you mean?'

'I mean, he used to take local girls down to the basement of the big house, under the pretence of explaining our aquaponics and hydroponics systems.'

She squeezes her eyes shut.

'Girls? I say. 'Or young women?'

'Young women,' I think. 'Eighteen, nineteen. If they'd have been younger I would have taken a knife to his throat myself.'

'When did you find out?'

'I don't know, really. I think I've been lying to myself for years.'

'But what happened to Elsa?'

Therese checks a peephole, scans the riverscape and then says, 'Honestly, I'm not sure, but she was his type. Abraham gave her gold, I know that much. At least two Kruggerrands and a Buffalo. Three ounces. Maybe that was designed to buy her discretion.'

'But that didn't work. She was going to tell someone, wasn't she?'

'I don't know. The CCTV camera footage of the alder trees was destroyed. The camera was taken down from its post before the police arrived. The post was removed. The hole where the post was driven into the earth was filled and topped with grass.'

'Andreas?'

She shrugs.

'I doubt Abraham killed her himself,' she says. 'He's too gentle. Too slight. My guess is that he ordered Linda Larsson to execute the girl.'

49

I receive a call from Thord asking me to confirm exactly where I am and who I am with. I tell him. He says he's at the entrance to Rose Farm but he can't get inside. He says he's coming to the cottage.

'The police are coming here,' I say to Therese.

'To Rosebud Cottage?'

'They're only a few minutes away.'

'Keep lookout until they get out here. Keep your eye on that peephole, keep watching the farm, but look the other way as well. Linda's capable; she could come out of anywhere. Until we're in a police precinct someplace, we are not safe, remember that. Linda, T-Bone, Andreas. They understand the territory. This is their land and the police don't know what they're dealing with. We can't rely on them like we could in Gavrik town.'

I touch my hearing aid, adjusting its position. Don't fail me now.

She sets up her rifle pointing the other way, upriver, and she clicks something on to her rifle scope.

'What is that?' I ask.

'What is what?'

'That thing?'

'Night vision. The light's falling. If Linda's wearing a headset then she can see us and I want to be able to see her. I don't imagine Chief Björn has this kind of technology in his police Volvos.'

I am tired all of a sudden. The adrenaline from the casket, from this escape.

'Things might escalate. If they all come at us, we must go down there.'

She points at the ground.

'What's down there? In the water?'

'No,' says Therese. 'This is built on a single, solid rock. It's not large, but there's a hole underneath. It's not a bunker and it's not even a basement, just a hollow. It's enough space for three men to hide, crouching in relative safety. If I give the word we have to get down there, yes?'

'Okay.'

All I see is floorboards.

'Police lights,' says Therese.

I sneak a look out of the corner of the metal shutters and I see one marked car out by the alder trees about three hundred metres away. One solitary car.

'Buckle up,' says Therese, adjusting her position.

'They're here to help.'

'Not them.'

She adjusts her rifle and I see a boat approaching, maybe a hundred metres away. The boat sits low in the water and it is covered in pondweed. It cuts through the reed beds and I don't know if it's electric or man powered.

Therese passes me her rifle.

'I can't shoot this.'

'Just hold it for a second.'

She moves a latch and lifts a trapdoor to the hollow in the floor.

The hole is lit with a weak battery-powered light on a sensor. The hole is the size of a septic tank. No windows. No escape tunnel. No ventilation.

'I'm not going down there,' I say.

'That's your decision,' she says. And then she takes back the rifle and picks a bullhorn off the wall and opens the steel door ajar and announces, 'Listen up. You come any closer and I will blow this river shack halfway to Karlstad. Keep your distance and we all come out of this unhurt. You try to approach and I will take decisive and irreversible action. You understand?'

Someone shouts something from the boat. I can't make out the words.

Thord's voice comes over from the cop-car loudhailer, 'We're here to assist you. Nobody needs to get hurt.'

'Don't come any closer,' says Therese. And then she picks a grenade off her belt and removes the pin and holds her hand down firmly over the trigger. She opens the door and she looks back to me and says, 'Cover your ears, Tuva.'

50

The grenade plops into Snake River and nothing happens.

Therese steps back and resumes her position, rifle trained on the boat, on T-Bone and Linda and Andreas.

And then the river erupts. A geyser of water flies up into the air and the whole hut shakes. River water rains down on the corrugated-iron roof and I hear yelling in the distance.

There are four dead fish floating on the surface of Snake River.

'Don't do anything hasty,' says Thord through his loudspeaker. 'We won't come closer. We'll call you.'

'Switch off your phone,' says Therese.

'What? No.'

She looks at me.

'They can use it against us. Give it to me.'

She doesn't point the rifle at me but she gives me a look that says I should not underestimate her.

'So I'm a hostage now? You bring me here to save me and now I'm a hostage?'

'You're not a hostage. If anyone's a hostage it's me.'

'What's happening?'

'You're free to go. Go on. Walk away.'

'I don't understand.'

'It's more complicated than you think,' she says.

'Go on then. Just me and you. What's so complicated?'

She picks up the bullhorn again and says, 'Don't come any closer. I'll send Tuva out in exactly one hour.'

'We understand,' says Thord. 'You need anything. Water? Food?'

'One hour,' she says, and then she locks the steel door.

'One hour?' I say.

'Get down into the hole.'

'What? Why? No.'

I won't be able to hear down there. Not in the dark.

'We're both going down into that hole. They might try to storm the shack.'

'Storm it? This isn't a movie, Therese. It's Constable Thord from Gavrik police. He couldn't storm us even if he wanted to.'

'I'm not talking about the police.'

A chill runs down my back.

I look through the hole in the metal sheeting and T-Bone is chatting with Chief Björn like they're old friends. Magnus is off to the side with Thord, and Andreas is towering over all of them.

'There's a lot you don't know,' she says.

I can see two grenades on her belt. Next to them is a pair of handcuffs and a large hunting knife and spare bullets for her rifle.

'You're not going to kill me?'

She smiles. 'Of course I'm not.'

'You're saving me?'

'I'm trying to save us both. And all of them out there. This is the only way I can think to avoid all-out war on Rose Farm.'

'So let's talk up here.'

'Down in the hole, Tuva. Both of us.'

'I can't do it.' My breathing starts to quicken. 'Not after the casket, not after that.'

She laughs. 'This is not the same. It's ten foot by nine foot. There's air. A light. We can take the stools down, come out whenever we choose. Trust me, it's a safe place where we can talk is all.'

Trust you?

'One hour?' I say. 'Then I can go?'

'Fifty-five minutes,' she says, looking at her watch. 'If you don't hurry up I'll need to tell them I'm extending it.'

'Okay, fine. I'll go down.'

She places the two stools down in the hole. I climb down. She climbs down. And then she closes the lid of the hole and we're down here in a chamber carved out of solid bedrock.

'What is all this about?' I say, my back hunched, my head touching the wooden hatch.

She looks at me and then she rubs her face with her palms. Rubs her eyes. She takes a deep breath and then she says, 'My name is...' she pauses, 'Abraham.'

51

The hole is cold but it's not dark. It's not rat-infested. There's a rucksack in the corner of the room, by Therese's stool.

'What do you mean *your* name is Abraham?'

Therese nods. Smiles. She looks like she's under the influence of a psychedelic substance. 'You need to record everything I say for posterity,' she says. 'For the historical record.'

'I have a Dictaphone?'

'That's fine. Use it. But I want you to record on your phone as well.'

'Why?'

'Why? Have you seen what's outside? All it would take is for Linda to persuade the police of something and they'll come through here guns blazing.'

'The police will not allow Linda or anyone else to do that,' I say. 'They're in charge.'

'They *think* they're in charge, Tuva, but they have no idea.' Her eyes look wild all of a sudden. Dilated pupils. 'Switch on your phone. Record all of this as a voice memo. That way, if we get executed in this hidey-hole the message will live on. Record my testimony and then if we get the chance you must send it to your boss at the newspaper.'

'Therese. I think we should talk to them.'

'Who?'

'The police. We can be calm, tell them we're coming out. Tell them to send a boat or something.'

'Oh, if only it were that simple, Tuva.'

She rummages in her rucksack and pulls out a small plastic bag and hands it to me.

It's a bag of wine gums.

'No, thanks.'

'But... but, I know you like them. I've seen them in your truck.'

I look at the packet and then I look at her.

'Did you plan all this? What's your aim here?'

'My aim?'

'Yeah.'

'My aim is to tell my side of the story, objectively, no bias, while I still have the opportunity. And the time. That is my sole aim.'

She picks off a hand grenade and holds it tight in her palm. The pin is still in. Her knuckles are white. The grenade looks old. Something from World War II, maybe.

'Okay,' I say, taking my phone from her, switching it on, my hands shaking. 'Talk to me.'

'This is why I brought you here. An independent observer, just like before. You'll send it to your boss?'

'Lena Adeola at the *Gavrik Posten*. Editor and co-owner. I will send it to her.'

'Okay, then.'

'Abraham?'

She puts her grenade back on her belt and then she makes a fist.

'My husband's Christian name is Abraham and he is a brilliant man. An artist. But I am the person they think is Abraham. Does that make any sense?'

'I don't know.'

'He is the man. But I am the leader. The true alpha. Rose Farm was my dream; has been for years and years. It was my plan to move here and build an operational community. I wanted us to be trained and prepared and cohesive. Ready for anything.'

'Is Abraham okay?'

'Oh, he's fine. He writes music all day and he practises on the terrace overlooking the river. He's completely detached from reality.'

He's not the only one.

'I brought in Andreas first. He's the comms and dog specialist. And then he brought in T-Bone who'd been living in the US. Kurt T-Bone McGee. He knows everything there is to know about food production and storage. Getting him here was a key part of the plan. If you're not raised on a farm then it's almost impossible to acquire all the necessary knowledge. I knew Kurt was who we needed to keep us all fed indefinitely. You can live without guns but you cannot live without food.'

I burst the wine gums packet and offer her one and she shakes her head so I eat.

It's dark down here but there is one LED lamp illuminating Therese's face. I can still see her lips clearly.

'Linda's my Number Two. She's a weapons expert, sure. Pretty much a sniper. But she's much more than that. A calm mind. You give Linda an order and she'll follow it out. Sometimes too efficiently. She's great on defences, designed the steep ditches and the fencing and the two-stage gate system. Private and public. And her café does decent business as well.'

'Did you buy the bullion or was that Abraham?'

'Abraham says paper money isn't really money, it's just currency. Fiat. Relies on trust. Whereas gold and silver, governments can't print it or manufacture it. You have to mine to get new gold, you have to invest money, labour and time. You can't just start up a printing press or type zeros into a computer. So Kurt, Linda, Ruby and Niklas, may he rest in peace, they paid into a centralised farm fund and we invested in precious metals. Abraham bought what he deemed was best value. Sometimes a year of buying silver bars from one dealer, then six months of buying gold coins from another.'

'Did you know Ruby would kill Niklas?'

'Of course I didn't know.'

'Did Ruby kill Elsa, or did Niklas kill Elsa?

'I don't know what either of those two did in their private time. I truly don't. But shooting Niklas like that, with her bow, was unnecessary. It was a key moment in our collective downfall and I will never forgive Ruby for it.'

'But why do this? I mean, with Ruby in prison, you and Kurt and Andreas and Linda could have rebuilt. Abraham's still here with you. You could still rebuild?'

'We're combat farmers,' she says, sternly. 'That is our philosophy. God-fearing, combat-ready farmers. It's a system that works. But it only works if there is complete trust in the group. If there is honesty. I thought we were prepped for life. The hydroponics, the fish ponds, the solar panels we'd invested in. We had all our bases covered. Except we underestimated the role of chaos. The free will of men to ruin it all.'

The phone buzzes in my hand.

'Ignore it,' she says.

'It's Thord,' I say. 'I'm going to answer it.'

She takes out the grenade again from her belt.

'You're not going to blow us up, Therese. Take a breath. I'm going to take the call.'

She clenches her jaw.

I accept the call and the phone stops vibrating.

And then she removes the pin from her grenade.

52

She looks at me and I look at the grenade in disbelief.

'Tuva?' says Thord through my phone.

Therese shakes her head.

I end the call.

'Put the pin back in,' I say. 'Now. Please.'

'No,' she says. 'I think I'll keep it out. Don't worry, it's perfectly safe as long as I hold it tight inside my hand.'

'You do not want to blow us both up.'

'Don't I?'

My heart skips a beat.

'I'm going to put my phone down now.'

She watches me do it.

We both sit back down on the stools. I know that if she were to drop the grenade in this hole we wouldn't have time to climb out and jump to safety before it exploded. Luka explained to us how they work back in the attics. How the shell of each grenade is uneven, like the skin of a pineapple, so it'll fragment into many pieces, essentially shooting shrapnel out at all angles. It acts like a bomb but also like a hundred bullets.

'I was a successful management consultant,' she says, her tone flat, her expression vacant. 'I gave all that up to move here and I never regretted it. I gave up a good lifestyle, a high income. All for the dream of living a self-sufficient life, away from high-population densities.'

I frown at her.

'I'm a perfectionist, Tuva. I like to be in control and I like to have things done properly. This place, Rose Farm, operated like a well-oiled machine for many years. We sacrificed and worked to build up our stocks. When we had solar installed, we worked towards building a hydro back-up. When we had our bug-out boats ready we started working on bug-out quad bikes and bug-out horses. We all have multiple disciplines. I'm a medic but I'm also the back-up comms person in case Andreas is ever out of action. T-Bone knows how to pressure-can food and grow wheat, but he also shadowed Ruby when she went on her water-filtration courses, and he knows how the wells and underground tanks work just as well as she does. You need backup plans, squared.'

'What?'

'You need backup plans for your backup plans.'

'What's your backup plan for today?'

She looks at the grenade in her hand.

'I hope you're not serious.'

'Right now, the plan is for me to tell you my story in my own words so you can write it accurately. A true record. I know how the mainstream media skew the facts; I've lived with that every minute of my life. If you report what I say honestly and objectively, which I think you will do, then you'll be blessed by the heavenly Father.'

Blessed by the heavenly Father?

'I always strive for accuracy,' I say.

'I know you do. That's why I chose you to be down here with me.'

What?

'This is still recording, right?'

I nod.

'I plotted this Rose Farm life from a cubicle in a fancy office near Stureplan. For years I would create excel spreadsheets to map out my ideal homestead. A fortress we could defend and thrive within.

Sun storms, EMP, fiat currency collapse, a dirty bomb, a plague, climate change, war. We could have managed here through much of that. If the shit hits the fan, or rather *when* it hits the fan, this place will hold up. The perimeter security, the food security. Multiple sources of water. The river for bugging out. I planned it all to the last detail from my office and then, when this place came back on the market, I jumped at the chance. Had to convince Abraham that this was the opportunity he'd been waiting for, to withdraw and work on his magnum opus. To finish his symphony.'

'Has he finished it yet?'

'He's very close.'

She looks like her hand is aching so she moves the grenade to her other hand and I flinch at the transfer.

'How did you find this place? I mean, it's not exactly just outside Stockholm.'

'That's why it's perfect. And anyhow, I always had an alert set for this farm. Even had three real estate agents in Gavrik and Falun prepped in case it ever came on the market.'

'Most Stockholmers would have trouble living way out here.'

'I'd always dreamed of living here again,' she says.

'Again?'

'I was born on this land, Tuva. I lived here for twenty-eight days before it was all taken away from me.'

53

The facts click into place.

'*Your* father?'

'Killed my mother and my brothers, yes, he did. But not like it was reported. He was a misunderstood man.'

Misunderstood?

'I'm sorry. I never knew.'

'Pappa was ill, you see. The papers said it was over money, over a business deal gone sour, over him losing face and not being able to pay loans or keep his family in the manner to which they had become accustomed. Nonsense. People see a physical ailment and they're sympathetic. But some problems aren't visible from the outside. Pappa was sick.'

'When did you find out about this?'

'My adopted parents, who are blameless, kind people, they told me everything when I turned fifteen. I was stunned. Broken. I'd never even guessed that they weren't my birth parents. My whole idea of myself shattered.'

She checks her watch and I see the grenade turn to its end, the hole where the pin should sit clearly visible.

'Time's almost up,' she says.

'Not yet,' I say. 'You wanted to move back here, to your home.'

'We have made it a home, haven't we,' she says. 'I think we have. It took Abraham and me years to build up our pack. But then, after much work and the establishment of training programmes and protocols, we had it almost perfect. A new family. And then…'

'Go on. I'm still recording. I'll send it all to Lena.'

'I want this to be accurate. Talk about pappa's troubles. Interview his cousin, Sven, if he'll talk to you. And do write about how hard-working and loyal everyone here was. Abraham, Kurt, Linda, Andreas, Ruby, even Niklas. We were an effective community. We had strength.'

I blink.

'And then it all turned upside down. And that was the fault of one person.'

54

'It's always been important that we train,' says Therese, her face casting an almost demonic shadow on the rock wall. 'We'd patrol the perimeter wearing plate-carriers and rucksacks, with planks of wood around our necks on rope. Each plank was cut to the same weight as a rifle or shotgun. And then, in the private space, away from the road, we'd practise drills through outbuildings and on Andreas's assault course. We'd train like a small militia. Developing muscle memory was core to our ideology.

She moves her grenade back to the other hand and I hear a helicopter pass overhead. I *feel* it.

'Police,' she says.

'Who ruined everything?' I say. 'Niklas? Ruby?'

'Oh, they ruined themselves,' she says. 'It was me that ruined Rose Farm.'

'What do you mean?'

'The best distance weapon is a firearm that you've properly trained with. The second best is a compound bow that you've trained with. The third best is a wrist-reinforced slingshot that you've trained with.'

'I don't understand.'

'If the government come for your guns, then at least you have a bow. If you run out of arrows then you still have your slingshot. If you run out of ammo for your slingshot it's still effective with smooth river pebbles. It's the ultimate backup weapon, especially here. Trust me, you don't want to get caught out with just a knife. Anything to avoid hand-to-hand combat.'

'What's this got to do with Elsa?'

She sighs.

'I was training down by the alders with my slingshot. Three XL rubber bands on a carbon-fibre frame. We buy them from South Africa through Ruby's contact, and then Linda tweaks them. I was training with stones that day. And lead balls.'

I move my hands to my mouth.

'You... *you* killed Elsa?'

'It was an accident,' she says, raising her hands in the air.

'Careful!' I say. 'Do not drop that.'

'I was aiming the lead ball bearings at a knot in the trunk of an alder. Those marble-size bbs are heavy enough to kill small and medium-sized game, if you're accurate. On that day I wasn't accurate enough. I often think back to that moment. If I'd had a rifle with a scope I'd have seen her. I'd have stopped. But aiming through the split branch of my slingshot I never saw her head. I just heard the dull thud of the impact as the lead ball impacted her temple. She went straight down.'

The hollow is heating up from the two of us, our collective breath, from the energy, the nightmarish potential energy of the unpinned grenade.

'I tried to save her,' she says, her words catching in her throat. 'But she was already stone dead. Her head was caved in a little and I couldn't find a pulse. I panicked. Not because of the accident but because of what we have here. *Had* here. The things we've built up and stand to lose. History repeating itself. The police and the newspapers would never have understood the extent of our supplies. They'd have arrested us all. Labelled us as survivalist lunatics and uncovered the connection to what Dad did in '87. Rose Farm would have been stolen from us all over again.'

'Did you tell anyone?'

She takes a sudden breath and says, 'No. Not even Abe. I've hardly slept since that day. I ruined everything for the whole pack.'

The helicopter hovers overhead.

'What about the cross? On her neck?'

She shakes her head. 'I don't know. I was trying to cover my tracks, I suppose. I thought there was no use in us going to prison for an accident, and if I painted that symbol then it might put the police off the scent.'

'It almost worked,' I say.

'It *did* work,' she says, pulling out a pair of handcuffs from her rucksack. 'If it hadn't been for you sniffing around, poking your fucking nose in. The police are clueless, Tuva. We'd have all lived on as normal here, if it wasn't for you.'

55

'Your hour's up. Put them on,' says Therese.

'We can both walk away from this,' I say, my voice trembling. 'I promise the story will be accurate. I give you my word.'

'Put them on.'

I look at the grenade and then at the cuffs. I place them on and she tightens them around my wrists.

'Send the voice memo.'

'Are you sure?'

'I'm done talking, Tuva. I've made my peace with what's happened. Send it.'

I send the voice memo to Lena's email, and I show Therese.

'Get up out of the hollow.'

We clamber out and look out through the peephole. Therese has her rifle in one hand, grenade in the other. The crowd consists of the wolf pack, what's left of them, and the police force, now swollen to more than six officers. A fire truck stands by and two ambulances are parked by the riverbank.

Therese moves a curtain and I expect to find more boxes and buckets of mylar-bagged food but instead there are ten large propane-gas canisters.

I can't catch my breath.

'You're not your father, Therese.'

'What would you know about it.'

'If you want to kill yourself, then I understand. I've thought about doing the same thing. But you don't have to kill me or them. You don't have to do that.'

'I don't *have* to do anything.'

'Your dad killed his wife and kids.'

'And all our horses. The whole stable.'

'I didn't know that.'

'And the family dog. An elkhound.'

'I'm sorry for what you've been through.'

'I take full responsibility for all of this,' she says, sternly. 'For everything I have done and everything I am about to do. I allowed you to think you'd protect us from over-zealous policing. I know your reputation. But I was mistaken. You played your part in our downfall, but I must take ultimate responsibility. The memo has been sent. The truth will out. Now, as leader, this falls to me.'

She places down her rifle and moves the grenade back to her other hand and I can see her palms are shiny with sweat.

The helicopter moves away.

I hear something.

'No,' says Therese.

I look through the peephole and there is a boat moving slowly towards us. Linda Larsson's rowing. Standing up at the front, like a galleon's figurehead, is a slight man with a long black beard. He's wearing white robes and his hair is shaved.

He is playing a violin.

'No,' she says again, quietly. 'Oh, no. Why, you fool.'

Therese starts to look around, as if for answers, the grenade held up close to her eye socket.

'We can all leave this,' I say. 'Alive. All of us. You included.'

She cries silently.

Her tears run down the body of the grenade and drip on to the rough pine-board floor.

'He's finished it,' she says, breaking into a smile. 'Listen. Abraham has finished his composition. His life's work. After all these years. Just listen to it, Tuva. Listen.'

The music grows louder as they approach. His face is without emotion.

Therese opens the door of the shack and dusk light pours in.

Abraham is playing.

The strings vibrate and music fills the river valley and it is haunting. Police watch on.

Abraham nods and puckers his lips and mimes a kiss to his wife.

She grabs the chain linking my handcuffs and jerks me out towards the door.

'We're going now,' she says.

We teeter on the edge of the shack and she pulls me in so close I can smell her sweat.

'Father, forgive us our sins...'

She goes to jump off the deck into the waters of Snake River gripping the grenade in one hand and my handcuffs in the other.

I kick out as hard as I can.

She takes her hand off the grenade trigger.

Screaming in the distance. Muffled warnings I can't decipher. Panic.

Therese tightens her grip on me, dragging me closer to the edge, closer to the water.

'No!' I scream.

She tugs again but I kick back. I get loose.

She falls into the water.

Abraham stops playing.

Silence.

56

It's been two days.

I've spent time in the police station explaining what happened. I've been followed by journalists, some of whom have respected my wishes, while others have camped outside my apartment building.

On the drive back to Gavrik that evening, sat next to Thord in the back seat of a police Volvo, I noticed that the snowberg had finally melted. The field was waterlogged but the white mass had gone.

Lena asked me over to her house for dinner last night. Most bosses would have suggested a meeting at the office, but she's not most bosses, not even close. Johan was also there, opening wine in the background, heating plates. He cooked roast chicken with baked potatoes and tarragon cream sauce. Lena told me after dinner, sipping sweet coffee in her garden, that she'd worried she'd never see me again. She said Lars and her chatted about group dynamics and how they can overwhelm the individual sovereignty of a person, of any person. It's not group insanity exactly, more like a wave of momentum that's hard to break free from. She even told me how she'd worked for a real-estate agent in New York before she started at her first newspaper. Told me how they had cult-like meetings each morning to fire themselves up for the day. Told me how her friends thought she'd been possessed. And then Lena talked to me about how she didn't want to lose her deputy editor. How she couldn't handle working each day everyday with just Nils and Lars for company.

She explained, in a very kind and circumvent manner, how, even if I didn't value my safety at the moment, my own life, that she did, she valued it very highly, and she'd rather I take better care of myself in future. That she'd help in any way she can.

I pass between McDonalds and ICA Maxi and join the E16 southbound. Seven hours to Gothenburg. The journey passes in a blur. Overtaking wagons loaded with spruce trees and trailers holding speedboats. Not noticing road signs. Just coasting in my Hilux, my brain on autopilot.

Driving past Lake Vänern, an inland sea more than a lake, and past Vänersborg, I ponder the meaning of shame. The point of it. If Therese had just explained to the police then, she'd have received a light sentence for killing Elsa. Perhaps no sentence at all. But in that split second by the alder trees, she made a poor decision. To conceal the truth rather than to offer it up. She was the architect of her own downfall. And in a way she took Ruby and Niklas down with her.

John Denver comes on the radio and I turn up the volume. Country roads, take me home. I turn the volume high and open my windows. West Virginia. Blue Ridge Mountains. I pass a sign to Gothenburg and I smile with complete happiness and then my lower lip starts to tremble and I bite down hard on it.

I overtake a couple in a 1970s red Saab. They're in their eighties, driving at forty, their car so far into the slow lane it's almost in the hard shoulder. Two lovers moving from here to there. A beautiful, gentle thing.

Thord tells me that Linda and T-Bone have taken charge of Rose Farm in the interim. The police have had access to all the buildings and caches; they've confiscated what they needed to confiscate and they left the rest. T-Bone's helping Abraham through his grief. According to Thord, Abraham Viklund is a quiet and intelligent man. A musical genius. But he isn't too good at looking after himself, day-to-day. Forgets to eat or sleep, that kind of thing. I can empathise.

I enter the industrial area outside Gothenburg and drive on.

This is the suburb.

I find the street.

The house.

I park outside and get out of my truck and stretch. I'm carrying my overnight bag.

She's waiting for me on the doorstep.

I walk over and my body feels weighed down with it all. If I could give my life to let Noora have hers, I would, a hundred times over.

Noora's mum opens her arms to me and I hug her. She kisses my forehead and she says, 'We heard all about it. My goodness, Tuva. Are you okay? Have you eaten?'

'I'm okay,' I say.

'Come inside. Come on.'

I step in and she closes the door. The house smells of fresh pine.

'You want to go through straight away, I know you do. Go on.'

'How is she?'

'Oh, you know. The same.'

The same. When someone is sick, people ask, 'How are they doing?' and they expect an automatic 'on the mend'. But having to reply 'no change' or 'not any worse' is so devastatingly sad. I do it at least once a week. You want to offer good news, that act of *giving*, to let someone walk away from the conversation with a nugget of hope. But sometimes you can't.

'I'll make tea. You go through, Tuva.'

'How are *you* doing, though?'

She looks exhausted all of a sudden. Beyond the make-up and the neat hair and pressed clothes, I see a mother who has lived through hardship and injustice, and now she's living through worse.

'I'm okay. Thank you for asking. I'll put the kettle on.'

She walks through to the kitchen.

I take a deep breath and try to compose myself. Sniff. Clearing of my throat. And then I walk through.

Noora's sat upright in an armchair, special cushions holding her in place

I walk to her and I cup her face in my palm, like I have done so many times in the past. I kiss her dimpled cheek and kneel by the chair and look into her eyes.

Noora's mum comes through with the tea.

'I remember the first time Noora made us tea,' she says, laughing. 'She must have been six or so. Came through with it on a tray. Cold water and a teabag and a spoon of salt. Her pappa drank his all up.'

I smile my love to her for sharing this story.

'Thord says hello,' I say to Noora, watching for a response even though I know there will be none. 'Even Chief Björn sends his best. Says you're to get back to work as soon as possible. Keeping your desk tidy for you. Says they need you in the station.'

'I'd say they do,' says Noora's mum behind us. 'Best officer they ever had.'

I take lemon-scented hand cream and squirt some on to my fingertip. I rub it into Noora's cool hands, working the balm into the creases and valleys of her perfect fingers.

'Tea's getting cold,' says Noora's mum.

We sit, talking, sharing news stories, things distant from here, just in case Noora can understand us, even though the doctors have said she cannot. It seems unbearably rude not to include her in the conversation. So we talk like she can hear us. We talk about politics and the weather and the May Day protests.

Later, Noora's dad comes home. We light candles and eat dinner together. They sleep in the guest room when I come to stay – a gesture of such kindness and generosity that I'm floored by it every time.

I have their bed and Noora has a specially-designed bed next to me.

I check she's comfortable and then I apply lip balm to her lips, my fingertip grazing her beautiful mouth. I kiss her forehead and climb into my bed. Our heads are half an arm-length apart and I know I don't deserve her. But since my near miss on the river, since the long drive down here, I feel different. Lighter, somehow. Lying here next to Noora, I feel like for the first time in a long time we are both at peace. Not fighting the world. Calm. It's quiet in the room. My breathing slows and I watch her face, the dimple in her cheek, and I whisper, 'Goodnight.'

Acknowledgements

To my literary agent Kate Burke, and the team at Blake Friedmann: thank you.

To my editor Jenny Parrott, and the team at Oneworld: thank you.

To my international publishers, editors, translators: thank you.

To Maya Lindh (the voice of Tuva): thank you.

To all the booksellers and bloggers and reviewers and early supporters and tweeters and fellow authors: thank you. Readers benefit so much from your recommendations and enthusiasm. I am one of them. Special thanks to every single reader who takes the time to leave a review somewhere online. Those reviews help readers to find books. Thank you.

To @DeafGirly: thank you once again for your help and support. In many ways your opinion matters to me more than anyone else's. I continue to be extremely grateful.

To Sweden: what a place! Thanks for welcoming me in.

To my family, and especially my parents: once again, thank you for letting me play alone for hours as a child. Thank you for taking me to libraries. Thank you for letting me read and draw and daydream and scribble down strange stories. Thanks for not censoring my book choices (too much). Thank you for allowing me to be bored. It was a special gift.

To my friends: thanks for your ongoing support (and patience, and love).

To Mary Shelley and Irvine Welsh: I read *Frankenstein* and *Trainspotting* back-to-back as an awkward teenager. The books blew my mind. Thank you.

Special thanks to my late granddad for teaching me some valuable lessons. He taught me to treat everyone equally, and with respect. To give the benefit of the doubt. To listen to advice even if you don't then follow it. To take pleasure from the small things in life. To read widely. To never judge or look down on anyone. To be kind. To spend time with loved ones. To keep the kid inside you alive.

To Bernie and Monty: what can I say? I'm lucky. You both make me happy. Thank you.

To every shy, socially awkward kid: I see you. I was you. It will get easier. I promise.

To my wife and son: Thank you. Love you. Always.

'Memorably atmospheric...compelling.' *Guardian*

'*Dark Pines* crackles along at a roaring pace.'
Observer, thriller of the month

'The tension is unrelenting, and I can't wait for
Tuva's next outing.' Val McDermid

'Memorably atmospheric...compelling.' *Guardian*

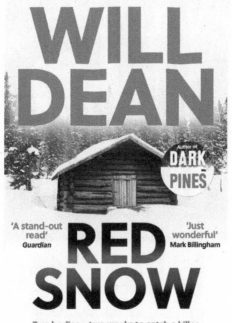

WILL DEAN

Author of **DARK PINES**

'A stand-out read'
Guardian

'Just wonderful'
Mark Billingham

RED SNOW

Two bodies – two weeks to catch a killer

'Just what crime readers want.' *Daily Telegraph*

'Tuva Moodyson is a wonderful creation.' *Daily Express*

'A cracking plot and a hugely likeable heroine.' *Grazia*

'A stand-out read.' *Guardian*

'Just wonderful.' Mark Billingham

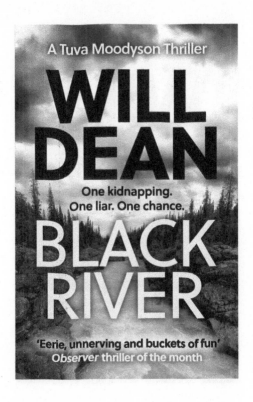

'A peerless exercise in suspense.' *Financial Times*

'BRILLIANT central character.' Ann Cleeves

'Eerie, unnerving and buckets of fun.'
Observer, thriller of the month

A Tuva Moodyson Thriller

WILL DEAN

BAD APPLES

'A delicious return to Tuva' Ann Cleeves

'Fiendish, funny, scary as hell. *Bad Apples* is the stand out in a truly outstanding series.' Chris Whitaker

'Unsettling from beginning to the very end but leavened with dark humour. A compelling thriller that devoted fans and new readers will adore.' Jane Casey

'A delicious return to Tuva.' Ann Cleeves

WILL DEAN grew up in the East Midlands. After studying Law at the LSE and working in London, he settled in rural Sweden where he built a house in a boggy clearing at the centre of a vast elk forest, and it's from this base that he reads and writes. Collectively the Tuva Moodyson books – *Dark Pines*, *Red Snow*, *Black River* and *Bad Apples* – have been selected for Zoe Ball's ITV Book Club, longlisted for the Theakston Old Peculier Crime Novel of the Year Award, shortlisted for the *Guardian* Not the Booker prize, and won Best Independent Voice at the Amazon Publishing Readers' Awards. The series is in development for television. Will is also the author of *The Last Thing to Burn* (Hodder; this has been shortlisted for the Theakston Old Peculier Crime Novel of the Year Award 2022), *First Born* and *The Last Passenger* (both Hodder).

Will loves to hear from readers. You can find him on Twitter and Instagram @willrdean and on TikTok as will_dean_author, and he posts regularly about reading and writing on YouTube as Will Dean – Forest Author.

#TeamTuva